EART-WARMING ROLE-PLAYING

GOLDEN SKY Stories

SNIFF
SNIFF

Heart-Warming Role-Playing

GOLDEN SKY Stories

Golden Sky Stories
Heart-Warming Role-Playing
By Ryo Kamiya & Tsugihagi Honpo

Japanese Version Credits

Planning: Ryo Kamiya, Emetaro Aiko, Radiwoheddo
Game Design: Ryo Kamiya
Authors: Emetaro Aiko, Kentaro Hayashi, Saint Marc
Illustrations: Ike, hira, Emetaro Aiko
Special Thanks: Harry, Tukasa Hashima, IWAKO

English Version Credits

Cultural Notes: Ewen Cluney
Editing: Mike Stevens, Grant Chen, Charles Boucher
Layout, Logos, & Graphic Editing: Clay Gardner
Special Thanks: Ryo Kamiya, Andy Kitkowski, Jon Baumgardner, Ben Lehman, Elton Sanchez, Tobias Wrigstad
Dedicated to: Bruce Stevens and Billie Bullock

The "Everyday Magic" section is by Ewen Cluney and is based on the discussion between Ryo Kamiya and South that appears in *Doko ni Demo Aru Fushigi*.

"About the Countryside" is by さうす (South) and originally appeared in *Tsugihagi Tayori Vol. 1*. It appears here in translation with the permission of the author.

This book was set in Fairfield and **Capucine** using Adobe InDesign CS5.

Starline Publishing
ISBN: 978-0-9899043-0-8

A Note on PDF Piracy: It is possible that you obtained the PDF of *Golden Sky Stories* through less than legal means. While we don't at all condone the draconian actions taken by many of the larger copyright holders against infringers, we did work very hard on this, so we would greatly appreciate it if you would consider making a purchase. Also, however you obtained this game, more than anything we hope you'll try playing it with your friends.

Table of Contents

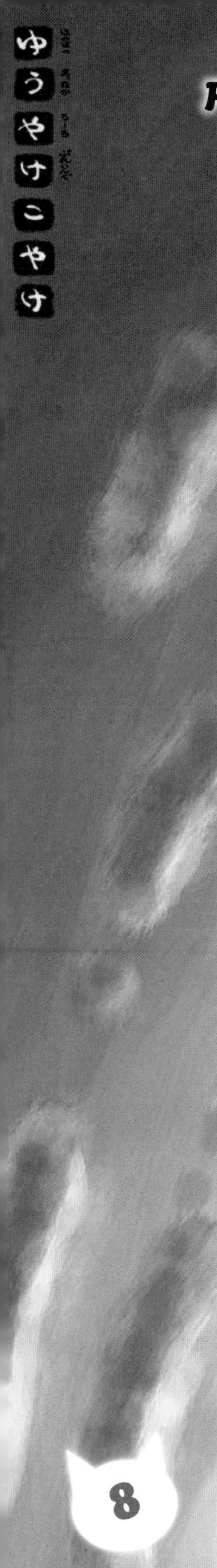

Foreword

To you who are looking at this book, thank you.
To you who bought this book, thank you.

This is a role-playing game rulebook. Role-playing game. RPG.

It's a game where you play the role of another person, another you, in another place, another world. That means that in order to enjoy this book, you need to create a place to serve as a stage, and this other you. Your other self and his or her friends will come together to talk, laugh, have fun, and occasionally feel sad or cry too, as you cut loose and experience life. Your other self will have all kinds of different experiences. Although these experiences will be indirect, you will likely still be able to feel them.

You control your other self. When he or she makes a decision, you decide through him or her at the same time. When he or she meets someone, you meet them through him or her. When he or she talks to someone, you talk to them through him or her.

Your other self can also do things that you can't. But on the other hand, she might not be able to do some of the things you can do. You can't do everything, and neither can your other self. The things that you can and can't do are part of what makes life enjoyable. Enjoy being someone different from yourself. Get a taste of a different way of life. That's the purpose of this book.

Now, there's another important thing: You don't enjoy these stories by yourself. You need to gather friends around you, so they can create their own other selves, who can in turn become friends with yours. The world is not for one person alone. The stories that come from this game are by and for everyone.

You might think that there are a lot of things that seem tedious. It might seem a burden even just to read this book. Preparing stories might seem troublesome. Your first try might not turn out how you'd like, leaving a bad taste in your mouth.

Still, the stories you create with your friends will surely be more wonderful than those made by others. There are some stories in this book, but please blow past them to spin the stories that are shining inside of you. Everyone has the power to create stories of their own. The games called "RPGs" are meant to draw as much of that out of people as possible.

May your stories sustain you. May it add flowers to the story of your life. That is what this humble author prays for.

This introduction has gone on a little too long, it seems. Please turn the page, and we can begin.

とても おいしい
太陽ミルク

ゆうやけこやけ

CULTURAL NOTES

Here and there throughout this book you'll find cultural notes intended to help Western readers better understand this game and its setting. However, please don't worry too much about cultural authenticity. For Japanese gamers playing Shadowrun*, Seattle becomes a fantastic, exotic locale, and* Golden Sky Stories' *rural Japan can be no less wondrous for you. This game is set in a Japanese countryside that's idealized even for Japanese players, with the aim of creating a more magical setting. Learning more about Japanese culture can be a great source of inspiration—and something interesting to do for its own sake—but the most important thing is to come together with your friends to tell heartwarming stories.*

There aren't really any anime series that quite capture the feel of Golden Sky Stories[1]*, but there are many different titles that can give you a better idea of what the Japanese countryside is like, not to mention giving you a better idea of Japanese mythology. Among these are* My Neighbor Totoro *(and many other Miyazaki films),* Petopeto-san, GeGeGe no Kitaro, Kamichu!, Natsume's Book of Friends, Mokke, Mushi-shi, *and* Wolf Children Ame and Yuki. When They Cry - Higurashi no Naku Koro Ni, *although far removed from the tone of this game, also has an exceptional portrayal of the Japanese countryside.*

GENDER

Although all of the sample henge you see depicted in this book are girls (as are most of the local gods), boy henge are perfectly fine, and can be every bit as charming in their own ways. Likewise, sometimes this book refers to a character as "he" or "she" because it makes the writing a little smoother, but you shouldn't feel obligated to have a character be male or female because of it. If you want to make the fox henge in "At the Fox's Shrine" a boy, or the child in "Crying In the Night" a girl, please do so!

[1] *Ike, who did most of the illustrations for this game, also does a manga called* Nekomusume Michikusa Nikki *("Catgirl's Wayside Grass Diary") that has a lot of the elements of* Golden Sky Stories *in it, though unfortunately, there's no English version as of yet.*

Spring is the season of beginnings.
The season of warm sleep.
The season when dreams begin.

Here you will learn what kind of game Golden Sky Stories is,
What you become and what you do when you play it,
What kind of being will take the stage.

You will come to know these things here.
Please read this part before your stories.

Spring

About Golden Sky Stories

In a Certain Town

Only a single rail line passes through it. A two-car train comes every hour, and no more. In front of the station are a row of shops not seen anywhere else. Many of the roads around the town are narrow, too small for cars to pass. Some of them are mere dirt paths, used by cats and rabbits more than people.

You can see open fields here and there. The rice paddies outnumber the houses. If you look into the distance, you'll see only mountains and trees. Narrow rivers flow from mountains, from ponds, gathering into one big river. The water flows in, the water flows away.

There are temples and shrines, empty and quiet. Bamboo groves filled with whispering wind. There are endless fields of pampas grass, flower beds, fields of lotus flowers and clover. There are ponds with lotus flowers, footpaths with blooming amaryllis, and stone walls sprouting morning glories. The mountains retain their caps of white snow, even when spring comes to the town.

The sky seems endless. At night there are no streetlights. Here the moon and the stars shine brightly on the town.

There are only a handful of traffic lights in the town. The tallest building is a three-story school.

The town is full of *sounds*. The sounds of leaping fish, of playing children, of the mailman's motorcycle, of the print shop's spinning machines. There are the sounds of dogs, cats, birds, and insects. There are sounds of flowing water, blowing wind, and falling rain.

Here, there are many things livelier than the people.

Here, the other living things outnumber the people.

This is the kind of town where you will create stories.

Where Things Besides People Live

There are a fair number of people in this town, and many other living things. They have lived among the people since long ago. These living things that aren't people exchanged words with them. You are an inhabitant of this town. However, you are not human. You're an animal. You are a henge. You are neither an adult nor a child, but an animal who guides the town. There are many things you can't do, but there are just a few things you can do that people can't.

You don't have the power to fight. You have just the tiniest bit of magical power. Well, sometimes it can't even be called magic; it's more like the ability to create a truly small opportunity. However, that tiny opportunity can change a person. And changing a person can save them.

People are strong creatures. They build towns, they make tools, they build houses to protect themselves and words to express their feelings. They're the only living things that make stories to remind themselves that there are henge like you.

Still, sometimes people become weak. Sometimes because of their words, sometimes because of their complicated hearts. People have the power to draw strength from within themselves, if only the opportunity presents itself. People can't create opportunities by themselves. You can help create that opportunity. You're not the only one who can help them, of course, but people can sometimes ensnare themselves. Since you're a henge and not a human, you can create the opportunities they need.

When someone is at an important point in their lives, when they stand on a crossroads, be there for them. It could become an important moment for you too.

In this town, neither animals nor people are living alone.

The Game

This is a game, and yet it isn't. It isn't a game where you fight with others. It isn't a game where you compete with others. It's a game where everyone works together to create a story. If you can tell a good story, everyone wins, and if the story is boring, then everyone loses. That's the kind of game this is.

The henge do not fight with weapons or magic. They don't seek out or expose great secrets. They don't save the world. They don't earn money. Stories about henge are simpler, but every bit as important. They save people not through money or food, but with their hearts. Such stories are waiting for you in this town.

Small quarrels might happen during these stories from time to time. Someone might even get a little bit hurt. But that doesn't resolve the story. Please, try to forget about other games, just a little, and play this one. Henge are special creatures, and yet they're not. They have the ability to be of some small help to ordinary people.

You can create a unique tale for this world. Try to make it a story that's warm and full of your own feelings.

There's one more thing you need to remember. The most important thing is to take an active role in the stories you participate in. Be active. Don't just think; try things out. When you get used to something, try out something new. Your stories will grow and become something wonderful.

The Henge

You are a henge. You are an animal with the power to take human form. You also have several powers that humans do not possess. Of course, since you are at your core an animal, you first and foremost live as one. You have no family registry, no house, no money, and no cell phone. You are ultimately an animal, even if you are one that can take on human form. You get your food as an animal, and since you appear fully clothed when you take on human form, you needn't worry about such things.

Of course, sometimes you might steal food while in human form, or display the weaknesses or predispositions of your species. The older people of the town usually know that there are henge who take human form living there. It's not a big deal. Even if you show up with your tail and ears visible, they'll be nice enough to pretend they didn't see. Granted, there are people who don't know, and they might be a bit shocked if they saw you. It's important to act like your animal type, but you don't need to look it up in *National Geographic*.

The merits and shortcomings that need to figure into your behavior are mostly laid out in the rules. Furthermore, the animals who can become henge do not all have the same traits. There are cats who are good at swimming, and foxes who are immune to the lure of fried tofu.

Henge can take on human form. Naturally, they can understand human speech even as animals. But what's a little…actually, *very* surprising to people is that they can also talk like humans while in animal form. They can of course talk with animals of the same type too (but please make do with human speech when talking to other kinds of animals).

Just why is it that henge can change? In the case of foxes it might be because they live so long. However, for other kinds of henge age has nothing to do with it. To the henge themselves, the ability to take on human form and other strange powers are something that just happens. Maybe all animals can change and have strange powers, and those that occasionally decide to use them to appear human are called henge. Whatever the reason, henge don't trouble themselves over it. They *are* the mystery, and they never give any thought to why they can change.

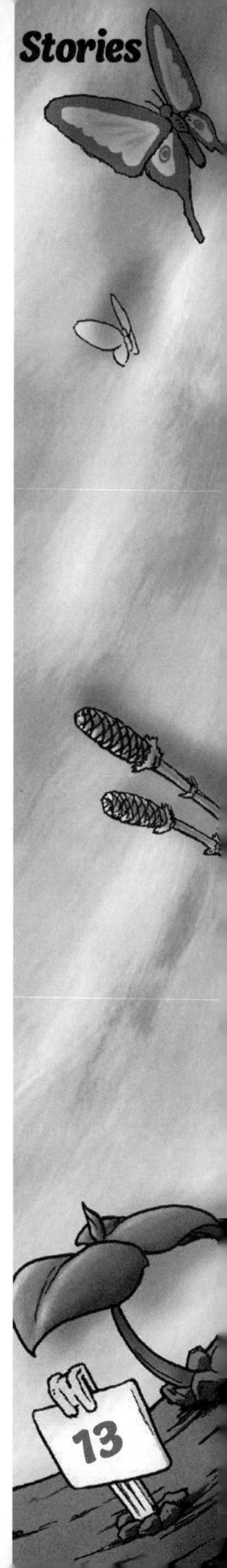

ANIMALS REAL AND MYTHICAL

The henge depicted in Golden Sky Stories are a curious mixture of Japanese folklore, real animals, and in some cases, pop-culture myths. In mythology, henge (a two-syllable word pronounced hen-gay, like a chicken that's happy, not a one-syllable word said like a stone monument in England) are a class of youkai (a Japanese term for fairies and similar supernatural beings), that are animals capable of taking human form and possessing other magical powers. This game isn't about the real animals or the actual myths, so the henge in it reflect the place they occupy in the Japanese psyche. It is also important to remember that in a sense henge are not mythical creatures that resemble animals, but simply animals expressing inherent abilities that they usually hide. Well into the 20th century (and perhaps even today) people attributed unexplained mischief to foxes or raccoon dogs and drew no distinction between regular foxes and "fox spirits."

Foxes are very prominent in Japanese mythology, and of all of the henge, they are the ones most defined by myth. In Japanese folklore they are long-lived and have potent magical powers. The foxes of myth can be dangerous, whimsical tricksters, or loyal guardians. There are even stories of fox-women marrying human men, though their tails sometimes give them away. In Shinto, foxes are associated with the god Inari, and they're treated as minor deities.

Raccoon dogs, or tanuki in Japanese, are a species of canines found in Japan and other parts of Asia, and while they're largely unknown to Westerners, to the Japanese they have every bit as much psychological relevance as foxes. They're so well-known in Japan that video game superstar Mario got to dress up as one in Super Mario Bros. 3. Raccoon dogs are cute, pudgy, fluffy little animals with markings kind of like a raccoon (but without the striped tails). In folk legends they're adept at transforming themselves.

Cats vary a bit in terms of how they're portrayed in Japanese folklore. They can be a symbol of good fortune, especially in the form of maneki-neko ("beckoning cat") figures, and they can be monsters, such as the bakeneko (dangerous monster cats) and nekomata ("forked cats" who grow a second tail). The cat henge in the game are more closely based on the real animals, and in RPG terms they have something of a thief/rogue role.

Dogs aren't too prominent in Japanese folklore, but where they do show up they show incredible loyalty to people, enough to transcend life and death, as in the story of Hachiko. There are tales of inugami, dogs that have died and returned as powerful protective spirits. In real life, dogs have lived alongside people longer than any other animal—there were literally cavemen with dogs—so their kinship with us runs very deep. Dog henge are informed more by perceptions of dogs in real life, but both reality and legends point to dogs being loyal to humans.

Rabbits and hares are the subject of a persistent pop-culture myth in Japan. Many people believe that rabbits are so dependent on others for love and affection that they'll actually die if they get too lonely. This isn't actually true, any more than the Western notion that they're obsessed *with carrots, but it forms the bedrock of the popular Japanese perception of the character of rabbits and gives rabbit henge a distinctive feel. Also, strictly speaking with the exception of the Amami rabbit only found on two particular islands, it is hares and not rabbits that are native to Japan. The Japanese word "usagi" covers both rabbits and hares (and even other lagomorphs like pikas), and in layman's terms the English words are easy to conflate. It is actually hares that appear in Japanese myths though, notably the White Hare of Inaba who so cleverly tricked a clan of sharks, and the hare on the moon, which is the basis of the henge's Mochi Pounding power. Non-native animals can still become henge though, so actual rabbits can be henge as well.*

***Bird** henge draw on folk tales of helpful birds, including the tale of the Crane's Debt, in which a crane takes on human form to become the adoptive daughter of an old man who freed her from a trap, and the Tongue-Cut Sparrow, who likewise rewarded an old man who showed kindness. There is also Yatagarasu, a sort of crow god that is a symbol of guidance. They are not related to the tengu though; these crow-men of Japanese folklore are the vengeful spirits of corrupted priests or nobles, and also do not actually transform as henge do.*

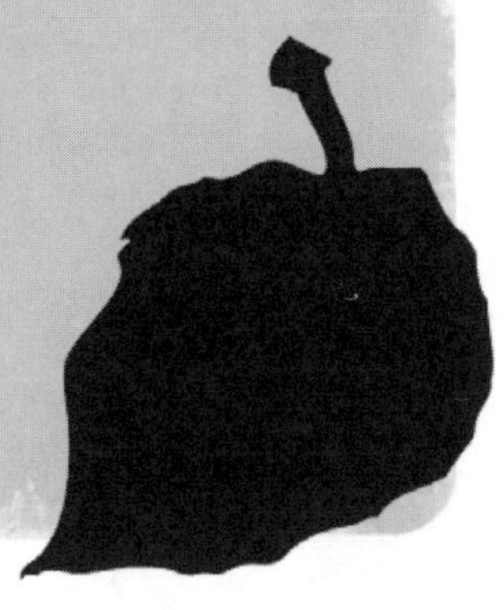

Humans, Animals, & Local Gods

Then there are the people who live in the town. They far outnumber the henge. The town is in the countryside and small, but there are still nearly ten thousand people living in the area. Even the old folks don't know everyone in the area. Only certain people, like the ones who have stores in town and who work at the town hall know most everyone. Henge can walk around the town without worry of being found out. Also, there are no street lamps, and little pedestrian traffic.

Most of the old people and the adults raised in the town know that there are henge around. A lot of people might know about foxes especially, but youngsters and people who just arrived from out of town probably don't know about henge. They might even assume that a henge is a kid from out of town, or a lost child.

Now, there are plenty of living things in the town that aren't henge. People can't talk with them, but henge can speak with them if they're the same type of animal. However, everyone is just doing their best to live their lives. You shouldn't expect them to help too much with information. Still, if you see them you might want to say hello anyway.

Anyway, there's henge, people, and... lots of animals. But there's one more group: the local gods. The local gods are actually fairly similar to henge, but they protect a particular place and don't leave it. They hardly ever take human form and live hidden in their own territory.

There are local gods for the forests, mountains, ponds, rivers, and so on. The gods are not usually animals with fur or feathers, but things like trees, fish, snakes, centipedes, or spiders, living things closely tied to the land. Local gods are worshiped by people and henge alike, but many of them are stubborn and eccentric, so they don't listen to just any request. They only really care about the things that live in their territory

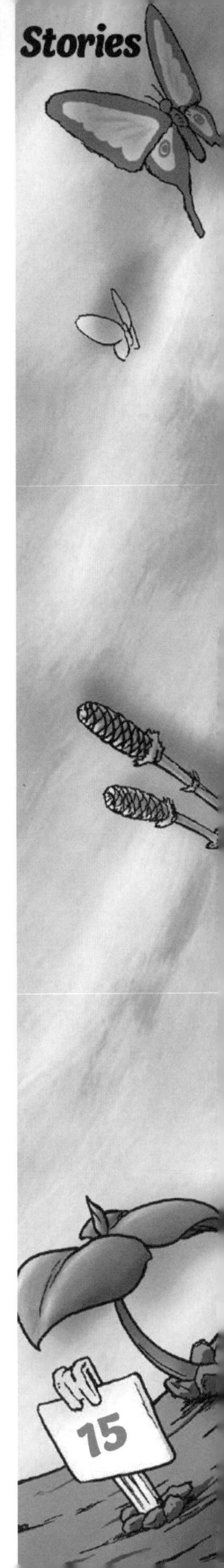

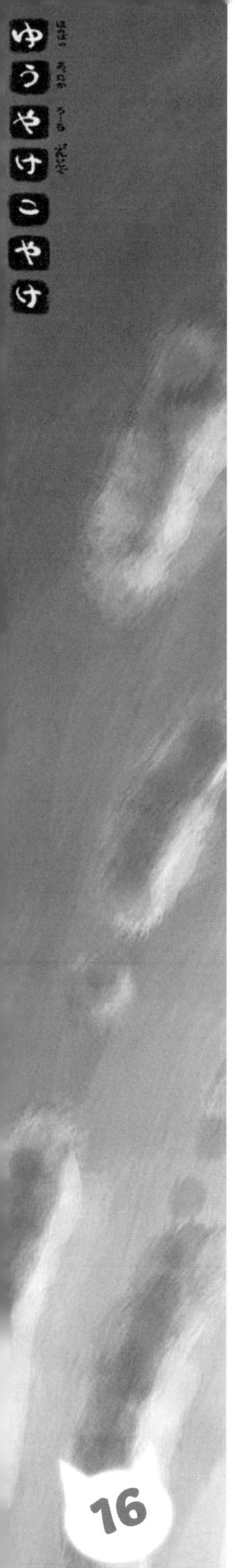

(including people and henge). For good or for ill, they pay no attention to anything outside of it. Local gods can converse with anything that lives within their territory. Also, since they have the power to take on human form, they can converse with people and henge.

That should be a sufficient explanation of the inhabitants of the town. We'll leave the fine details to the stories where they come up.

The Narrator

In the explanation of the rules that follow, the word "narrator" is used a lot. The narrator is a person who becomes the axis of the story's progress. Think of being the narrator as like being "it" in tag or hide and seek. Running or hiding can be fun, but isn't it also fun to be the one doing the chasing?

The narrator's role is very different from that of his or her friends. However, just as you can't play tag without someone being "it," this role is vital to bringing the story together. Many parts of it are difficult, but even without participating as a henge, there's still fun to be had.

Still, don't just leave the narrator role to one person all the time; take the initiative and become one yourself every once in a while. You'll no doubt come to understand things you didn't before.

Now, the narrator doesn't get to participate in the story as a henge. However, he or she does set up the larger framework of the whole story. The narrator decides—in a general way—the story's setting and contents, and the characters that will appear. The other participants don't really get to decide on the overall contents of the story. It's something only the narrator can decide. Some people will find it fun to make these decisions, while others will think it's a bother.

Since you have this book in your hands and you're reading it, why not try being the narrator for your friends? The rules for being the narrator are in the Autumn chapter. Try it if, rather than always participating in someone else's story, you might want to have others participate in yours. Please read on a little bit.

MASTER OF THE GAME

While this game is unconventional in a lot of ways, it takes a typically Japanese view of the role of the Game Master/narrator. In Japanese tabletop RPGs, the GM generally has a very strong, authoritative role in the game, and there aren't really any games that have changed this the way that some English-language RPGs have. How much the narrator sets the rules and how much goes to group consensus is ultimately up to the people playing, but whatever you think is the sweet spot, your goal is always to have fun with your friends. A skilled narrator can be a great leader, guiding the group to weave wonderful stories together, but it can also be nice to let everyone else offer their ideas. The rules often say that you must have the narrator's permission to do something, but the narrator doesn't have to always be deciding everything alone. Take suggestions, take votes, and so forth to enrich your stories with everyone's ideas.

Various Henge

Now, in the following pages we'll introduce six types of animal henge. When you create your other self, you'll have to pick one of these. Each of the six types of henge is introduced by a single representative. These girls are just examples, however, so it's perfectly okay to create ones that are different. Your henge can be a boy, and there are many possible personalities besides those introduced here.

In any case, please read about what your chosen type of henge is like. You might even learn something you didn't know about the actual animals.

My name is Suzune Hachiman, and I am a **FOX**. In human form I am a girl of a mere ten and one, but I have lived over three hundred years. There are youngsters who say I'm conceited and secretive, that I dress strangely, but you mustn't believe such thoughtless words.

Oh, you want to know about **fox henge?** We foxes have lived in the town far longer than any other kind of henge. We're closer to the local gods than the other henge. Not a few of my kind have shrines of their own like me. It is our special privilege to have power over great mysteries, and to bring forth phenomena that some call gods.

Still, as we are so great, we are poor at handling trivial matters. I say that's really the work of other henge. When dealing with the requests or worries that people bring, it's often a virtue to let other henge show their capabilities.

Foxes as animals? For me that's going back some time. As you can see, I'm covered in this beautiful fur, and my body measures a little over two *shaku*[1]. My tail is more than a *shaku* or so, which is more than three *shaku* in all. We don't often need to show ourselves before humans. We must seek prey in our territory, protect the family, and raise children in a den inherited from our parents. The way of the fox is to fulfill our duties as animals to become like a fox spirit.

You think I'm **pretty?** It's only natural. In animal form I have beautiful fur and well-proportioned limbs. In human form I have an alluring beauty. Hm? Did you say "cute"? You should choose your words more carefully! Do not speak thusly to your elder! *Hmph!*

And now you want to know about my **clothes?** Out of date?! No, it's your attire that is strange. Don't say such rude things! These clothes suit me perfectly. Don't lump me together with those who chase the latest fads to excess.

I was once a **hunter.** I'd catch rabbits, birds, and mice and eat them. Since I learned how to change, I've been able to eat people's offerings. However, I haven't forgotten how to be a hunter. Don't think I'll lose in a race.

A child's heart? Maybe I have grown up too much…? Sometimes things seem unbearably dazzling.

The Japanese word for **isolation** is "*kodoku,*" and the first character of that is the word for orphan, *minashigo*, which looks very similar to the character for fox[2]. It's not a coincidence that I'm… by myself. I wonder if all foxes are this way? **sigh**

A fox's den is a complicated labyrinth. In order to protect us from enemies, it has many exits for emergencies, and some dead ends as well. Only the foxes that built it or were raised there know the way through a den. Naturally, my den in this forest is like that too.

There is of course the matter of **seductive** foxes. There are various kinds of foxes. However, I am certain there are as many among the rabbits and cats who are attracted to humans as there are among our number. Though we are long-lived, we cannot be so content as the local gods. We… crave human company because of boredom. Please don't think badly of us for it.

---

1 *Shaku are an archaic unit of measure from Japan. One shaku is about 30cm, or one foot. This length was decided in 1891, and before that it would vary from place to place, but we'll assume that Suzune's shaku is the 30cm one.*

2 *These are* 孤独, 孤, *and* 狐, *respectively.*

I'm Riko, a **RACCOON DOG!**
When I become human I'm a 13-year-old kid, but as a raccoon dog I'm already 3, you know? People say I'm naïve and get carried away too easily and like to take my time and stuff, but I've been able to change for a year now, so I'm already a veteran at it! Such thoughtless words.

Ahem! For **raccoon dog henge**, the most important thing is being able to change. We can change into all kinds of different things. We can turn into scary monsters, or tools, or vehicles, and we can even look just like someone we know! We can also turn leaves into money… Oh, but we never do anything bad with these powers. As much as we can play tricks, there are others who can play tricks on us, so… I'm a good girl, so I don't go trying to scare people.

As animals, raccoon dogs are adults by the time they're two years old. We're only about 60 centimeters long, which isn't all that big, you know? Eheheh… A person could carry one of us in their arms. We live in thickets or dens, or sometimes under old houses. Raccoon dogs don't really have "territory," so everyone gets along like a big family! Sometimes we go into town to look for food, but only at night, so… Eheheheh… We don't meet anyone besides the cats.

We might **look kind of like raccoons**, but we're not. Look: my tail's shorter, and I'm nice and fluffy. Ummm… And, well… I didn't want to mention this, but, um, I'm a little more… plump. ***blush***

So, about my **glasses**. I have these black rings around my eyes, right? So it's like I need them to be able to relax. Eheheh… A lot of raccoon dogs wear glasses like me… right? ***glances around***

A long body and stubby legs...? Please just drop it. ***pout***

Eheheh... I can **climb trees** too. I mean, I love persimmons and stuff, so I have to climb the trees, or the birds will eat them first.

So, when **winter** comes, raccoon dogs grow a thick, fluffy coat and get fatter too. So when we take human form we wear thick clothes and gain some weight. D-D-D-D-D-Don't ask my weight! ***sweat*** I'll be nice and slender in the summer, okay?

Huh? I'm not "**slow**!" ***cries*** Oh, who told you that? I mean, I know that if I was in a foot race with other henge... ***mumble mumble*** but... I think I'm pretty average for an animal.

In Japanese there's that word "***furudanuki***," for an old raccoon dog, and some raccoon dogs live to be over a hundred. I know some of them know a lot and can drink booze and stuff, but... they're not all that different from me, you know. I hope I can be more reliable than that when I'm older, you know?

I'm Kuromu the **CAT**, and as a human or a cat I'm 15. I'm more than enough of an adult, so don't go treating me like a kid just because of how I look. Hm? Even though I'm an adult I have a cat-tongue, can't swim, and I'm selfish? Well, duh. I'm a cat.

So, about **cat henge**. Well, you know, even if we're henge, a cat is still a cat. Sure, we can change and talk, but otherwise we're about the same. We just do whatever we want. Some like to stick close to people, and others never stay in town for long. That's weird even for a cat? I'm just me.

So if I like someone I'll help them, and if I don't like them I won't. If I want something, I'll take it, and if I don't, I'll leave it where it is. Everyone says I'm whimsical, but what did you expect?

Now, as far as **cats as animals** are concerned... What, you've never seen one before? Some cats get really fat, but they're still small enough for a person to pick up. We're supposedly descended from the mountain cats of Libya, but really, who cares? Some people keep cats as pets, but we still just do whatever we want. People can give us food if they want, but I can find my own food by hunting and such.

Of course there are **things I like and dislike**. Even people are particular about what they eat. Sometimes I like something... and sometimes I don't. You don't need to ask about that!

Purring is kind of a rare, special thing for an animal. But whatever.

My body's soft? More like the others' are too hard, right?

Cats' fur comes in lots of different colors. There's lots of breeds too. I'm all black, but there's also tabby cats, striped cats, white cats, brown cats, and so on. Personally, I like my own black fur, I suppose. We always like ourselves, so of course we like our own fur, right?

You can tell how a cat's **feeling** by their tail, right? If it's sticking up I'm in a good mood, if it's swishing side-to-side I'm in a bad mood, and so on. If I like someone, I'll rub my tail against them. Oh, and if the hairs on a cat's tail are sticking out, making it look bigger, don't come close. They're telling you to stay away.

I don't want to be treated as a **pet**. I hang around because I want to. After all, I don't think you're special. Don't get any funny ideas, okay? And stop staring at me while I'm "sleeping." I'm actually awake.

Don't start on those myths about **monster** cat spirits, or two-tailed cats, or what happens when a black cat crosses your path, or witch's familiars, or gods. Someone just made all that up. Don't treat me like some kind of monster. No matter how long we live, a cat is still just a cat. We do what we want, but that kind of talk just makes trouble.

I'm Koro Tanaka, a **DOG**, and I'm five. Wuf? Oh, when I change I'm… uh… ummm… about twelve! And, um, everyone says I'm clumsy and stuff, but, you know, my master gave me a collar, and he says I'm "honest." Ehehe.

So, about **dog henge**. We're dogs, so we're all near people. I have a master, but some don't, but we all still live around people. Since we're always living near people, we like them. All dogs really like people, you know? Out of all henge, we're the ones who get along with people the best. Some dogs can be scary, but they still want to be friends.

Oh, also, a fox told me that a lot of other henge are afraid of us. I just want to be friends with everyone, but… I guess it won't work because I have a human master?

As for **dogs as animals**, if I tried to tell you everything I'd go on forever. Some are big, some are small, some are fluffy, some have long hair. But we all try to get along. Sure, sometimes we bark or howl, and I can talk too. Oh, also, also, we're good at following scents. I just sniff and sniff and off I go!

Huh? What's a "**pedigree**"? I dunno. It's nothing to do with me. I get along well with some dogs and not so well with others. Maybe my master has one?

Whee! **Around and around** I go! I keep chasing my tail, but I can never seem to catch it! Maybe if my tail was long, like a cat's… I can't stop thinking about it. Grrrrr… TAIL! Around and around…

I love **going for walks**! We all love walking! Let's go! Come on!

Ummm… Yeah, we do kinda **pee on things**. I'm sorry. I, um, can't help it. I know I should stop, but I just can't. Ohhh, please forgive me!

We have a lot to do with **how people live**. And our lives always have lots of people in them! It's a mutual thing. Eheheh. Having everyone with you is way better than being alone.

Some dogs **live in houses**. I live outside and I have a dog house, but I keep seeing other dogs watching me through windows. I wonder if they get to go for walks too. Someday, I wanna go inside a house.

So, **wolves** are, like, our ancestors. They're big and strong and scary. I'm not scary at all. Um, there aren't any wolves around here anymore. But deep in the mountains there are still some who became local gods. I wonder if, like, my grandpa's grandpa was a wolf too?

I'm Amami the **RABBIT**. Um, um, I haven't turned one yet, but when I'm a human I'm about 7 years old. Still a kid? No I'm not! I get lonely easily, I'm impatient, and I'm spoiled? So what? Will you be my friend? I hate being alone!

The thing about **rabbit henge** is, we can make all kinds of dreams come true. Including mine, incidentally. Heeheehee. Huh? I can't? H-Hold on! What's wrong with wanting friends? I can transform them and I can make them healthy. Let's be friends! Please? We all get lonely really easily, so you have to be nice to us. And when someone as adorable as me tells you to do something, you'd better listen. Ignoring me is strictly prohibited! Let's play!

Rabbits as animals? I don't really wanna talk about it. Well, I'm just a cute little bunny, right? Hey, don't look at me like that. Okay, so we learn to run when we're really little, and hares turn white in the winter, and we eat grass, stuff like that. Huh? We eat our own poo? I don't know anything about that! Don't say such rude things! Especially to a girl!

The rabbits with **red eyes** are just the white ones kept in schools and stuff. Wild rabbits have black eyes, even when their coats turn white in the winter. Oh, and I'm a white rabbit by the way.

Heeheehee. Aren't these **frills** cute? Other henge don't really think about fashion, but I am a girl after all. I've got to wear something cute. ***twirls and poses*** Human girls are always careful about what they wear. I won't lose to them!

My feet don't have **pads** on them. I'm a rabbit. If you want to touch those, then why don't you ask a cat?

My **legs are fat**...? I think I must've misheard you. Why don't you try saying it again? Oh, by the way, aren't my legs pretty? I'm *really* fast, you know. And I have an amazing kick. It's really something! ***angry, strained grin***

It seems like **I do nothing but run around?** Listen, a delicate girl like me is always facing danger! I can't take it easy. I have to live facing forward with everything I've got!

Carrots have nothing on cabbage. Or spinach or lettuce. I love stuff that's leafy and crisp. I think you understand, but I'm a vegetarian, so don't feed me any meat or fish, okay?

They say the **rabbit in the moon** is making rice cakes, but he must be really lonely. I mean, I like making rice cakes too, but it's way better to make it where everyone is doing it together and having fun, right? I don't like being alone at night, so I always spend nights with someone. I wonder if the rabbit in the moon is okay?

I'm Sarah, a **BIRD**. How old am I…? I'm not sure. I'm a bird brain. Haha, I am a bird after all. I'm also a bit night-blind, and kind of delicate when I'm not flying. I can cause trouble for everyone? But, I can fly. I am a bird.

Bird henge… only really understand the wind and the sky. It seems even when we look human we still say weird things sometimes. Heehee. I can't remember what it was I said. But there are things I can't say because you'd only understand if you can fly… I guess. It'd be nice if everyone could fly.

I like people because they're interesting. Although I do forget a lot and may be causing trouble. But we do know a lot about things you can only see from the sky. So, I'm big and wide and… I don't know how to explain it. I cause trouble, but I've also helped out sometimes… I think. Wait, yes. Yes I have. Heehee. I remembered.

As **animals, birds…** well, there's lots of kinds of birds. There are crows, sparrows, herons, ducks, and other birds that can fly who become henge. I'm a canary. Heehee. I escaped from my cage… I think. There's a lot to eat in this town. I live here without fighting with the other birds. We have different ways of living here, but we all fly in the sky… So we're friends.

Singing… we always, always sing. We weave our songs into the wind. We become one with the wind. While we sing, we become one with the whole sky. Tiny little me covers the whole town. If you want to cry, you should sing instead.

Flightless birds might also become henge, but… they probably couldn't fly in the sky or use the wind like I can. I've never met one. Have I forgotten? Maybe.

Yeah, **the sky** is so big. Even if we all spread our wings and fly, we won't bump into each other. Being blown by strong winds can be scary, but… as a henge I can create my own wind. In the wind and the sky my head becomes quiet… I forget things, but it feels good.

Beaks… are dangerous, so don't touch them.

Also, there are these **migratory birds** who come to town sometimes. And some bird henge too, though since they won't be staying long they stay away from people. Even if I ask them to play, they just want to talk and won't play. The migratory birds seem to know me, but I don't remember… Sorry.

We can't fly in **the night sky**. But there are birds that can. Someone said that. Was it me, maybe? I never could fly at night, but I heard some can if they become henge. I can't. Because I'm a bird. Huh?

One time someone called me an **angel**. I don't know much about angels, but I'm just Sarah, and I don't think I'm an angel. I'm a bird. Maybe angels are birds then? I don't remember what they said, but it was different from what I said.

A Sample Story

Now let's look at an example of a story so you can see what kind of tales you might spin. This is just one example. However, many of the stories you can spin are like this. It all begins with a warm meeting between henge and someone from the town.

An Evening Encounter

It was evening, on a small path. The path was surrounded by fences and a hedge, but it wasn't paved. There was a small patch of open land, where there were two animals: Riko the raccoon dog, and Kuromu the cat.

Riko waved her tail happily and said, "The sunset is so pretty!"

Kuromu watched from on top of the fence and said nothing.

As the two of them watched the sunset, a boy came running down the narrow path. He was still a child, and he was running as fast as he could. Riko walked out, hoping to talk to him, but he was startled by the sudden appearance of a raccoon dog. He cried out and fell so that Riko found herself squished underneath him.

Still a cat, Kuromu had run up to the boy and yelled at him without thinking. "Jeez! What're you doing?!"

The boy panicked at the sudden sound of a girl's voice, and as he started to pick himself up, he realized there was a raccoon dog knocked senseless underneath him. He let out a scream and jumped up off of her.

She stood up and cocked her head. With a puff of smoke, Riko the raccoon dog transformed into a girl wearing glasses. Right in front of the boy. Of course, if you'd looked carefully, you'd have noticed the girl had a raccoon dog's ears and tail.

"Hey, are you hurt?" asked Riko.

Kuromu stayed quiet, but held her head.

The boy rubbed his eyes and sputtered. "Huh? The r-raccoon dog…? What?"

"Are you alright?" asked Riko. She wiped the dust off of the dumbfounded little boy. Seeing that both of them were okay, Kuromu stayed in cat form and watched from the sidelines.

The little boy looked away from Riko, who was right next to him. Riko smiled as she got a better look at him; he was cute. Kuromu tilted her head to one side and let out a quiet, curious mewing sound.

The boy still seemed confused. "Huh…? Um… Uh…"

"Meow," said Kuromu, as she stepped out to where he could see.

"My name's Riko," said Riko. She picked Kuromu up, and passed her into the boy's arms. "And this kitty here is Kuromu, you know? She's my friend!"

Kuromu wasn't terribly happy about all of this, but she decided to remain silent for the moment.

The boy took a deep breath and said, "Uh… Um… I'm Naoto. Naoto Sawada." Naoto spoke falteringly, nervous as he was talking to an older girl like Riko. He gently petted Kuromu.

Riko gently patted him on the head. "Naoto, huh? Nice to meet you, Naoto!"

Being petted, Kuromu couldn't help but close her eyes and purr. With Riko patting *his* head, Naoto couldn't help but blush. Riko and Naoto talked a little. Kuromu stayed in Naoto's arms and listened carefully. Time passed as they continued talking. Suddenly, they heard a voice. When they looked up, the sky has become quite dark.

"Naoto! Where did you go?" called a girl's voice.

Riko blinked. "Huh?"

Kuromu looked around, suddenly alert.

"H-Hide!" whispered Naoto.

Riko glanced towards where the voice had come from and back to Naoto. "But… But… Isn't that a friend of yours?"

Panicked, Naoto hid behind something in the clearing. Kuromu hopped out of his arms and found her own hiding place. That left Riko by herself.

Before long, a girl came down the path, from the same direction as Naoto.

"Huh? Is that Naoto's big sister?" Riko bustled towards a girl who looked a little bit older than Naoto. "It's dangerous to be out walking this late, you know? What's wrong?" she asked as casually as she could manage.

The girl was a bit startled by the sudden voice and let out a yelp. However, perhaps because of how dark it was, she didn't realize that Riko was a raccoon dog.

"Umm…" said Riko, worried that there was no reply.

Kuromu, having just changed into human form, popped out of her hiding place, startling the girl yet again. "What're you doing?" asked Kuromu. "It's pretty late."

"Well, I'm looking for a boy. He's about this tall." She held up her hand at around her shoulder's height.

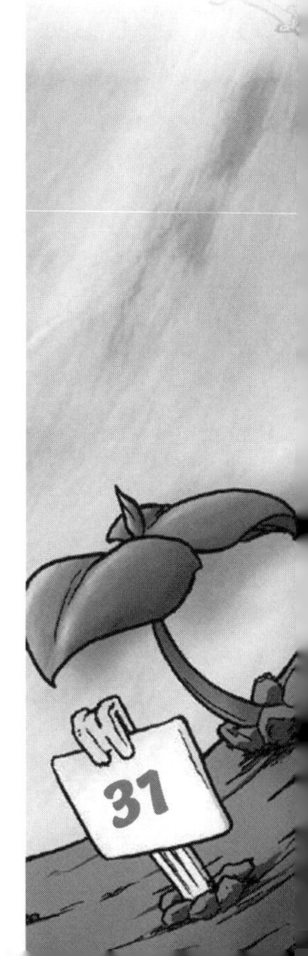

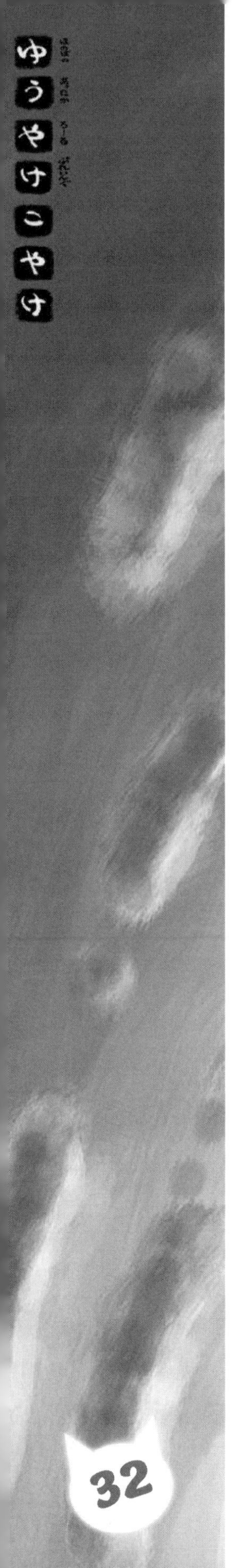

"Well, I don't know anything about Naoto," said Riko.

Kuromu's eyes went wide. "H-Hey!"

"Nope, Kuromu hasn't seen Naoto either, right?"

Kuromu shook her head.

The girl seemed a little offended by all of this. "Look, if you know where Naoto is, please just tell me! Don't hide things from me!"

Getting that kind of look just made Kuromu feel like being stubborn. "Well, I'm not sure we can really help you."

Kuromu snuck a glance at Naoto's hiding place. The girl wouldn't be able to see him in the dark.

Flustered, Riko went on. "B-But… I mean… We don't know anything about Naoto, and he wants to hide right now…"

"Stop it!" Kuromu snapped.

The girl called out into the bushes. "I know you're hiding, Naoto! Come out right now!"

With their animal eyes, Riko and Kuromu could clearly see Naoto keeping his head down.

"What do we do?" whispered Kuromu.

Riko looked at her friend with wide eyes. "H-How did she find out?"

"Naoto! Come out right now!" yelled the girl.

Riko took a deep breath and tried to talk to her. "Um… Um, um… Naoto is scared right now. Maybe you could tell us what's going on?"

"Who are you anyway?" demanded Kuromu.

"I'm just looking for him because he ran away! I've had enough of that moron!" The girl pouted for good measure.

"Hmm. So did you do something he'd run away from?"

"Who knows? Maybe he was too embarrassed from being made fun of? Hmph." The girl turned her face away from them, but finally let out a sigh and said, "Fine. If you know where Naoto is hiding, then you can tell him he should come home. And also… he might be able to hear this right now, but… tell him Yuka isn't really mad at him."

Kuromu mulled things over. The girl slumped her shoulders and started plodding back the way she came. She seemed very sad.

"Please, wait," Riko called out as she followed after the girl.

Meanwhile Kuromu headed for Naoto, who was still hiding. "What happened?" she demanded.

Naoto was suddenly confronted with another girl. Somehow, he realized that this was the black cat from before. Something about Kuromu's haughty expression reminded him of the cat.

"N-Nothing!"

Kuromu the black cat stared directly into Naoto's eyes. She was using her special power as a cat to take a peek into Naoto's heart, because she wanted to know the real answer to her question. In Naoto's heart, she saw what had happened before he came here running.

Although Yuka was taller than Naoto, they were actually the same age. They had been good friends for a long time, since they were both even smaller.

On the way home from school they were holding hands and talking pleasantly. Some of their classmates spotted the pair and started making fun of them. Naoto and Yuka walked away as fast as they could. They suddenly didn't feel quite so good about holding hands, and they let go. Still, they kept walking together.

One of the older people they met in the town said they looked like a big sister and her little brother. Naoto was short, and Yuka was tall. Since he was embarrassed to look younger than her, he ran away.

Kuromu stood in front of Naoto and spoke in a low, whispering voice. "You didn't have to run away over something like that. Why don't you go after her and apologize? She's heading home now, you know."

He whispered back, "But, even if I do

apologize… I won't get taller. And she's way more responsible, and…"

Meanwhile, Riko clung to Yuka's arm and cried out for her to wait.

"Let go!" shouted Yuka. She dragged Riko along as she tried to head home.

"Are you gonna go home without Naoto? He seems lonely, you know?"

"Listen, Naoto—"

Yuka pushed Riko away a little too hard, and made her fall down and scrape her knees.

"Oh! I'm so sorry!" cried Yuka.

"Owww!" sobbed Riko. "That hurt!"

Kuromu hurried over to Riko, who had burst into tears. "Oh, jeez. You…"

Yuka was turning red. "I'm sorry! I'm always…"

"Oww… But still, you were worried about me too, you know?" Riko smiled as she wiped away the depressed Yuka's tears. "You're actually really nice, huh?"

Naoto worriedly watched the two of them from his hiding place.

Kuromu sighed. "Riko's always such a klutz, you shouldn't worry about it too much."

"Grr, Kuromu! Don't be so mean!" hissed Riko.

Yuka pulled band-aids out of her bag and carefully applied it to Riko. "I'm really sorry…" She still looked depressed, and she got ready to leave.

"Um, wait a moment," said Riko. "Please, you really should talk things over with Naoto."

Kuromu rolled her eyes. "Why didn't you say that to start with?"

Undaunted, Riko continued. "You don't have to worry about me scraping my knee. But, you know, I think it's really sad that you two are fighting."

Yuka nodded. "I know. Me too."

Kuromu let out a long sigh, and motioned for Naoto to come out. Timidly, Naoto did finally step out into view. Yuka wasn't sure what kind of face to make, but she seemed troubled. Naoto wanted to rush over to her, but his legs didn't want to move. The two children stood apart, watching each other.

Riko whispered into Kuromu's ear, "I think the only thing we can do now is give them an opportunity!"

Kuromu quietly turned back into a cat and rubbed against Naoto's legs. The feel of a cat's soft fur has the power to melt away people's fetters.

With his own stubbornness melting away, Naoto picked up Kuromu, who was rubbing against his legs, and, hanging his head, walked towards Yuka. "It's dark and stuff. Let's go home."

"Yeah."

"I'm sorry, Yuka." Naoto took hold of Yuka's hand, and gave it a squeeze.

Without a word, Yuka squeezed his hand back.

"Meow," said Kuromu.

"Isn't that great, Naoto?" said Riko.

He nodded. "Yeah. Thank you, Riko."

Naoto turned to look back, but there was no sign of Riko. It was as though it had all been a dream… except for the raccoon dog's tail sticking out of her hiding place. Kuromu looked skyward and shook her head.

Yuka looked confused. "Huh? Where'd she go?"

"We'll have to remember to thank them later," said Naoto as he petted the black cat in his arms and he carefully lowered her to the ground. Kuromu disappeared into the night.

"Hurry and tuck that in!" Kuromu whispered to Riko.

"Huh? What?"

The raccoon dog tail they'd spotted also disappeared into the night, and the two children went back home.

The next day, Naoto and Yuka came to the same spot around noon.

They both called out "Hello!" to the seemingly empty patch of ground, and rummaged through their bags.

"I'm not Riko at all, you know?" A raccoon dog emerged, speaking as she came out. There were band-aids on her legs.

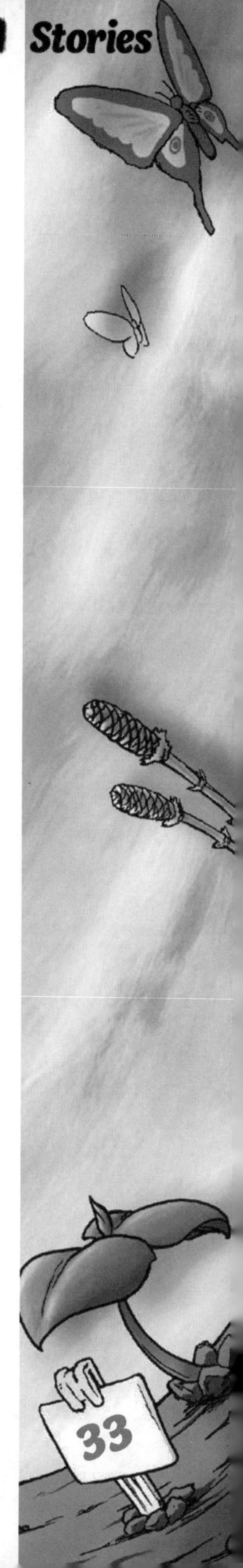

The black cat on the fence seemed irked at her companion's foolishness, but said nothing.

"Hi there, Riko," said Naoto.

"Uh oh, I've been found out…" Before their eyes, Riko changed into human form with a puff of smoke.

Yuka held out the thing she'd been looking for in her bag. She'd brought rice balls, a can of tuna, and a bottle of hot tea. "I'm really sorry I hurt you the other day."

"I'm fine, you know? I am a raccoon dog, after all, so I'm stronger than a person." Riko laughed as she gobbled down a rice ball.

Naoto looked up at where the black cat was perched on the fence. "And thank you too, Kuromu."

Try as she might to stay aloof, Kuromu couldn't help but be drawn by the tuna. She stayed in cat form, and chowed down on her beloved fish.

Riko tried to eat the rice ball a little too fast, and it got stuck in her throat, and Kuromu's cat tongue meant that the tea was too hot for her. Still, the two children and the two henge ate together and their friendship deepened.

This is the story of how two children and two henge from a town in the countryside met. We can only hope they'll become even better friends tomorrow.

Riko's BIG Mistake

Part 1

Riko seems troubled.

Riko: Aaaah! Oh no! Oh no! This is terrible! (flustered)

Elder Turtle: Well, well. If it isn't Miss Riko! What might have you so flustered?

Riko: Ohhh! Elder Turtle! Thank goodness you're here, you know? I have a big problem!

Elder Turtle: Oh? Well, if you think an old man like me can help, ask away.

Riko made a big mistake, you know?

Riko: Well, the thing is, this girl named Kikuna has to move away, you know?

Elder Turtle: Oh?

Riko: But, Kikuna, she said she doesn't want to move away!

Elder Turtle: I see…

Riko: So, I went to see Kikuna's dad to tell him they shouldn't move…

Elder Turtle: I see…

Riko: So, I turned into a big monster, and said, "If you move away, I'll eat you!"

Elder Turtle: Hohoho. Quite the stubborn one, you are.

Riko: But then, her dad fainted and she started crying… Ohhh, what should I do? (cries)

Riko learns about stories.

Elder Turtle: Well, let's see. Even

if one person sees something as unfortunate, someone else might not, or they might see it as truly horrible. Do you understand?

Riko: Yes. Like, Suzune is almost always okay no matter what happens, but if I eat her fried tofu she gets really, really mad, and then really calm, you know?

Elder Turtle: Hohoho, that's true. Even when they're talking about the same thing, different people make different stories.

Riko only saw what she had done.

Riko: Stories?

Elder Turtle: Yes. Even for the same events, people won't always tell the same stories. How someone lives, their dreams, their connections, all of those things come together when they create stories.

Riko: It… It sounds really hard, you know?

Elder Turtle: Well, why did that child not want to move? Did you ask her that, Miss Raccoon Dog?

Riko: Oh my gosh! I didn't ask her at all!

Elder Turtle: Miss Raccoon Dog. Getting rid of something painful might look easy, but… Turning a painful story into a happy one? That's the most important thing. You mustn't rush it.

Riko hurries, for the sake of a happy story.

Riko: Yes! I'm going to go ask Kikuna why right now! Elder Turtle, thank you so much, you know?

Elder Turtle: Hohoho, good luck making that girl's story a happy one!

Summer is a season that overflows with life.
It's the season when the sprouts of spring become leaves.
It's the season when dreams begin.

Here you'll find the specific rules of Golden Sky Stories:
How to create henge to be your other self,
And how you and your friends can play together.

These things are explained here.
You'll come here many times as you enjoy your stories together.

夏 SUMMER

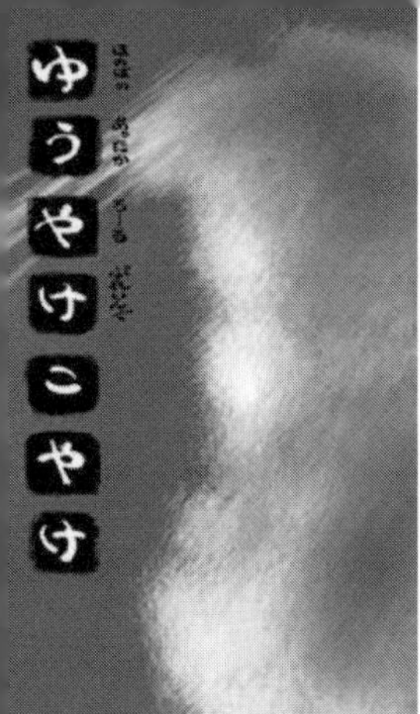

How to Make a Henge

Let's create the henge that'll be your other self.

0 What Kind of Henge?

You might want to just read ahead and jump into creating a henge, but first you'll need to read the explanation of the world, or at least ask the narrator to explain it for you.

If you know what kind of henge you want to create, if you have some kind of image in mind ahead of time, you won't get lost along the way. Do you want to guide other people who get lost? Or keep walking while getting lost together? Or watch freely from a little ways away? Having a general idea of the direction you want to go will be very helpful when you make your henge.

1 What's Your True Form?

First, choose one of the six available animals to be your henge's true form. Each animal has different abilities, but it's more important that you pick one that fits the kind of henge you want. Below are some basic explanations of what the different kinds of animals are like:

Fox (Kitsune): Among the animals, foxes are the ones with authority closest to the gods. Even within the town, they stand above the other animals.
Raccoon Dog (Tanuki): Raccoon dogs are the animals most skilled at transforming. They can change into many different things, not just humans.
Cat (Neko): Cats are whimsical and selfish animals. They can do many different things, but they have trouble making friends.
Dog (Inu): Dogs are the animals who get along with humans best. They are especially good at making themselves useful to people.
Rabbit (Usagi): Rabbits are prone to loneliness and have mysterious powers. They're particularly good at making friends, even with people they've just met.
Bird (Tori): Birds are among the most mysterious of animals, and the furthest removed from humans. They can do all sorts of things with the sky and the wind.

Once you've picked your henge's true form, write it down on your henge record sheet under "True Form." Next, find your henge type in the next section, and record his or her six *Basic Powers*, as well as the number next to each one, which is the cost in *Wonder*. You might want to jot down what each power does, or you could photocopy that page of the rulebook; we don't mind.

2 What Are Your Weaknesses?

Animals have various weaknesses. All animals have them, so there's no such thing as an animal without any. These weaknesses mean there are more things they can't do, and that they'll fail at things you might not expect.

Please select at least one of the weaknesses from your animal type to be your henge's weakness. However, in exchange for each weakness your henge gets the corresponding additional power. If you want more, you can pick up to three weaknesses and thereby get extra powers, but you can't have more than three weaknesses. Also, certain weaknesses require the narrator's permission. Please be sure to read the descriptions carefully before you choose.

Once you've figured out which 1 to 3 Weaknesses you want for your henge, write them down on the record sheet under "Weaknesses" and "Additional Powers." You can still tell many great stories with only one Weakness. Also, your henge might have some hidden weaknesses that could be revealed as you experience more stories. You can just leave the extra spaces blank for now.

3 What Are Your Attributes?

Please divide 8 points between the four attributes. With the exception of Adult (see below), each one has to be at least 1, but no more than 4. As a rule of thumb, 2 is average, 1 is low, and 3 or more is exceptional. For example, a henge with Animal at 3 would win most of the time against normal animals. Likewise, if a henge's Henge attribute is only 1, he or she will be an unskilled henge who has a hard time transforming and using special powers compared to others.

When you assign attributes, Adult is the only one you can have at zero. This means that a henge isn't really ready to deal with human calmness and does not exhibit knowledge of civilization. A henge with Adult at 0 can't use electronics, and would have to be taught even something as simple as making a phone call or turning on a light switch. If you set Adult at zero, you have to be well aware of this.

Henge represents the strength of your henge's special powers, and his or her knowledge of the gods and the other henge of the town. It also indicates your status among your friends.
Animal measures your henge's strength, stamina, agility, senses, etc. It is everything to do with physical strength and animalistic power.
Adult is how well you can hide your feelings, read the feelings of others, use machines, act with finesse, and so forth. This is very high for human adults.
Child represents how well you can express your emotions, wheedle your way into getting what you want, get others to protect you, and just plain have fun.

Once you've decided on how to arrange your henge's attributes, write them down on the record sheet under "Attributes."

4 What Kind of Human?

Next, it's time to decide the human form your henge can take. Unless they use a special power, a henge can only take one specific human form. You'll need to decide the age, manner of dress, and overall appearance of that human form.

A henge's gender always stays the same when he or she takes human form, but there is no such limit on age. A dog might be very old in dog years, yet change into a high school or college age human, while a fox that has lived for centuries could look like a small child. However, in order to easily deal with humans, it's best for henge to look like they're between the ages of 8 and 18. If you want your henge's human form to fall outside that age range, you should ask the narrator for permission.

Unless a henge has a weakness that makes demands on his or her clothing style, he or she will wear clothes that fit the current era, or at least clothes that won't cause undue fuss when walking around the town. (Though henge can change clothes after transforming…) Also, if the narrator allows, henge can wear stuff besides clothes and shoes. This could be a cap, accessories, or a simple prop.

Still, there aren't any particular rules for deciding on your henge's appearance

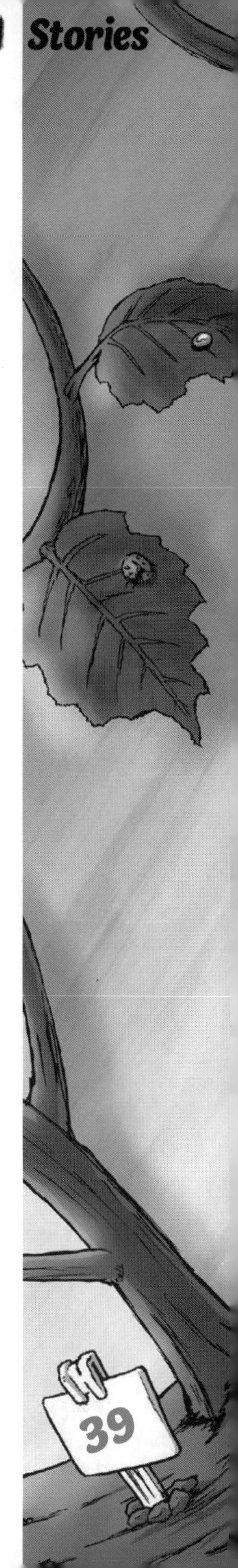

per se. Cats and dogs of breeds from foreign countries might well dress like people from those countries. If you're stuck on your henge's human appearance, first take a look at the illustrations in this book.

Once you know what you want, write it down on the record sheet under "Human Form." However, if you write too much, you could have a hard time keeping track of it. Try to write this description so that the narrator and your other friends can easily understand it

5 Finishing Up

Now it's time to decide your name, gender, and age. You'll most likely have figured out your character's gender along with his or her human form, and have a good idea as to his or her age, but there are some guidelines for names, noted below.

Please decide, then write them on top of the record sheet.

With that, your other self is complete. Listen to the narrator, and enjoy your stories.

HENGE NAMES

As henge are basically animals, they have simple names. In Japanese these should be names written in katakana or hiragana. Here are several examples. Some have notes on what they mean in parentheses. If you're stuck, you can just pick one from the list, or make up something similar.

Ami	Buchi	Buu	Cha
Gin *(Silver)*	Grey	Haa	Hachi
Hachiko *(Famous Dog)*	Hanabi *(Fireworks)*	Hina	Hiro
Hoshi *(Star)*	Ichigo *(Strawberry)*	Jiro	Koro
Kuma *(Bear)*	Kuro *(Black)*	Kuu	Maki
Mao	Maru *(Round)*	Mayaa *(Cat in Okinawan)*	Mii
Mikan	Mike *(mee-kay; Calico)*	Mona	Moro
Naru	Nene	Nono	Nori
Nya *(Meow)*	Piyo *(Tweet)*	Pucchan	Pochi *(Dog Name)*
Poyo	Riru	Runrun	Ruu
Sakura *(Cherry Blossom)*	Shippu	Shiro *(White)*	Shirokuro
Shuu	Sora *(Sky)*	Taiga	Tama *(Cat Name)*
Taro	Tora *(Tiger)*	Ume	Uni
Uno	Wata *(Cotton)*	Yuno	

Pet Henge

Henge such as dogs and cats who are kept as pets can have whatever kinds of name humans might give them, from cliché pet names to ordinary people names to exotic Western names. Some henge kept as pets adopt their owners' family name; see the section on People in the Winter chapter for examples of Japanese names.

Fox Names

Foxes, especially those who have their own shrines, can have flowery, archaic Japanese full names passed down through the generations. You can use Japanese names culled from history, ancient stories, and so on. Here are some examples:

Female Names: Ayame, Kagami, Kuzunoha, Murasaki, Oiwa, Okuni, Shino, Shion, Shizuka, Suzume, Suzune, Yaegiri

Male Names: Bashou, Chuuemon, Danjuro, Genjuro, Hiromasa, Monzaemon, Munefusa, Nakamaro, Osamu, Seimei

Family Names: Abe, Chikamatsu, Hachiman, Hiiragi, Ichikawa, Minamoto, Murakami, Nakatani, Sonozaki, Taira, Tamano, Yoshida

THE ROAD LESS TRAVELED

This book has a lot of things in it that show henge who are all girls helping children with problems. While this game lends itself very well to these kinds of stories, the signature henge are just six possible examples, and the stories in the book are only a tiny fraction of the ones you could tell with this game.

Although all the sample henge are girls, boy henge can be every bit as charming in their own ways. You can also have henge who are a bit older (up to 18 years old in their human forms) and who do more adult things. You can also go in all kinds of different directions to make henge different from the sample ones. Kuromu is one possible cat, but you could just as easily make a cat henge that is an inquisitive, energetic kitten, a prickly mother cat with kittens of her own, or a fat, friendly tomcat.

While children are a natural subject for the kinds of stories that Golden Sky Stories is about, you can of course deal with more mature themes too. A boy lost in the woods might be a good basis for a story, but a grieving widow or a crabby old man can be just as good. You can even do stories about romantic love, whether a teenage couple having issues, or the spider goddess pining for a man who's scared of spiders. If you want to go in that direction, your henge can have family—parents, children, and more besides—and even lovers.

Of the animals, foxes are the closest to the gods, and in the town they occupy a position higher than any of the other animals. As a result, foxes are the most skilled at influencing other henge, but they're lacking when it comes to moving about themselves. They are not the best choice for those who wish to be proactive. Many foxes think much of themselves, wear strange clothing, and because of the many secrets they hold, keep their distance from people.

However, as fox henge have much to do and tend to run all over the place, they tend to be important as leaders. It is their place to calmly think things through, and sometimes to give everyone an adult opinion on matters.

FOX POWERS

Alluring (0)

You have a mysterious charm that can confuse the opposite sex. When a fox creates a new connection with an Impression Check, if the other side is a person or henge (but not an animal of a different species) of the opposite sex, the strength of the connection from them is increased by one. You can also pick the contents of the other side's connection.

Oracle (6)

You can make someone sleeping nearby have whatever dream you like, and they'll think it was their own dream. If your Henge attribute is higher than the person's Adult attribute, you can make them hold back on doing something they were planning or go ahead with something they were holding back on. However, to use this power you must explain the contents of the dream to the narrator. If the narrator finds a dream problematic or contradictory, he can ignore its intended effect.

Fox Fire (6)

This makes it appear as though there's a ball of fire on the tip of your tail. However, you can only use this power in the evening or at night, and only while your tail is out. For the rest of the scene you can use it to make people who see it flee in fear or draw closer out of curiosity. If they can make an Adult check that beats your Henge attribute, they can react however they like, but if you win, you can make them run away or draw closer as you please.

Invisibility (8)

You can make your body transparent. Others can only see the fox if they can beat her Henge attribute plus 3 with a Henge check. This lasts until you decide to turn it off or the scene ends.

Fake (10)

You can turn an object into something else, living or inanimate, of similar size. This lets you change the object's outward appearance to whatever you want, and it will be fully convincing in its looks. However, a rock turned into a person couldn't move, and a broken car turned into a new car wouldn't run. Only the appearance changes, while its abilities (or lack thereof) stay the same. Things changed in this way go back to normal when you cancel the effect or the scene ends.

Fairy Rain (12)

You can cause a light rain to fall in the immediate area. This rain will come down regardless of whether there are any clouds, and it can come day or night. While in this rain, henge can take human form at no cost and they can use Wonder and Feelings interchangeably (i.e. they can use Feelings for powers and Wonder for checks) This lasts until the end of the scene.

WEAKNESS

Fried Tofu

You just love *abura'age* (fried tofu). When you see it, your transformation comes partially undone. If you were in full human form, your tail comes out, and if your tail was already out, your ears come out too. If both were out, you'll revert to full animal form.

Secret

You have a very strict rule against letting people see your true form. If someone does see your full fox form, your connections to both that person and the town lose 1 strength.

Pride

You take an arrogant attitude towards humans and other henge. When others want to increase their connection to you, it costs them an extra 2 Dreams.

Strange

You speak and dress in a way that's out of touch with the times. Because you stand out so much, you can't really hide, and if walking around town in human form, you'll draw everyone's attention.

Cold

You have difficulty showing emotions, and you come off as cold. Reduce the strength of connections from others gained by Impression Checks by 1.

Bluff

You are always exaggerating your abilities. You must spend 2 points of Feelings just to be able to spend Feelings to raise your attributes in a check.

ADDITIONAL POWER

Liar (8)

You can make a person believe a lie you've just told them. If they can't beat your Henge attribute with an Adult check, they'll be tricked. They'll go on believing your lie and acting accordingly until they find very clear evidence to the contrary.

Old Friend (6)

In your long life, you've come to know many people. When you first meet another henge, you can have them be someone you've known a long time, and when meeting a person, they can be someone you met when they were a child. (This also works for local gods.) This only works when meeting for the "first" time. Also, you must tell the narrator how you met.

Shrine (0)

Humans have made a shrine dedicated to you. A fox that has a shrine can have up to 10,000 yen (about $100) of actual money until the end of each story. Also, people will not chase after or harass the fox, though they can still be Surprised. You can also speak to local gods as an equal.

Float (4)

You can float through the sky at a leisurely pace. You can move this way at about the speed a person can walk, and getting up that high gives you a +2 bonus to checks for searching for things. The effect lasts until the end of the scene.

Marriage Knot (4)

By coldly scolding one person in one scene, you can create a stronger connection to another. You can reduce the strength of one person's connection to you by 1 in exchange for strengthening your connection to someone else. This can raise a connection from 0 to 1.

Present (8)

You can give a human an object with a special power in it. Pick any one power of yours or a friend's to put into it. If used properly, they can use that power (with their Wonder/Feelings). You can decide what form the present takes and how it's used, but it shouldn't be too big or useful for anything else.

Raccoon dogs are the animals most skilled at changing form, even among the henge. They can change not only into a human form, but into monsters, specific people they know, and inanimate objects like rocks or even vehicles. Fallen leaves can become money, and the very scenery itself can change around them. In any case, whether it's a human form or something completely different, raccoon dogs are the most skilled of henge when it comes to transforming.

A raccoon dogs' role is to use their powers to get through difficult circumstances by bewitching people and transforming themselves. Their calm, warm demeanors can also help set the mood.

RACCOON DOG POWERS

Money (2)

You can make leaves, acorns, and so on appear to be money. It only works in the evening or at night, and the "money" will turn back into leaves and such at dawn.

Bogey (8)

You can change into a monstrous form to scare humans. People and henge who see you like this will be Surprised. When you use this power, you get a special +1 bonus to Henge for causing Surprise. You can decide what kind of monster you turn into.

Become Anything (8)

You can turn into a tool or a natural object, such as a teapot or a stone. Also, if you change back suddenly you may be able to Surprise people. If you pay double the cost (16 points), you can become something big enough to hold several people, like a car or a shack. However, this power does not let you become liquid, gas, flame, or living things.

Copy (10)

You can change into a copy of a person you know. You can't change into someone you don't know. Also, once you've changed, if you talk to someone who knows the person you're copying, you have to beat their Adult attribute (or the strength of their connection to that person) with a Henge check, or they'll realize you're a fake.

Tanuki Drumming (12)

You can call your other raccoon dog friends and have everyone drum on their bellies together. This can only be used in the evening or at night. People appearing in the scene who hear the drumming sound have their Adult attribute go down to zero, and electronics and other civilized devices stop working. This effect lasts until the scene ends.

Dream Vision (16)

You can surround someone with illusions and enchant their senses. One person is completely ensnared by these illusions, and they'll believe they're in a completely different place. Other people can, of course, see reality, but the victim has to beat your Henge attribute with their Henge or Adult attributes to break through the illusion. This power lasts until you cancel it or the scene ends.

WEAKNESS | **ADDITIONAL POWER**

Cowering
You are timid and easily scared. Any time you are subjected to Surprise, you'll faint, regardless of your check result. Your transformations won't come undone when this happens, but you won't be able to move unless someone carries you.

Swell (8)
You can make your body become massive to Surprise people. People (and even henge) who haven't seen this power in use before can be Surprised by it. If this is the case, you get a bonus of +2 to your Henge attributes for Surprise checks.

Gullible
You just can't figure out when you're being tricked, even when you're in the middle of tricking someone yourself. You never suspect you're being lied to, and even if you as the player fully understand that a lie has been told, your henge will have to believe it.

Carelessness (6)
You can calm people down by showing your clumsiness. You can only use this power when you've gained Dreams for being clumsy. Everyone who saw your clumsiness (though no more than three narrator characters) gets 2 points of Dreams.

Glutton
You love to eat, and if you don't get a proper meal, you can barely move. Furthermore, if there's food in front of you, you have to stop and eat until you're full or the food is all gone, even if you have other things to do.

Stomach Worm (8)
When your stomach is empty, you can make it emit a soothing rumbling sound. When finishing one scene without eating anything, you can use this power during the next scene. If anyone present has a Protection, Affection, or Family connection to you, you can increase their connection to you by 1 (to a maximum of 4).

Carried Away
You get easily carried away when people flatter you. You have to attempt to make checks, even if they're difficult, and even if you know you'll fail (for example, even if your participation isn't necessary).

Tanuki Dance (12)
You can do an odd dance for the enjoyment of others. People who see you dance must make an Adult check of 4 or higher, or they'll drop whatever they were planning to do and burst into laughter. Everyone who laughs in this way gains 3 Dreams.

Relaxed
You move slowly and you just can't help it. You can't put your Animal attribute above 1 when you create your henge, and if you want to raise it for a check, you have to spend 1 extra point of Feelings.

Rest (0)
You can take it easy in order to increase your power to change. You can gain 6 points of Wonder at the end of a scene you didn't participate in.

Teasing
You like to tease people all the time. You get blamed for most of the strange incidents around the town, and because of that, your connection from the town can't go above 2.

Mischief (0)
You like doing mischief, and everyone loves you for it. When you Surprise someone, you can gain as many points of Dreams as there are other participants (including the narrator).

Cats are whimsical, selfish animals. They're quick to act, with little regard for words or for danger. They can sneak in quietly, read people's hearts, quickly hide themselves, and so on. They're talented at acting alone and finding things and thoughts that are hidden.

On the other hand, cats aren't very good at making friends. They're poor at forming bonds with people. They tend to pretend not to notice people, unless they're really in trouble, in which case they'll help... Such is the role of cats.

CAT POWERS

Kitty (0)

You are an ordinary cat, the kind people see everywhere. Even when you are in your animal form, you will not Surprise people who see you, and they will not find your presence strange.

Fuzzy (4)

By taking a friendly attitude and rubbing against someone, you can remove the fetters of a person's heart. While you stay close to someone during a scene, that person's Adult attribute drops to zero.

Peek into Hearts (6)

You can read the heart of another. This mainly lets you hear what someone is saying in their head, not what they're feeling or what's true. Still, it lets you find out what someone's real intentions are from their heart rather than their mouth.

Stealthy Feet (8)

You move around neither leaving any traces nor making a sound. No one in the scene will notice your presence at all; no check is possible. Unless you speak or do something that will overtly make noise, this effect will continue until the scene ends.

Cat Paths (10)

You can use paths that only cats can see to appear and disappear unexpectedly. This lets you enter or leave a scene when and where you want, regardless of whether it's already in progress. This even works if you're doing something different in another scene taking place at the same time.

Friends (14)

You can call the other cats in the town to help you out. This will bring out a number of cats equal to the sum of your Henge and Animal attributes, times two, until the end of the scene. However, with so many cats in one place, you cannot use your Kitty power. If you and your friends don't do a good job of hiding, you'll probably Surprise people you meet.

WEAKNESS	ADDITIONAL POWER
Skittish You are naturally curious and have a strong hunting instinct. When you see something smaller than yourself, or something you don't really understand, you'll go after it. And yet, when its movements or reactions turn out to be something unexpected, you'll be Surprised. (Make a Child check; the narrator sets the required number.)	***Cat Burglar (8)*** You can take something from someone without them realizing it. You can steal any one item that someone in your field of vision is carrying or wearing. You can even steal articles of clothing, but you can't steal vehicles or other things that a cat couldn't carry.
Lazy You're particularly sensitive to heat and cold, and a rather lazy cat. You can only spend 1 point of Feelings for checks relating to actively moving your body around.	***Sleeping Soundly (0)*** You can participate even when you're doing nothing. If you appear in a scene but spend it sleeping, lazing around, yawning, etc., you can automatically get 10 points of Dreams. However, you can't get this effect if you make checks, use other powers, or proactively engage in conversation. (The narrator judges what qualifies.)
Cat Tongue There are a lot of things you can't eat. You can't have hot (temperature-wise) things, citrus fruits, squid, or raw onions. If you eat any of these things by mistake, you're automatically affected by a level 7 Surprise.	***Feigned Innocence (4)*** This lets you hide your true character and put on an excellent act. Declare that you're using this power before you make the check. When you use it, you can use whichever attribute you like for a check, rather than one designated by the narrator or the rules.
Can't Swim You're one of those cats who can't swim and hates water. If you enter a bathtub, pool, or a large body of water, you're automatically affected by a level 7 Surprise.	***Acrobatics (4)*** You can move as though you're practically flying. When it comes to athletic stuff, if you make an Animal check, you can pull off things that seem impossible. (Except, of course, for swimming.)
Selfish You're very independent and moody. Even if you and someone else have Connections of 5 to each other, you'll still only get 5 points of Feelings/Wonder each.	***From the Shadows (6)*** You can be anywhere and catch sight of anything. If you use this power, you can declare that you've seen something that happened before in another scene or story, even if you weren't there. However, you can't use this for things that happened before you were born.
Shred When you see a *shoji/fusuma* (paper sliding door), poster, etc., you can't help but go at it with your claws. When you come across something like that in the town, you'll forget what you were doing and start scratching.	***Menace (8)*** This lets you use a cat's mysterious dignity to menace and drive someone away. Make a Henge check. If you beat their Adult or Henge, they'll flee the scene. However, you cannot use this on a friendly henge.

Dogs are the best at getting along with humans. More than any other kind of henge, they think like people.

Dog henge can do all sorts of things. A dog's special abilities are for protecting people close to them. They can take someone's place, put a friend at ease, and howl to drive off a stranger, all to protect someone important to them. Of course, for a dog, the most important thing is finding that special person.

A dog's role is to be a bridge between the other animals and people. Your other friends can't help but think like animals, so try to help them understand what people think and feel.

DOG POWERS

Doggie (0)

You are an ordinary dog, the kind people see everywhere. Even when you are in your animal form, you will not Surprise people who see you, and they will not find your presence strange.

Sticking Close (4)

When you come to like someone, you can help them calm down. You can even use this at the same time as an Impression Check. When you're both appearing in the same scene and you use this power, they receive Feelings equal to the strength of your connection to them.

Petting (6)

Being petted makes you happy. When someone is in the same scene as you and pets you, you can gain Feelings equal to the strength of your connection to them. You can't just decide to use this power; you need someone participating in the scene to actually pet you.

It's All Right (6)

By licking someone's face and such, you can make them feel better. This lets you cheer them up after they've been Surprised, lost a quarrel, or otherwise had something get them down.

Substitution (8)

When it looks like someone is in danger, you can take their place. If you use this power, you can enter a scene even if you weren't participating in it before and put yourself in the line of fire. If it does turn out to be something dangerous, the narrator may have you get hurt and receive thanks for this act of sacrifice.

Howl (10)

By suddenly barking and giving chase, you can scare off other henge. When you use this power, if your Animal is higher than someone's Adult, they will be Surprised. Henge who are Surprised by this power will return to their true animal forms regardless of their current state.

WEAKNESS	ADDITIONAL POWER
Collar You have a master, and you cannot disobey this person. Regardless of the strength of your connection to him or her, you cannot go against your master.	**Home (0)** At the start of each story, you have a connection with your master with a strength of 2 each way. You can only raise this connection after a scene where your master has appeared. Please discuss with the narrator the kind of person your master is.
Clumsy You're not very good at doing things efficiently or taking care of yourself. Your Adult attribute has to be zero, and you can only use 1 point of Feelings on a given Adult check.	**Perseverance (4)** You have the ability to persevere through pretty much anything. If you use this, you can ignore Surprise. (You must declare that you are persevering.) Also, you can use this power to persevere through your own Weaknesses.
Honest You're a very honest dog who just can't lie. Throughout every story, you can't tell lies at all, not even lies that would be kind.	**Sorry (8)** You're such a good kid that for the most part, if you apologize, you'll be forgiven. By using this power, people will forgive you for almost any non-fatal mistake, but your words and attitude must be properly apologetic.
Shy You are a bashful dog who has trouble with getting to know new people. When making an Impression Check, reduce the strength of the resulting connection by 1. However, this only applies to people you're meeting for the first time, so you can make a normal Impression Check if you have a Thread to that person.	**I Believe in You (6)** You can stay true to your feelings and you keep on believing in someone special to you. You can use this power at the end of a scene. When you use this power, everyone you have connections to receives Feelings equal to the strengths of your connections to each of them.
Naïve Being such a pure, innocent dog, it's not in your nature to distrust or dislike others. You cannot show dislike or distrust towards others during stories. (There's room for a little bit of give and take, but you still can't seriously think of people that way.)	**I Love Everyone (0)** You truly love the whole world from the bottom of your heart. You start each story with a connection to "Love For Everyone" at a strength of 3. (You do not get a connection back.) You can only raise this special connection at the end of a story. Also, if the Narrator approves, you may well be able to start a connection from "Everyone."
Scary You are a scary dog with a large body, and perhaps a fearsome bark. When you make Impression Checks, the strength of the other person's connection to you is reduced by 1. However, this only applies to people you're meeting for the first time, so you can make a normal Impression Check if you have a Thread to that person.	**Go Away! (8)** By barking and chasing, you can scare someone and drive them away. Make an Animal check. If it's higher than their Animal, they will leave the scene. However, you cannot use this against friendly henge.

Rabbits succumb to loneliness easily, but are especially good at making friends. Their abilities make them good at strengthening connections, getting people with whom they have connections to do favors, and doing favors in return. They're also adept at getting along with people they've just met.

A rabbit with no people around can't do anything. It is their role to form connections with many people, to be friends and have fun, and to make happy stories. Rabbits exist to make others—and surely themselves—happy.

RABBIT POWERS

Cute (0)

You have a certain charm that makes everyone find you cute and loveable. The cost in Dreams for others to strengthen a connection to a rabbit is reduced by 1.

Mochi-Pounding (1+)

Mochi is a kind of rice cake made by pounding rice into a paste. Japanese people traditionally make it during New Year's with a big wooden hammer to pound the rice, and Japanese folklore says the rabbit in the moon spends his time pounding mochi.

Perhaps because of some inheritance from him, you can make mochi. If you get someone to eat it, they'll gain Feelings equal to the amount of Wonder you spent on making the mochi.

Lop-Eared (3)

By letting your ears droop, you can look depressed and get others around you to worry about you. You can only use this when you've failed a check. When you use this power, you can gain Feelings equal to the strength of your connection from one other person who is currently in the same scene.

Help Me (6)

You run into someone you know by coincidence. This lets you cause one person with whom you have a connection to appear in the current scene. However, what that person actually does when they arrive is up to the participant or narrator.

I Dunno (8)

You can keep secrets and tell lies without arousing suspicion. When you use this power, you cause one person to stop suspecting you. Even if there is definite proof, they will not suspect you unless someone gets you to admit it. This effect continues until the end of the scene.

Moonlight (20)

You can draw power from the moon and cause animals to become human and humans to become animals. You can only use this on a moonlit night, and only on those who want to be affected. Henge lose their Base Powers (but not Weaknesses/Additional Powers), and humans gain some of those animals' Weaknesses and Additional Powers. Those affected by this will not return to their normal selves until either the rabbit chooses to end the transformation, or the story ends.

WEAKNESS	ADDITIONAL POWER
Loneliness You're prone to loneliness, and you hate being alone. You can't act separately from someone else. You have to always be with someone.	**Friendship (0)** You're good at getting to know people, and you're naturally lovable. Reduce the cost to strengthen your connections to others by 1 Dream.
Crybaby You're very easily brought to tears. You are easy to Surprise, and for Surprise checks your attribute drops by 2. Also, unless you lose consciousness, you will cry very loudly when you are Surprised. This stays the same in human form.	**Please (6)** You can make requests with tearful eyes and get someone to listen. If the person's Adult is higher than your Child, they can refuse. However, if the request is self-destructive, the narrator can choose to ignore it.
Lovesick You are particularly prone to falling in love. When you make an Impression Check with someone, you have "Love" as the contents of the connection formed, regardless of strength. Unless your partner strongly tells you otherwise, you cannot separate yourself from them.	**I Love You! (12)** By proactively appealing to the person you love, you can heighten the feelings between the two of you. This raises the strength of a connection from someone else to you by 1. You can only use this power on a given partner once per story.
Impatient You're very prone to panic, and are always in a rush. Because you're so flustered, you do lots of pointless things. Whenever you want to use a power, you have to spend 1 extra point of Wonder.	**Dash (8)** You're very, very quick when you run away at full speed. You can interrupt any check to flee from the current scene to somewhere safe. You can also take one unresisting human or henge with you as you run away.
Meddling You can't help but stick your nose into other people's business. You're too sympathetic to others' problems and tend to adopt their way of thinking. Whenever you're in a scene with someone who has a connection to the person to whom you have your strongest connection, the contents of your connection will change to become the same as that other person's.	**Remember (6)** You can make it so that you and someone you've met have previous memories together. This lets you increase the strength of a connection someone makes to you via an Impression Check by 1.
Spoiled Rather than doing things yourself, you'd much rather find a way to get someone else to do them for you. With the exception of Impression Checks, you cannot make any checks unless all of your friends have tried and failed.	**Let's Play! (8)** You pass the time playing with someone. When you're not appearing in a scene you can play with others who are also not in the scene. When you use this power, you and anyone who played with you can spend Dreams to increase connections, and gain Wonder and Feelings like usual.

BIRD POWERS

Surveying the land below from high in the sky, birds are the most mysterious of henge, and the most distant from humans. Their outlook is a little different even from other henge, and they have their own peculiar way of thinking.

Birds can fly through the air with ease. Furthermore, they can make others fly, and spread rumors on the wind. Despite these abilities, they have many weaknesses. They're very forgetful, they can't see at night, they have difficulty walking, and they have more trouble understanding people than most.

When a bird flies through the air, it makes people take notice, even if the bird had no such intention. That is the role of the birds.

Little Bird (0)

You're an ordinary little bird, the kind of animal that people see all the time. Even when you are in your animal form, you will not Surprise people who see you, and they will not find your presence strange.

Wings (2)

You have wings that let you freely fly through the sky. You can also carry things that are smaller than yourself. Furthermore, when you are running away or searching for things, add 2 to your attribute. However, you cannot use this power when you are in full human form. This effect lasts until the end of the scene.

Wind Song (4)

You can call on the wind to blow how you wish. If you use this power, you can make the wind blow in an unnatural direction, such as making a piece of paper in the air move how you want. You can cause sudden, powerful gusts too, but not so strongly as to damage things like a typhoon.

Gift of Wings (8)

You can make it so that a human or another henge can fly. You can only use this on people and henge with whom you have a connection. Whoever you use this on can effectively use a bird's "Wings" basic power by spending 2 Wonder or Feelings until the end of the scene.

Rumors (10)

You can spread rumors through the town. However, you cannot spread rumors that are directly hurtful to someone or that deviate too much from the truth. There is no numerical significance to using a rumor, but depending on what it's about, it can potentially help someone (but that doesn't mean you can go speaking ill of people).

Down Pillow (12)

By embracing someone with your downy feathers, your hearts become closer. This strengthens that person's connection to you by 1. However, you can only use this power while you have wings, and you can only use it on a given person once per story.

WEAKNESS	ADDITIONAL POWER
Night Blindness You can barely see at night or in dark places. You can't make Animal checks at night at all.	***Found It (10)*** You have sharp eyes that let you see exceptionally far. If the narrator agrees, you can use it to find an object or person you need to locate in the area. (Actually getting to the thing or person once you've spotted it is a separate matter, however.)
Eyeball You have a weakness for eyeball patterns. (In Japan, these are used like scarecrows.) Any time you see a large eyeball pattern (large concentric circles of different colors, etc.), you're automatically affected by a level 7 Surprise. Needless to say, you can't get close to things with such patterns by yourself.	***Flock (14)*** You can get many other birds to come help you. This will bring out a number of birds equal to the sum of your Henge and Animal attributes, times two. However, with so many birds in one place, you cannot use your Little Bird power. If you and your friends don't do a good job of hiding, you'll probably Surprise people you meet.
Bird Brain You tend to forget things very quickly. You cannot do knowledge-related Adult or Henge checks at all. Even if you as the player remember things, your bird henge will forget.	***Trust the Wind (4)*** You go into action putting your trust into luck, and come out on top. When you use this, you gain 3 points of Feelings.
Delicate You're not very good at doing things on the ground. Whether in animal or human form, you cannot do any checks relating to physical activities (especially with Animal) unless you're using your wings to fly.	***Tranquility (6)*** By embracing someone, you can give them peace of mind. If someone is Surprised, has lost a quarrel, or is otherwise troubled, you can cheer them up and bring them out of that state.
Chatter You are quick to tell people what you know. At the conclusion of each story, you must tell everyone with whom you have a connection what you've found out (except the town, of course).	***Listen Up (4)*** You can inform your friends of things you've realized or seen even when they're far away. When you use this, you can relay information even to people who are not appearing in the same scene. You can also use this to cheer up people who are in another scene from far away.
Distant You are distant from the mundane world, and you think differently from humans. The required result for Impression Checks goes up by 2 for both you and people making connections to you.	***Twilight (20)*** You can cause night to fall suddenly. This works regardless of the time the narrator has described. Until the current scene ends, it becomes night, and henge can use their powers at half the usual cost.

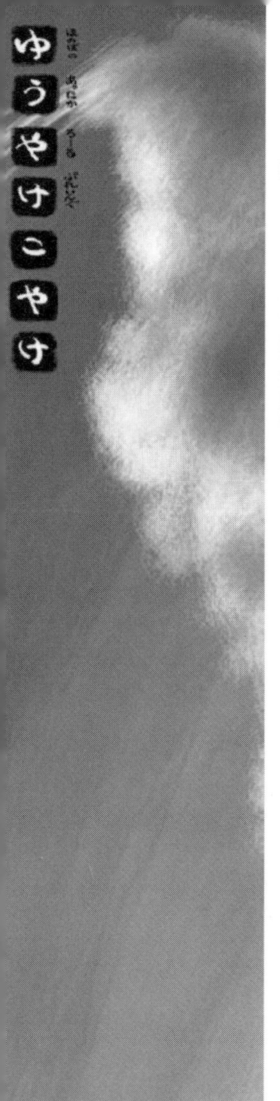

How to Enjoy Stories

Before the Story, Connections

So, by now you should have everyone's other selves all ready, and the Narrator should have a story prepared.

But hold on just a moment, please.

Before you start your story, you need to determine how everyone is connected. The henge are not going to be unfamiliar with each other. They live in the same town, they know about each other's existences, and they've spent at least a little time together. Basically, the henge who participate in stories together are friends.

Introduce your henge to the other players, so that everyone knows about each other's henge well. If you explain how you want your henge to be seen ahead of time, he or she should be able to play the role you want in the story.

Now, once the introductions are done, it's time to set up your henge's "Connections" to the other henge and to the town.

Connections

Connections show the depth and contents of your henge's bonds with people, henge, and others, and to the town itself. They also show how you think of them, how much you treasure them, and how they feel about you. This is where you decide these important things.

Please look at the Connection Contents table on the next page for information on what connections can contain, and decide on your henge's connections to the town and the other henge. This is something you get to decide yourself, and the other party can have a completely different type of connection to you.

Once you've recorded all of your connections, show them to the narrator and the other participants, and make sure no one objects to your choices. For example, having a rivalry with the town would be a little weird. Explain why you set each connection the way you did, and be sure everyone can agree before moving on.

Also, certain Weaknesses and Powers may let you have connections to things other than your friends and the town.

The strength of connections depends on how many people are participating. First, the connection to the town always starts at a strength of 2 for everyone; please make sure two boxes are filled in on the character sheet. Connections to your friends' henge are set at a strength of 2 if there are two of them, or a strength of 1 if there are 3 or 4.

The narrator might decide to have the henge start with a connection of strength 1 or 2 to another character who is important to the story, but unless he or she says otherwise, you'll only have connections to the other participants' henge at the beginning.

Once you've figured out the contents and strengths of the connections, you'll need to record them on that part of the record sheet. The contents and strengths of a connection will constantly change, so you should write them in pencil so you can erase and re-write later.

CONNECTION CONTENTS TABLE

Contents	Description
Like	You like them, for whatever reason. *Note:* The strength of this kind of connection can only go as high as 2. If you want to raise it to 3 or higher, you'll have to change its contents.
Affection	You like them. You're lonely when they're not around. You want to be with them.
Protection	You want to protect them. You feel you need to be there for them.
Trust	You trust them. You go to them when you need help.
Family	You've lived with them for a long time. You understand them very well.
Admiration	You want to be like them. You want to be like that too.
Rivalry	You don't want to lose to them. You see them as a rival. You see them as competition.
Respect	You think they're amazing. You think they're great.
Love	You're in love with them. You love them a lot. Just thinking about them makes your heart pound. *Note:* This kind of connection must be of strength 2 or higher. If it has a strength of 1, you'll have to pick a different contents.
Acceptance	You accept them; you give them a place to belong. *Note:* This is only for the town and local gods. You must have the narrator's permission to select it.

If the Narrator allows, you can have connection contents not on the table above. However, please keep in mind that connections always come from a positive relationship.

Stories and Scenes

Once you've got your connections, the story can begin. The curtain rises on the first scene.

A story is organized into several "scenes," and by progressing through scenes, the story begins, develops, and comes to an end. Only the narrator knows how many scenes are prepared for a given story. Try to do the very best you can in each scene.

When the time or place changes, the narrator can bring a scene to a close and move on to the next. The participants cannot end a scene. Only the narrator can end a scene. However, before the narrator creates a new scene you can say, "Before that I'd like to have a scene about such-and-such." Naturally, it's still up to the narrator to decide whether or not to include the scene you suggested into the story. If the narrator's decision bothers you, consider discussing it after the story is over.

If everyone splits up to search for something, or otherwise acts separately, there will of course be scenes where you don't get to appear. That doesn't mean there's nothing for you to do however. If you read the rules carefully you should understand what it is you need to do.

In this game, stories are essentially about helping out someone who is in trouble (though the narrator may present other kinds of stories at times). You meet someone with a problem. You learn of their difficulties or worries, and you find some way to resolve them. Henge have powers that can help them solve problems that might arise during a story, and sometimes these powers can even help them to be loved.

These stories progress as they stretch across a number of scenes. Furthermore, there are things for you to do between scenes, and after the story ends. Let's go through these things one by one.

Things You Can Do In Scenes

A story starts with its first scene. When this first scene begins, the narrator sets out when and where it takes place and will probably name which henge can appear in the scene. (Usually all of them can appear.) From there you can do any of the following seven things in each scene:

❶ GET WONDER AND FEELINGS

You do this at the very beginning of each scene. Each henge that appears in the scene receives points of Wonder and Feelings based on the strengths of his or her connections.

Wonder comes from a henge's bonds towards others, so it is used for the special powers that he or she can use for the town or other people. At the start of each scene, a henge receives Wonder equal to the total strengths of his or her connections from themselves towards others.

Feelings come from the bonds others feel towards a henge, so they are a very precious thing carried in one's heart. At the start of each scene, a henge receives points of Feelings equal to the total strengths of his or her connections from others towards themselves.

You'll often use these points during scenes, but when the scene changes, you can keep your leftover points. These are added to the new Wonder and Feelings you get in the next scene. For example, if you had 6 points of Feelings left at the end of a scene, and you received another 8 at the beginning of the next, you'll have 14 total. If you don't use up those Feelings in the next scene either, you'll have even more. The same goes for Wonder.

However, when the story's final scene ends (the narrator will tell you when the final scene is starting), you can't save any of your Wonder or Feelings for the next story. Because of that, you shouldn't be stingy with these points; try to use as many points of Wonder and Feelings as you can before the story ends.

❷ TALKING AND TAKING ACTIONS

These are the most important things you can do during scenes. You are participating not as yourself, and you need to speak and act as an animal, as a henge. Stories progress through the speech and actions during scenes. In order to resolve problems and worries, it's important to talk to and work to heal the people involved.

Henge are not called merely for power in a fight or briefly looking cool. They must use sympathetic affection and kindness for mutual understanding through talk and suggestions. Try to speak and act kindly and affectionately so that other participants, including the narrator, will be pleased. Remember, even if a henge is acting or speaking for his or her own sake, he or she can still help and heal others. Also, rather than acting on your own, you should actively talk to the people the narrator presents and your friends' henge.

However, speaking of things one can normally do, henge do have Weaknesses. Participants need to keep their henge's Weaknesses in mind as they act and speak. The description of each Weakness explains how it affects the rules, but there are many that add things you can show through words and actions.

❸ AWARD DREAMS

You can do this regardless of whether or not you're participating in a scene. You can give "Dreams" to the henge and people belonging to other participants—including the narrator—based on their actions and dialogue.

"Dreams" let you show your appreciation to others when they do or say things you find appealing. Receiving Dreams lets both participants and the narrator strengthen connections. Unless henge strengthen their mutual connections, they won't be able to get a good supply of Wonder and Feelings. If that happens, it may become difficult to satisfactorily finish the story.

All of the participants can award Dreams, except the one doing the thing in question. Watch what the other participants do and say, and whenever they do or say something you think is neat, you can give them a Dream. For one bit of speech or action you can give only one point of Dreams. Since each person can give one point of Dreams for one thing that happens, you can potentially get one point of Dreams each from everyone else. This applies to the narrator as well. If you like one of the narrator's characters or descriptions, you can give him or her a point of Dreams. This is important, because otherwise the narrator cannot improve the other characters' connections.

Admittedly, it can be difficult to know what's "neat" enough to give Dreams. You can award Dreams according to your own sensibilities, but please keep the following two points in mind:

- You thought something said or done was cute.
- You thought something said or done helped or healed someone.

Furthermore, it's up to each participant to figure out how he or she will perceive speech and actions. Even if everyone else is giving Dreams for something, you can still refrain. Likewise, even if no one else awards Dreams for something, you can still award one if you feel you should. Don't follow what everyone else is doing, and don't give or withhold Dreams just because someone has a lot of Dreams or only a little. In other words, you should give Dreams based on your own feelings.

Keeping track of all of the Dreams being given and received by writing down numbers would be troublesome, and sometimes it'd be too easy to forget. As noted in the section on initial preparation, you can use some kind of cards or marbles to keep track of Dreams. The "To Become A Narrator" section that follows explains this in more detail.

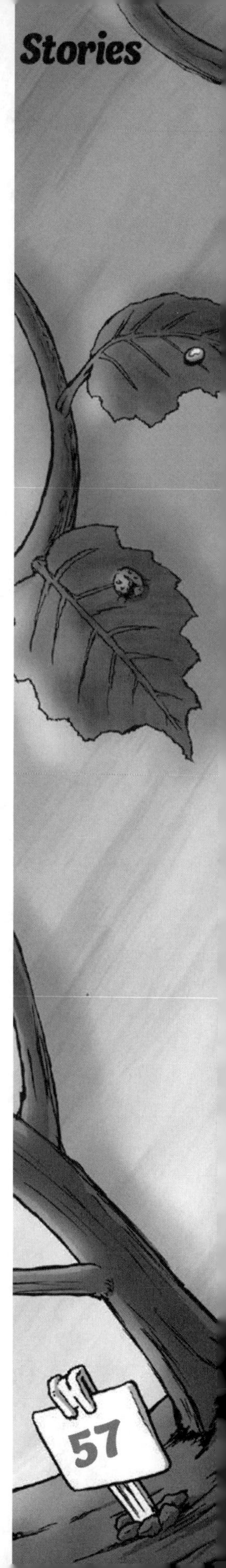

❹ ACTION CHECKS

Although it goes without saying, despite being fictional characters in a story, your henge won't succeed at something just because you say they're going to do it. Of course, if it's something anyone can obviously do, or something that animal can obviously do, you can have your henge do it just by saying so. But there are things that aren't like that, right?

For example, if something happens far away, you don't know for sure whether a rabbit's ears or a dog's nose will help them notice it. In a situation where something unexpected happens, whether you can react calmly cannot be settled just by saying you did. Even a bird would have a hard time flying to where she wanted in a typhoon. When someone is trying to do the opposite of what you want to do, you can't just say "did it" without indicating who did it. The same goes for when you have a contest and need to determine a winner.

That's why you have attributes. We can determine whether or not you can accomplish something based on your attributes. This is called a "check." When the time comes for a check, the narrator announces which attribute it will use, and what total result is required. If your attribute is equal to or higher than the required number, you'll succeed. In other words, you'll accomplish what you wanted. Also, when you're competing against someone else, compare each other's numbers. If they're the same, it's a tie. Otherwise whoever has the higher result wins, even if it was only by 1 point.

However, there are lots of times when you can't succeed just with that, right? When you need to put in some extra effort, or when other people are there to cheer you on, you can do better than you might think. This is where Feelings are important. All kinds of Feelings can help you succeed where you might not otherwise.

If you spend Feelings equal to the amount you're short of the required number, you can increase your attribute for that check only. You can spend as many points of Feelings as you like on a single check, but you can only use as many as you currently have. Basically, you can't borrow points ahead of time, or get them from friends (unless a Power lets someone transfer or grant points of Feelings).

If both sides are using Feelings to compete, they keep raising their attributes until someone can't or won't use any more. Of course, if you're sure you can't win, you can just not spend any Feelings and accept defeat.

Also, if you want to avoid Surprising someone, or you want to be deliberately clumsy, you can spend Feelings to lower one of your henge's attributes. Every point of Feelings you spend this way lowers your attribute by 1.

Sometimes there are things you can't do if your Adult or Henge attributes are too high. That's a time when you might want to do this.

ACTION CHECK GUIDELINE TABLE

#	Guideline
2 or Less	You probably don't need to do a check.
3-4	Well, I'm sure you can get by.
5-6	You can manage if this is something you're good at.
7-8	Normally, this'll be impossible.
9+	No way!

Just remember, creating stories isn't about winning or losing, or even about having the story go how you want it to. Checks are an important rule, but if you worry too much about what they do, you might forget something more important.

5 USING WONDER

Henge possess mysterious powers that let them do things humans can not. By using these powers, they can accomplish various things that humans can't.

In order to use these Powers, you need the energy of Wonder gained from your

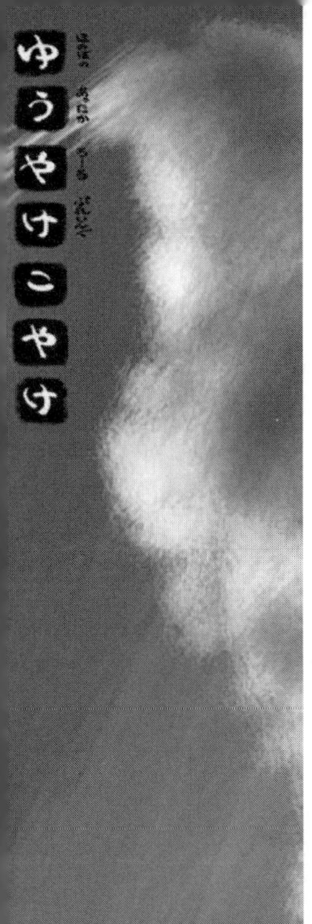

connections to others. Think back to when you first created your henge and picked out an animal type and weaknesses. At that point you should have gotten Basic Powers, plus the Additional Powers paired with your Weaknesses. The numbers you wrote down next to the names of the powers are how many points of Wonder you have to spend if you want to use them. Since some powers require a check too, be careful of how they work and how many points of Feelings you have when you use Wonder.

You can use as much Wonder as you like, but you can only use as much as you currently have. Basically, you can't borrow Wonder ahead of time or get any from your friends (unless a Power lets someone transfer or grant points of Wonder).

❻ TAKE HUMAN FORM

This is another mysterious power that all henge possess. Since henge are still animals, it's because they have this power that they can show themselves to humans. Henge can change instantly, so fast that the time it takes for someone to blink, or a little bit of cover is sufficient. If you think you need to change, do it whenever you think is right, without hesitation.

In order to change, you need to use Feelings or Wonder. You can use some of each, but regardless, the amount you need depends on the time of day and the form you want to take. Also, even if a scene takes place immediately after the one before it, you still need to pay the Feelings and Wonder for changing at the start of each scene. Be careful of the time of day and the situation in each scene.

Also, you can always use all of the Powers on your record sheet, regardless of what form you're in, except those that specifically say otherwise. The same goes for Weaknesses too, so please be careful.

The table below gives the cost of transforming. The cost is a combination of the time of day and the form you want to take. The time should be self-explanatory, but let's explain the form part.

Taking on a completely human form is rather expensive. However, you can reduce the cost by letting the tail or the tail and ears of your true form show through (and if you reveal your ears and tail in the evening, you can transform for free). Which form you will use probably depends on where you are and who you're dealing with. For example, if a fox were to go around in broad daylight with her tail showing (6 points), she'd likely stand out. On the other hand, if she's meeting a friend at dusk or on a road at night, showing her ears and tail shouldn't be a problem. However, please note that unlike other kinds of henge, birds reveal their wings rather than their ears or tails when they change.

One more thing: If you've taken human form, you can revert to your animal form instantly. You don't have to use any Feelings or Wonder for this. If you're confronted with a situation that you can't deal with as a human, you might want to do this, assuming anyone around knows you well enough to know about your true form. Regardless, whenever you change into human form again, you'll have to use more Wonder or Feelings.

TRANSFORMATION COST TABLE

Time of Day	Form (Except Birds)	Form (Birds)
Morning/Daytime +4	Completely Human +4	Completely Human +4
Evening +0	Tail +2	Small Wings +2
Night +2	Ears and Tail +0	Wings That Look Like They Can Be Used to Fly +0

7 CREATE CONNECTIONS

To a certain extent, how you feel about someone you've just met depends on how he or she behaves at the time. When you meet someone with whom you don't yet have a connection and you have a chance to talk to them and see how they act, you'll start to form an impression of them, right? That doesn't necessarily mean that's what the person's really like, but it would not be an exaggeration to say that your opinion of them is formed at that moment to some extent. It's just like that in a story too.

When characters meet during a scene and talk for the first time, they can make "Impression Checks" regarding one another. This is a check for creating connections from someone you've met for the first time during a scene (usually a character introduced by the narrator). Here's how it works:

First, the henge selects which attribute he or she wants to use to appeal to the newcomer. Pick one attribute based on how you want to show yourself to them. Then it's time for the check. A result of 4 gives you a connection from them with a strength of 1, while a result of 8 gives you a connection from them with a strength of 2.

However, you can't use an Impression Check to create a new connection if the other person doesn't want to make an Impression Check back. Be sure to remember this. Also, although an impression check lets you create a new connection, you don't get any extra points of Wonder or Feelings right away. You can get them at the start of the next scene.

In any case, the contents of connections like this are roughly determined by which attribute you use to appeal, as noted below.

- **With Henge:** Admiration, Respect
- **With Animal:** Affection, Trust
- **With Adult:** Admiration, Rivalry
- **With Child:** Protection, Affection

Note: If you're both using the same attribute and your result is less than theirs, the contents of their connection to you will automatically be "Like."

Things You Do Between Scenes

There are also certain things that participants can do between scenes. You can strengthen connections to all of the participants that appeared in the last scene and/or reconsider the contents of those connections.

1 STRENGTHEN CONNECTIONS

By spending the Dreams they earned during scenes, henge can strengthen a connection to someone else. However, you can only strengthen a connection with someone who appeared in the previous scene. If they didn't appear in the last scene, you can't strengthen your connection. Also, only the other party can strengthen his or her connection to you. A henge can only improve his or her connections to others.

Naturally, if you have Dreams left over, you can hold onto them for the next scene. You don't have to force yourself to use them up right away, and you might want to save them up to get particularly strong connections.

If someone does strengthen their connection to you, don't forget to write it down on your henge record sheet. Connections aren't something you create by yourself. You need the other person to think about you too.

COST TO STRENGTHEN CONNECTION

To	Costs
1	5 Dreams (0 with Impression Check)
2	5 Dreams (0 with Impression Check)
3	5 Dreams
4	8 Dreams
5	12 Dreams

❷ CHANGE CONNECTION CONTENTS

Now, another important thing you can do between scenes is change the contents of your connections. You don't have to merely Like someone indefinitely, and sometimes Admiration can change into Love. If, after a scene ends, you think the contents of one of your henge's connections has changed, ask the narrator. If the narrator gives permission, you can change its contents.

Once that's all out of the way, you can move on to the next scene. It might seem a bit troublesome to do all of this stuff to end a scene, but if you get used to it, it'll go by quickly. It might take a little time at first, but please make sure you do it all properly.

Ending a Story

After finishing several scenes, the story has finally ended.

However, hold on just a minute. Aren't you going to tell stories with your henge again? You could have opportunities to use them again. If so, you might also want to make notes about that henge so you don't forget today's story, for the next one.

Henge can still get Dreams during the last scene, but they can't keep leftover Dreams for the next story. Instead, you should use as many of them as you can to strengthen connections. Total up the strengths of all of your connections towards others except the one to the town (don't count connections from others, or Threads). This is how many points of Memories you get for this story. Please see "Other Things" to find out how to use Memories.

Once you've written down your Memories, it's time to change all of your Connections, except the one to the town, into Threads. For Threads there are "Threads From You" and "Threads To You." Write down your Connections To You and Connections From You on your henge record sheet. Threads have contents too, just like Connections. Write down the contents so you don't forget, and keep the precious Threads for later. See "Other Things" to find out how to use Threads.

Once you've gotten your Memories and Threads, your story is finished.

Other Things

This is a supplement to the rules. If you're telling your first story, you don't need to worry too much about these things, but as some henge powers relate to these, we do recommend you read through this section.

PRODUCTS OF CIVILIZATION

Although henge can take human form, they still need to make checks for most anything to do with machines. Henge don't possess any such technology, after all. They don't have cell phones or money, and they can't drive cars. Just making a phone call requires a check.

Please act based on the fact that such actions do not suit the henge.

SURPRISE

Ordinary people tend to be shocked by the sight of a henge changing form or using other strange powers. Henge even manage to surprise each other sometimes. When henge do such things around people who don't know much about henge, or in front of people without realizing it, they can Surprise them.

When henge unthinkingly do unnatural things, the narrator can have people around them suffer "Surprise," which will probably remind the henge that they've done something strange. If it's a particularly desperate situation, you might want to first ask them if they really want to do such a thing.

People who've been Surprised will scream, run away, and so on. Henge might sometimes want to purposely surprise people who are bad or who are causing trouble. However, you definitely shouldn't go carelessly scaring your friends.

If you deliberately try to surprise someone, you need to make a check. Compare the henge's Henge attribute to the victim's highest attribute; if the henge's Henge attribute is higher, the victim is surprised. How they react exactly depends on the margin by which your result exceeded theirs.

SURPRISE TABLE

#	Effect
1-2	The person cries out then and there.
3	The person runs away as fast as they can.
4	The person is paralyzed and can't move.
5+	The person faints and falls down.

FIGHTING

Fighting is not a good thing. You really mustn't fight. But sometimes it happens anyway. When it does happen, make a check with either Animal or Adult. Using Animal means you're scratching and biting, while using Adult means you're punching and using weapons. Whoever gets the higher result wins, and the loser can run away or get knocked down. However, and we can't stress this enough, you need to avoid trying to solve problems with violence as much as possible.

Horseplay among good friends is one thing, but you mustn't go picking fights with people you don't know that well just because you don't like them. Even if you do win the fight, nothing good can come of it.

If your connection to the town is 3 or higher, it will drop to 2 if you get into a fight.

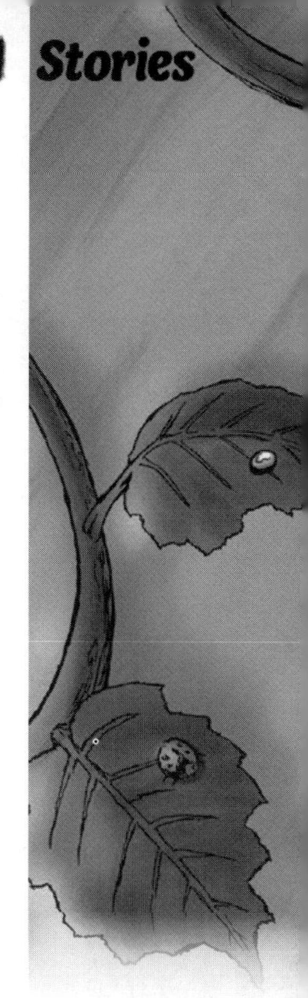

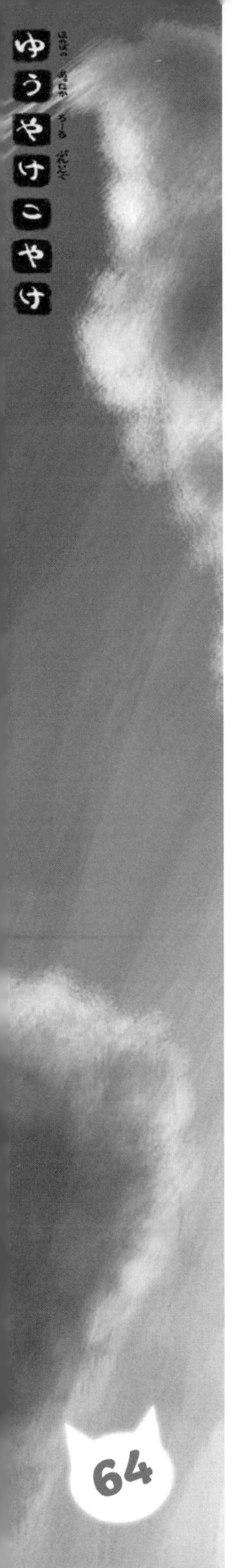

WEAKNESSES

Because henge are still essentially various kinds of animals, they all have weaknesses that they just can't help. How many weaknesses depends on the individual henge, and the more they have, the more special powers they can use. However, sometimes those weaknesses can keep them from moving forward.

A henge can spend a total of 6 points of Wonder and/or Feelings to briefly overcome a weakness. However, this only lasts through a single action. If you find yourself needing to overcome a weakness several times during a scene, you'll have to keep paying 6 points each time. For example, if a cat with the Can't Swim weakness wants to swim to the other side of a river, get something, and come back again, she'll have to use 6 points on the way over and 6 on the way back, for a total of 12.

If a henge just can't overcome a weakness at all and can't spend the 6 points, the participant can remove the weakness with the narrator's permission. (But he or she must have the narrator's permission!) If a henge does remove a weakness, he or she also loses the power that was paired with it. Also, if a henge winds up without any weaknesses, he or she must pick a new one. You can only remove one weakness per story.

YOUR CONNECTION TO THE TOWN

All henge start with a connection to the town they live in, but this works a little differently from other connections. It always starts at a strength of 2 on both sides, with the town's connection towards the henge having "Acceptance" as its contents. It represents how much your henge is a part of the area where he or she lives. If "the town" seems too abstract or stiff, you can think of it as a connection to "everyone." It's not the physical location that creates the bond, but the community, the people who live there.

Your town connection does not become a Thread or contribute to the amount of Memories you earn at the end of a story. However, because the town remains a constant from one story to the next, unlike the henge and people, it is the only connection that remains unchanged at the end of a story.

It is possible for a town connection to rise in strength, to or from the henge. Henge who are feeling particular affection or gratitude towards the community can possibly strengthen their connections to it. Likewise, the narrator can strengthen the town's connection to henge who do things that make the whole community take notice. If a henge's connection to the town does get stronger, it stays stronger into future stories.

STRONG CONNECTIONS

It often happens that both sides of a connection reach a strength of 5.

When a connection forms a line across the henge record sheet, those on both sides of the connection receive a total of 10 points each of Wonder and Feelings at the start of the next scene as a special reward.

If you have one of these strong connections at the end of a story, both sides get two Threads to one another (use two boxes for threads). These two Threads can have the same contents, or they could have different ones if their relationship is more complex.

SHOWING UP

If the narrator hasn't let you appear in a scene and you think you could, or you want to, you should ask the narrator directly. It's up to the narrator to decide whether a henge can appear in a given scene, but you shouldn't let a good opportunity pass you by.

You might also wind up taking part in a different scene that takes place at the same time and place, but you'll want to play together as much as you can.

MEMORIES

Henge are stronger than usual when they have lots of memories to draw upon. You can use your points of Memories

as Wonder or Feelings when you need them during stories. However, once you use them they're gone, and you don't get them back when the scene changes.

You can keep the Memories you have at the end of one story for the next. Also, the new Memories you gain are added to the ones you didn't use. For example, if you have 10 points of Memories and you only use 2 during the course of a story, you'll have 8 left. If you earn another 12 points during the next story without using any, you'll have 20 points to use.

THREADS

When a story ends, all of the connections you've created, except for the one to the town, become Threads instead.

A Thread is an unforgettable "connection" that endures through multiple stories, even if the other person doesn't appear in a given story. Regardless of how many threads you have, they don't directly influence the story. However, if you encounter someone with whom you have a Thread in another story and you're able to interact with them again, you can turn the thread into a new connection with the same contents and write it down on your henge record sheet, with its strength increased by 1 for each Thread you have with them. (Don't forget to check their threads to see the ones they might have back to you.) If you do turn a thread into a connection like this, you lose that thread. However, you get to create a new thread at the end of the story.

For example, at the start of a story, a connection with a friend typically starts with a strength of 2, but if you had a story with them before, you start with a connection at 3 (or 4 if you have two Threads with them). Furthermore, if the narrator has you make an Impression Check for a character he or she has introduced, the connection is strengthened by the number of Threads you have to them.

Threads are a weaker version of connections, but they can be very important if you continue telling stories for a long time.

Part 2

Kuromu isn't really interested in hearing about how to save friends.

Kuromu: Hey gramps, you seen Riko?
Elder Turtle: Hohoho. A little kitty this time? Quite a lively day, this is.
Kuromu: So she did come by here. Riko was saying something about some kind of mistake.
Elder Turtle: I see… So you want to help her, eh?
Kuromu: Well, whatever. What would you do if one of your friends was troubled?

What does knowing someone's story have to do with it?

Elder Turtle: Well. I see. If it was me, first I would come to know of their story. And I would ask that friend what that story means to them.
Kuromu: Just ask?
Elder Turtle: Hohoho. If you're having a hard time, it helps if someone else knows about it. It's painful to keep a story to yourself. The burden is less if you split the story with someone else.
Kuromu: Hmm… I guess so.
Elder Turtle: Of course. However, you've got to be careful, haven't you? Even if you think what she did was

foolish, it might still be painful for her. You can't just dismiss it as "no big deal." Listen to your friend; find out why it's so difficult for her.

But what if it was just too much for her to bear?

Kuromu: But, if you're really at your wit's end, what good will having someone listen do?

Elder Turtle: When that happens, it's time to break down the painful story.

Kuromu: That sounds… violent?

Elder Turtle: Hohoho. You're not breaking the thing itself. You're breaking the story that's causing that person such pain. For example… Ah, I know. A story that says, "This is my mistake, so I have to fix it by myself." If a story like that is causing your friend pain…Then you need to break it, and that could help your friend.

Kuromu: I get it. You're not busting the thing itself, but you have to get rid of that painful story.

Elder Turtle: Hohoho. And if the story that goes "No one will help me" is causing someone pain, you should do your best to help them. If it's "I'm lonely," be their friend. Only a good friend can break down a painful story.

You have to turn sad stories into happy ones.

Kuromu: Thanks, old man. I'm going to head out now.

Elder Turtle: One last thing. I need to tell you how to look for the best kind of story. That's where you change the story's meaning.

Elder Turtle: It's the same story from the same person, but if you change its meaning, a painful story can become a happy one. The story, "I have to fix this by myself" doesn't have to be a story of loneliness. It can become, "I have the confidence to fix this with my own strength" instead. If you do that…And, you've already left, it seems. Youth is so wonderful…

Everyday Magic

According to designer Ryo Kamiya, *Golden Sky Stories* is part of a genre called "everyday magic," a distinction it shares with a much older Japanese RPG called *Witch Quest*[1]. Everyday magic stories are heartwarming stories about everyday life with some magic to make them a little more interesting, a little more wondrous.

Non-Violent Role-Playing

If you've played many other role-playing games, you're probably used to telling stories with violence. *Golden Sky Stories* is a game without fighting. This isn't because we think that stories with battles are bad, but rather because stories without them can be good in their own ways.

Telling stories without any violence may be hard if it's not what you're used to, but most stories you read or watch probably don't actually have the characters resolve problems with violence. The henge in your stories might have to deal with a bully or someone who's very stubborn, but there are no "villains" per se. If someone is doing something bad, it's because they either have what they think is a good reason, or they're not thinking about the feelings of others. If that happens, your goal isn't to prove that they're wrong or that they're weaker than you, but to put all your heart into showing them that there's a better way.

This game doesn't lend itself to having an ending prepared in advance because the resolution of a story depends on changing people's minds and opening their hearts. The henge need to not only solve problems, but meet someone and become friends with them. (Though the two can be the same thing!) The appeal, the catharsis of completing a story in *Golden Sky Stories* is that you work towards finding a way to make people happy. And it should be possible to make everyone happy.

One thing that helps is for everyone to be on the same page at the start. In a fantasy RPG, if a group of adventurers are in a tavern and find someone is offering them payment to clear out a dungeon, the narrator is basically saying, "This is the hook for the story I planned. Go here and we can get started." Stories in Golden Sky Stories are based on the idea that someone is troubled and the henge get to help them, so the participants can come to the table with that in mind. When the first scene starts with the henge running across a crying boy, the participants know that this will lead them to the meat of the story.

Little Stories

Golden Sky Stories is a little game for little stories. It's hard to fully grasp just how small the scale of a *Golden Sky Stories* story is supposed to be just from hearing the game's concept. Fantasy adventurers can go on great journeys that last months or even years, and encounter hundreds of people and other things along the way. *Golden Sky Stories* is a role-playing game where a typical session is about events that might take place over the course of an hour or less, and involve two to four henge and one to three narrator characters. Henge might walk from the forest into town, but that's about the limit of their mobility. They are never far from home.

What you gain from telling such small stories is intimacy. Your henge, and the handful of people they meet, can all become good friends, and that's the main thing you're there to do. Your henge won't really leave the town, but if you keep playing regularly, you can really get to know the town and its inhabitants.

[1] *Witch Quest is an RPG about young witches and their cat familiars, very much in the vein of* Kiki's Delivery Service. *The game was originally created by* Adventure Planning Service *and published in 1991. It is currently being published by a fan group called* Majo no Kai.

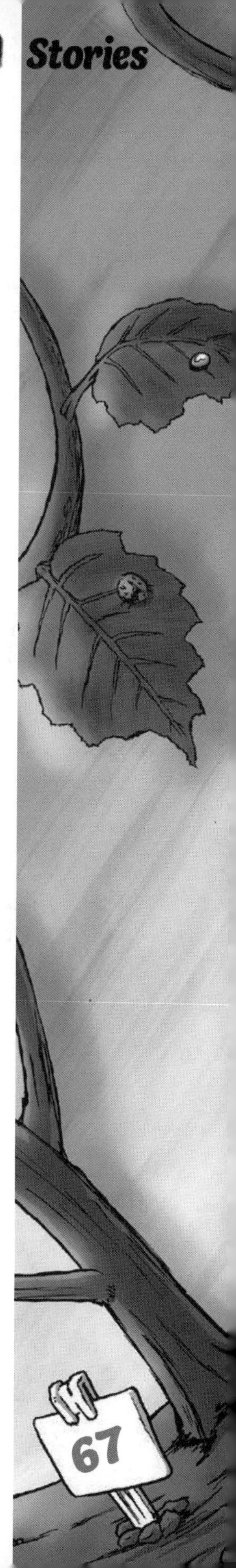

All of this is also important because of the way the rules are structured. As written, the rules limit the number of characters basically because the balance of the various point pools starts to break down if you have too many. If the henge have more than 5 or so connections each, they wind up with enough Wonder and Feelings that they can likely power their way through any obstacle put in their way.

Finally, stories in *Golden Sky Stories* are small in terms of what's at stake. There's no need to put henge into desperate situations where they have to fight for everything they hold dear. That's some other game. You don't need a "conflict" per se, so much as a "wrinkle" that the henge can help straighten out. When you put together a story, it's a truism that the protagonists should be absolutely necessary, but for this game that isn't necessarily the case. While the henge can solve problems, a lot of the time what they do is more to nudge people in the right direction and make things work out better and sooner. The boy and girl from "An Evening Encounter" probably would've patched things up eventually, but thanks to Riko and Kuromu they did so that evening rather than letting it drag on, and they made two new friends along the way.

Autumn is the season of ripening,
The season when flowers give the blessing of fruit.
The season that brings dreams.

Here you'll learn about the narrator's role in Golden Sky Stories.
What should a narrator do?
How do you tell stories?

Take in what's written here.
From here, you'll create your own stories.

秋 AUTUMN

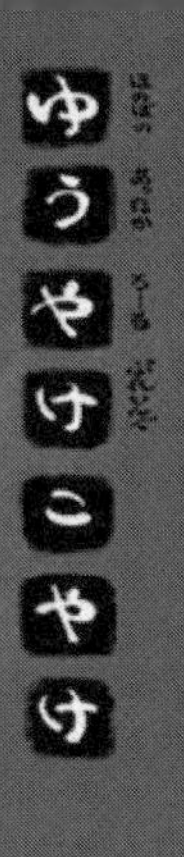

To Become a Narrator

Preparing to Narrate

To play *Golden Sky Stories* both the narrator and his or her friends need to prepare. There are several things you have to prepare in advance, but none of them cost money. Start with the things below. The narrator doesn't have to do these preparations alone. Everyone can lend a hand.

NARRATOR AND FRIENDS

You don't create stories alone. As the narrator, you'll need some friends to participate. For this game, a group of two to three players is best. You can go as high as four, but five is too many. It becomes hard for one narrator to keep track of everyone, and there are only so many places for henge to take part.

THIS BOOK

In order to create stories, you'll need the rules in this book. Even if you're sure you can remember most of the rules, when you're starting out you might want to copy the pages with the important ones, and keep the book handy just in case.

HENGE RECORD SHEETS

These record sheets are for writing down the henge that are the players' other selves and characters the narrator wants to introduce. You need at least as many sheets as there are participants. There's a henge record sheet in the back of this book and on our website (starlinepublishing.com); you can make as many copies as you want for playing the game.

PENCILS

You need to be able to write and erase all kinds of things on the henge record sheets. Pencils are best, whether regular or mechanical, and you'll need erasers to go with them. Don't use pens or anything else that you can't erase later.

CARDS/MARBLES

Keeping track of who's given who how many Dreams using numerals can be difficult, and sometimes you might just forget.

We suggest using cards, marbles, or some such to represent Dreams. Put your cards or marbles in the middle of the table; participants take them from there to give them to others, and put them back when they spend them on strengthening Connections.

However, the more stories you enjoy, the more cards or counters you'll need. Try to have as many on hand as you can.

A TIME AND PLACE

First, the person who will become the narrator needs time to read this book. Then you need a time and place for everyone who'll be playing to gather. Try to find a place where everyone can assemble for a few hours and where you can make a little noise.

GENTLE FEELINGS

Don't forget your gentle feelings towards the characters that appear, and your friends...

The Role of the Narrator

As the narrator, you do not participate in stories as a henge like your friends, but you get to do many things they do not.

1. Create a Town
2. Prepare a Story
3. Drive the Story
4. Be a Referee
5. Portray Other Characters

The narrator can do all of the things listed above. Or rather, he or she *must* do them.

The narrator bears the important role of guiding the story. In order to make the story more wonderful, everyone should try this at least once. You should come to understand things you wouldn't if you just participated as a henge.

Now, let's explain these duties in detail.

CREATE A TOWN

Don't think of this as a difficult task. First, come up with a name for the town. You can just take a Japanese family name and add "Town" on the end, or you can just use the name of a real Japanese town. This is will be the town you use to play in as the narrator.

Next, decide in broad terms the natural world that surrounds the town. This doesn't have to be too detailed either. You can just go off of an area you know well. Is there a big river? Is there proper electricity? Is the sea nearby? Is there a train station? Is it surrounded by mountains? Does a lot of snow fall in the winter? Or does no snow fall there at all? Be sure to tell everyone about things that make the town unique.

How far is the post office from the train station? What kind of playground equipment is there in the park? Everyone can make up these kinds of fine details during stories. If someone wants something to be in the town, the narrator decides if it is.

Over the course of the story, everyone will be asking the narrator questions like, "Does the park have a see-saw?" and "Does the town have a convenience store?" The narrator should take the needs of the story into account, but can decide however he or she wants. However, you should think about the long term, and make notes about these things as you go along. It would be troubling for the people of the town if it kept changing every time a new story started.

As the narrator, you create a town for you and your friends. Make a town that will make everyone happy. If you're having a hard time making a town that you like, feel free to use Hitotsuna Town from the Winter chapter.

PREPARE A STORY

This is the narrator's most important job. Stories don't just spring out of nothingness. You need a rough outline for the story.

First of all, if you're being the narrator for the first time, try using the stories at the end of this chapter or the example story towards the beginning. Then, once you're used to it, try using the "story fragments" scattered throughout the *Winter* chapter to help create your own stories. Of course, if you can create your own story, go ahead and use it.

When preparing for a story, you only need to set up as much as you yourself find necessary. In other words, you don't have to write a detailed summary like the stories in this book. Of course, if you feel it doesn't have enough detail for you, you can add more.

Now, a story needs to have someone who is troubled. They can be an animal, a henge, or a local god rather than a human if you like.

Someone is troubled by *something*.

That is the basic story for this game. This "something" can't be someone's evil intentions or something that has to be exterminated. A lot of the time it will be something where other people or even

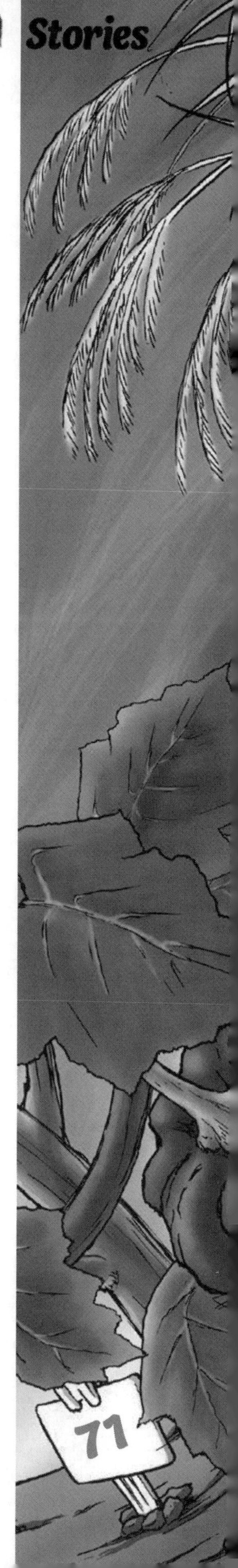

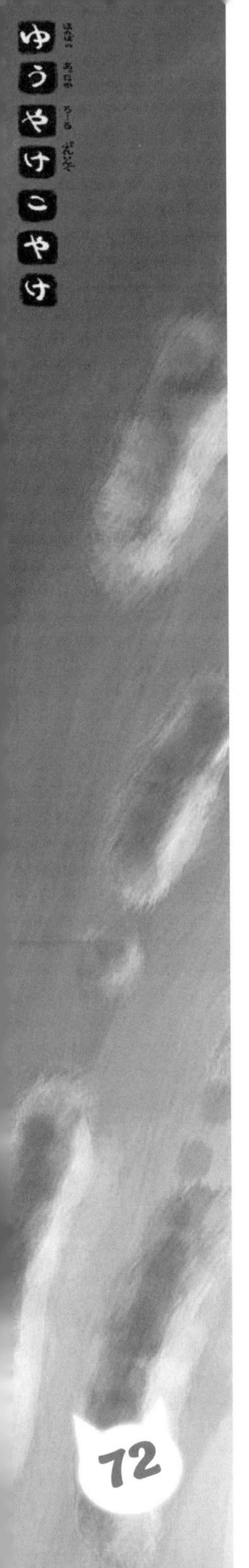

the troubled person can do something about it. However, that means that "saving" someone takes on a different meaning. Look at the stories and story fragments in this book, and think about the same kinds of easily solved problems. Put simply, once you figure that out, the story is ready. The role of the henge is to give that troubled person the power to move one last step forward. That means that in a sense the narrator's job is to find a troubled person, and bring him or her and the henge together.

As the narrator, once you've gotten them to meet with the troubled person, guide them towards finding a way to help that person. Give the henge who were so kind as to help out a sense of relief at the end. This is the narrator's most important job and most important responsibility.

It's also necessary to decide on the when and where, as well as what kind of places the henge will have to go to resolve the situation. That will determine how many scenes make up the story. One story should have about four or five scenes. Look at the example stories in this book to see how it's done.

Even if a story occurs entirely in one place, there will still be plenty of opportunities to change scenes. Otherwise, there won't be any Wonder or Feelings for that story.

These are the most basic rules for preparing a story, but unlike those who participate as henge, the narrator has a set number of points of Wonder and Feelings. Instead of gaining Wonder and Feelings as the scenes progress, the narrator gets 10 to 20 points each of Wonder and Feelings to spend per scene. Even if you have points left over, you can't save them for later.

As a rule of thumb, it's 10 points each of Wonder and Feelings for a normal story, and 20 for a story with henge and/ or local gods.

The amount of Wonder and Feelings set for the narrator doesn't change even if there are lots of characters appearing. This rule is actually to lessen the narrator's burden. This also affects how the narrator's characters influence the henge's connections. Once participants are more used to the rules, you can tell them about this rule.

DRIVING THE STORY

Narrating the story is also the narrator's job. You have to tell your friends about the story's time and place, the season, the weather, people's footsteps, etc. However, if you're not used to this, remember you don't have to describe every little detail.

You could start off by saying, "It's autumn, a dim twilight, and you're in the park. Since the sky's dark, the children have all gone home and no one else is here."

After that, everyone could well ask what kind of place the park is, what it's usually like. Even if they don't ask, you should still add or change the description when it's necessary or convenient.

"It's started raining over the park."

When this happens, everyone will probably start looking for somewhere to take shelter from the rain. If you think of that ahead of time, you could tell them that there is a good place to take shelter or wait until they ask you.

"When you get underneath the slide to get out of the rain, you find an envelope there."

Thus, through answering the participating henge's questions, you can drive the story forward. Of course, they may well not ask questions, or they might do things you didn't expect. When that happens, you'll have to do your best to play it by ear and move things forward. If in the above example, the henge had decided to leave the park, you could say:

"At the entrance to the park, you spot a damp envelope."

Or, if you can't think of something else, you could have everyone make a check (in this case, probably on Animal), and say to the one who got the highest result:

"As you're leaving the park, you realize that there's an envelope underneath the slide that looks like someone forgot it."

That'll also make it easy to keep the story moving forward.

Thus, once the story moves from a playground in the evening to another location, it's time to move to a new scene.

When you change the location, you need to change scenes, and often the time as well, from morning to day, day to evening, evening to night. That means you need to prepare several scenes for the story. However, sometimes the participants will want to do scenes that are different from your plans, or you might even feel that different scenes are necessary, in which case you'll have to improvise as best you can.

The narrator's job is to drive the story forward, but that does not mean you should restrain the henge's actions. Try to figure out how to move the story you prepared forward while still respecting the judgments and actions of the henge.

BE A REFEREE

Another important job for the narrator is deciding what attributes henge use for checks and the required attribute numbers for those checks. Look at the part on checks to see how to set up checks and their required numbers. Sometimes you can figure out what attribute to use for a check by getting everyone's opin-

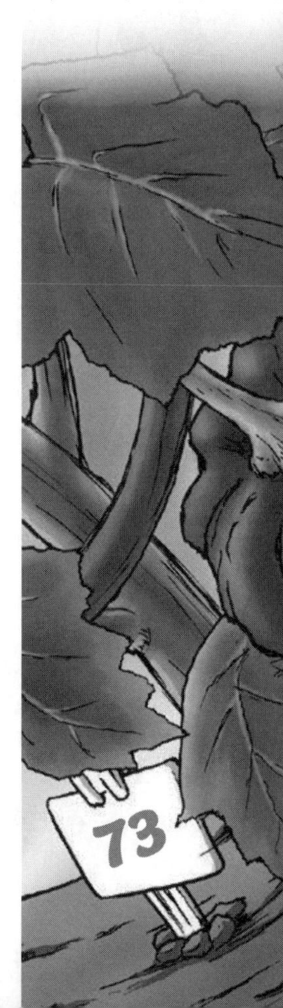

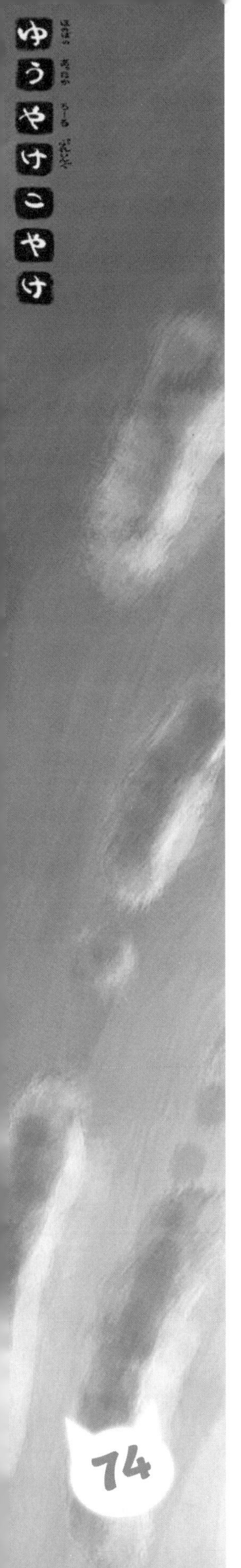

ions. It still falls to the narrator to decide which attribute to use. If you have a really hard time picking one, you can list off two or more possible attributes and let the person making the check pick one.

Also, as the narrator you mustn't forget to watch the henge's speech and actions, and take the initiative in awarding Dreams. If the narrator doesn't start handing out Dreams right off the bat, it may take longer for the players to get into it. Try to start giving out Dreams early, so that the participants can learn from your example.

There's one more thing, which the narrator needs to do in secret: Keep a good grasp of the henge's weaknesses.

Before you begin a story, take a look at each henge record sheet, and make some notes. Each henge should have at least one weakness. You don't have to know their weaknesses in every last detail, but you definitely need to have some idea what they do. When henge try to do things that would go against their weaknesses, make sure they haven't forgotten and remind them that they can't do such things.

Naturally, participants should be sure to remember their own henge's weaknesses, and if they use them well you can reward them with Dreams.

PORTRAY OTHER CHARACTERS

This is the most important thing for the narrator. You have to portray troubled people in an appealing way.

A troubled person (or henge, animal, or local god) that the henge can help out forms the heart of a story. Thus the troubled person has to be someone that the henge will want to help. Playing the part of that kind of person is the narrator's job. This is perhaps the most difficult part of the narrator's role.

You can draw on comics, novels, TV shows, movies, etc. to help polish your skills, and try your hand at playing a henge to actively work to improve your acting ability. Work hard to create a "troubled person" that the henge will find appealing and that you yourself will enjoy playing. You can learn what to do from the Dreams you receive from everyone else too. If you get a Dream, then the players find it appealing, so keep doing whatever it is you're doing, but don't overdo it, or they'll get bored.

The narrator also has to portray the "extras," passers-by who happen to be in the area. If they don't have any particular connection to the story, you just need to let the participants know that those people do in fact exist, but sometimes there are multiple people who are important to the story. When that happens, you need to be able to skillfully portray all of them. Still, until you're more used to being the narrator, it's better to avoid getting too caught up in things, and instead concentrate on thoroughly portraying the central character.

This might seem like a foregone conclusion, but take care that you portray your characters in such a way that the henge do not ignore them.

Also, don't forget to create connections from these characters.

If you can portray them in an appealing way, you'll get plenty of Dreams between scenes. You don't need to keep track of which Dreams were awarded for what character.

Please use your Dreams to strengthen your characters' connections between scenes. The participants' henge aren't the only ones that form connections, after all. Try to put yourself in that person's shoes as you decide whose connections you want to strengthen.

An Actual Story

We've now explained all of the rules you need to create stories. However, there are things that are difficult to understand with just an explanation, things you wouldn't get if you just jumped in and tried to play. In order to avoid at least some of those problems, let's take a closer look at the "An Evening Encounter" story from the *Spring* chapter. This will show you how it was actually played. Please use this as an example when you create your own stories.

First comes the preparation before the story. Suzune has prepared a place, and picked a time that is convenient for her two friends to play *Golden Sky Stories*. The story in the *Spring* chapter begins right away, but in reality they had to prepare first once they had gathered together.

Creating Henge

Suzune: All right, let's begin the story. I shall be the narrator, and you two shall create henge. Write on these record sheets. (She hands each of them a henge record sheet.)

Riko: Uh, okay. Thank you!

Kuromu: So, what do we do?

Suzune: Well, first pick what kind of henge you want to be. You have six kinds to choose from. (She opens this book to the henge introduction page and shows them.)

Riko: Wow, there's a lot! (gawks)

Kuromu: (stares) … I'll be a cat.

Riko: Woah, what? So fast! (worried)

Suzune: There's no need to rush. But don't dawdle too long either.

Riko: Uhhhh… Okay, I'll be a raccoon dog!

Suzune: Very well. Now that you've decided, pick your weaknesses. Pick at least one from the six choices. If you want several, you can have up to three. (She hands photocopies of the henge powers to each of them.)

Kuromu: Do you get something for taking lots?

Riko: Every weakness looks like it'll make things difficult, you know?

Suzune: In exchange, you get the corresponding power. You have to take the weakness to get those powers.

Riko: Woah! So if you have a lot of weaknesses you can do a lot of different stuff?

Kuromu: Hmm… Okay, I'll take Cat-Tongue, Can't Swim, and Selfish. That gives me Feigned Innocence, Acrobatics, and From The Shadows, right? (She writes them on her sheet.)

Suzune: Yes. Exactly.

Riko: Umm… Uh… Okay, I'll take Gullible, Carried Away, and Carefree, you know? That gives me Carelessness, Tanuki Dance, and Rest. (scribble scribble)

Suzune: Well, well. Both of you took three. Can you really keep track of them all?

Riko: Uhh… I'll do my best, you know?

Suzune: Very well. Now, you'd best write down your basic powers. That's from what kind of henge you are.

(The two of them write for a while.)

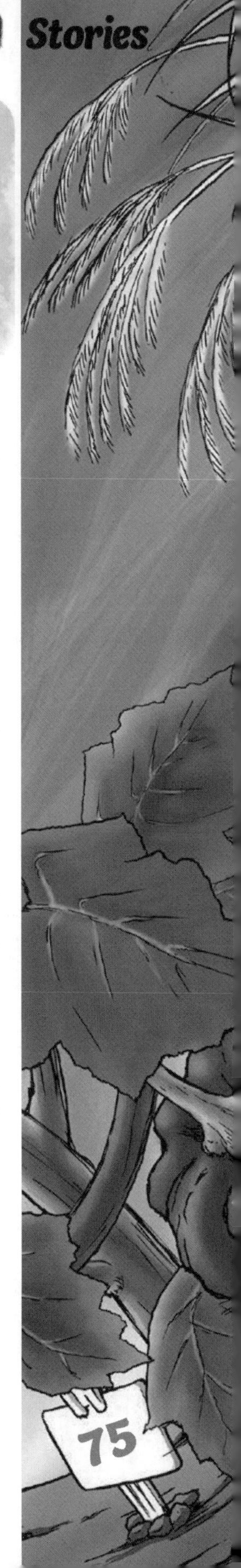

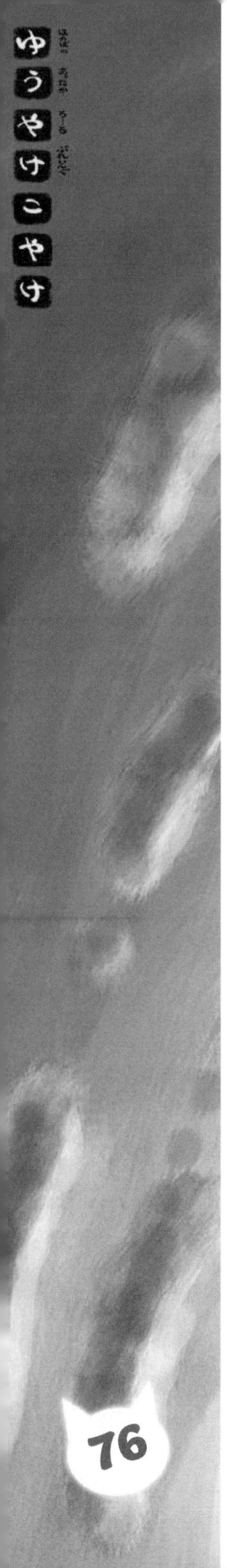

Riko: Done!

Kuromu: Yup. Finished.

Suzune: Next you pick your attributes. Divide 8 points any way you wish. However, they have to be at least 1, and no more than 4. Remember that, all right? However, you can put Adult at zero if you wish.

Riko: Um, I need the Henge attribute for this power... (while looking at her powers)

Kuromu: Hm. Henge 2, Animal 3, Adult 1, Child 2.

Riko: Wow! That was so fast, you know? Too fast! (worried)

Kuromu: I can't help it if you think it's weird. If you're that lost, why not have them all be 2?

Suzune: I... I suppose. You needn't think too hard about how you choose.

Riko: You think so? W-Well... um... I'll have... Henge 3, Animal 1, Adult 2, and Child 2.

Kuromu: ...Are you really that much of an adult?

Riko: I-It's fine, you know?

Kuromu: Whatever. (looks away)

Suzune: Come now. The henge you're making aren't yourselves. Play them how you want.

Riko: Okay!

Kuromu: Hmm... So we're done now?

Suzune: No. Next you have to decide what shape you take when you take human form. This includes how you dress and how old you are. Naturally, this is where you also pick your gender.

Kuromu: What would a cat look like in human form...?

Riko: When a raccoon dog changes...? Hmm...

Suzune: Well, you can take your time to consider this part. This is very important for a henge.

(The two of them both think about it for a while.)

Kuromu: Hm. Okay, like this. (see Kuromu's picture)

Riko: And I'm like this, you know? (see Riko's picture)

Suzune: Hmm. So you're both girls. Well, we're just about done. Decide on your names and ages.

Kuromu: We can pick however we want?

Suzune: Well, only foxes and animals with owners have surnames.

Riko: Oh, that's how it is? And I guess we can't pick ages however we want either?

Suzune: Well, you can up to a point. It'd be odd if you were thousands of years old, but... well, as long as it's less than a hundred years.

Kuromu: No one's going to be that old.

Riko: Okay, my name's Riko. I look 10 when I'm in human form, but I'm actually 3 years old.

Kuromu: Hm. I'm Kuromu. I'm 15, both in real life and when I change.

Riko: For a cat, 15 means you're like an old lady, you know?

Kuromu: I'm a cat henge. What about you? You're only 3. Are you sure you can change?

Suzune: Come now, are you trying to start a fight? Have you finished writing everything down?

Riko & Kuromu: Yes, Suzune.

Setting Up Connections

Riko: So, now do we begin the story?

Kuromu: (pointing at the henge record sheet) I don't know what goes here, but there's a lot of space left, isn't there?

Suzune: I'm glad you noticed. Well. The main things you write there are the connections to the characters in the story.

Kuromu: But right now the only characters in it are me and Riko, right?

Suzune: Right. So right now, each of you write the other's name down. When you meet people during the story you'll write their names down. Go ahead and write the town's name down too. The town is called Hitotsuna Town.

Riko: Okay! So for the other person's name I'll go ahead and write Kuromu. (scribble scribble)

Kuromu: And I'll write Riko. (scribble scribble)

Suzune: Once you're done writing that, pick the contents of your connection. Pick one of these to show what you think of them. (She holds up the connection contents table.)

Riko: What should the connection to the town be? Home?

Kuromu: Well I'm putting Like for the town. I might head for another town if I get tired of it. Well, I'm comfortable there anyway.

Riko: Well, I'm putting "Family," you know? I'm good friends with everyone in the town, you know?

Suzune: Alright. And what about each other?

Riko: I'm putting Like for Kuromu-san, you know? She's kind of hard to get close to.

Kuromu: Riko, huh? I guess it'd be Protection. Someone's got to keep her out of trouble.

Riko: Yay! You're really a nice person, Kuromu!

Kuromu: Enough. You don't think I'm bad?

Riko: Not at all, you know? You're definitely good! (grins)

Kuromu: … (pft)

Suzune: Hmph. Come on now. We can tell you're playing around. Your connections are all at 2. Go ahead and fill in the boxes.

Riko: Okay! (scribble scribble)

Kuromu: … (pouts)

Suzune: Alright. Now that that's done, we're finally done with the preparations and we can begin!

Riko & Kuromu: Okay!

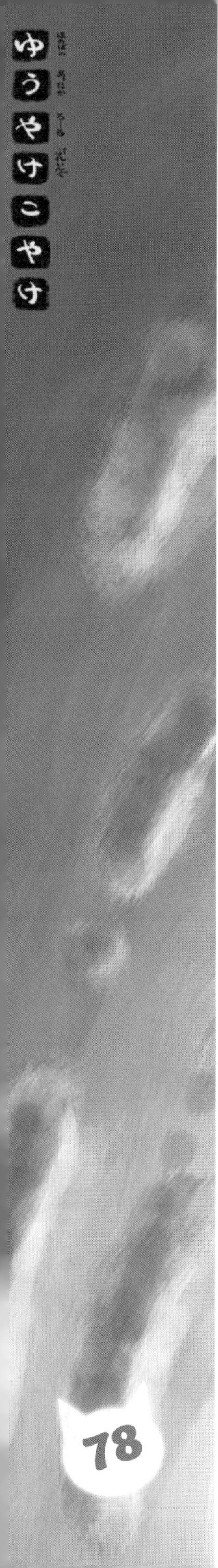

Now let's begin this story. In preparing this story, Suzune has allowed herself 10 points each of Feelings and Wonder per scene. It only concerns people, and it won't require many checks, so that should be plenty.

Scene One

Suzune: Now it's time for the first scene. It's the evening. You're on a dimly-lit path surrounded by fences and a hedge. It's a patch of open land overgrown with weeds, and the two of you are watching the sunset.

Riko: I wave my tail and happily say, "The sunset is so pretty!"

Kuromu: I don't say anything and just look around from on top of the fence.

Suzune: Well, I'll give Riko a Dream.

Riko: Yay!

As the narrator, Suzune passes her a playing card, so that it will be easy to count later. The number of playing cards each player has represents how many Dreams she's accumulated.

Suzune: Now, while you're doing that a boy comes running up the path.

Kuromu: What's the boy look like?

Suzune: He's smaller than either of you. He's probably a third-grader. He looks well-mannered.

Riko: I sort of trundle over, and rub against him.

Kuromu: But you're a raccoon dog!

Riko: I sure am, you know? When I get close to him I'll be like, "Um…"

Suzune: I see. Well, since a raccoon dog is approaching a human, the boy is Surprised.

Riko: Aaah! Is that what happens?!

Kuromu: Normally you would be surprised.

Suzune: So, the boy goes "Aaah!" and slips. If you can't make an Animal check of 2 or better, you'll get caught up in it, Riko.

Riko: Uh oh! My Animal is only 1!

Kuromu: But, you can use some Feelings to make it, right?

Suzune: Right. Since you have the Relaxed Weakness, you'll have to spend 2 points of Feelings to make your Animal temporarily go up to 2, and you won't get caught up in his fall.

Riko: Umm… Uhh… I think I should get caught up though, you know?

Suzune: Okay. The boy falls on top of Riko.

Riko: Squish! I'm seeing stars, but I'll let my soft body cushion him, you know?

Kuromu: Wow. That's cute… Have a Dream.

Suzune: I'll give her a Dream too.

Riko: Yay! Now I have three, you know?

Kuromu: (Ack. And I have none.) A-Anyway, I'll panic, and say, "Jeez! What're you doing?!" and rush over while still in cat form.

Suzune: Well, well, well. Suddenly hearing a girl's voice, the boy panics and springs to his feet.

Kuromu: I'm getting a little worried here. I'll just try to sound like a normal cat. "Meow."

Here both Kuromu and the narrator get one Dream each. You don't have to say anything when awarding Dreams. They're using the cards to represent Dreams, and it's best to award them without interrupting the story's progress. There's nothing wrong with passing the cards without saying anything. From here on out we'll omit the awarding of Dreams from this transcript.

Suzune: Well, even with the cat that came out from the side, the boy is more Surprised by the raccoon dog with rolling eyes underneath him. Without thinking, he cries out.

Riko: Uh oh. That's not good, you know?

Kuromu: You should've changed into human form first.

Suzune: So, what will you do?

Riko: Umm… Uhh… This boy is surprised, and I'm goggle-eyed and panicking too, so I change into a girl right in front of him. Since it's evening it won't cost anything if I leave my ears and tail out, right?

Kuromu: What?!

Suzune: Well, well. That'll really Surprise him. What's your Henge attribute, Riko?

Riko: It's 3, you know?

Suzune: Let's see now… Well, that's how it goes. It goes up by 2. The boy's highest attribute is his Child of 2. I think I'll add 2 to Riko's Henge and we get 5, so he's Surprised by a margin of 3. He tries to run away? (But that'll make things difficult for me here…)

Riko: Oh no… Then I'll spend 3 points of Feelings to lower my Henge down to 2. Hey, I'm not scary? See? I smile, and wipe the dust off of him, you know?

Suzune: (Wha…?) Very well. The boy is still confused, but he stops screaming, and isn't trying to run away.

Kuromu: Oh man. Could you try to think ahead a little? I angrily glare at Riko.

Riko: I don't even notice Kuromu doing that. I say, "Hey, are you hurt?" to the boy.

Suzune: The boy says, "Huh? The r-raccoon dog…? What?" He's flustered and he rubs his eyes.

Kuromu: Jeez. I don't believe this. (sighs)

Riko: "Are you alright?" I say calmly, as I wipe the dust off the boy.

Suzune: Well, with Riko right there next to him he gets embarrassed and turns his eyes away from you.

Riko: Aha! He's so cute, you know?

Kuromu: Nice. Still pretending to be a normal cat, I tilt my head to one side and watch, I guess.

Suzune: The boy tries to say something to Riko, but he's too flustered. Would you two like to make an Impression Check for this boy? If so, which attribute do you want to use to appeal to him?

Riko: Umm… Eheheh… Okay, since I made such a mysterious appearance, I'll use Henge, which is a 3.

Kuromu: Since I showed up as a cat, I guess Animal? He should see me as a cute kitty. I have a 3 too.

Suzune: All right then. I see. The boy has a Child of 2 towards both of you. If you spend Feelings to get up to 4, you can have a strength 1 connection from him with whatever contents you want. I'm going to use some Feelings myself. His connection to Riko will be Admiration, and to Kuromu, Affection.

Riko: Okay! Then mine will be Affection, you know?

Kuromu: Mine will be Affection too. I'm purring and rubbing against him.

Somehow or other, they get to introducing themselves. They learn that the boy's name is Naoto, and they introduce themselves to him in turn.

This is abbreviated in the Spring chapter, but the three introduce themselves in more detail and make small-talk. They talk about elementary school, Riko suggests they find an open patch of ground to roast sweet potatoes, but everyone stops her… We needn't include all the details of this idle chatter, but don't forget such things when you tell your own stories. There's nothing wrong with just chatting if everyone participating enjoys it. Rather than just cutting it off, the narrator should enjoy such chatter. As long as everyone including the narrator is having fun, there's nothing in the rules against this. (But if someone does want to move the story ahead, do respect their opinion.)

Of course, take care not to go on so long that you start wasting the time you set aside for the story.

These kinds of discussions can result in something really wonderful, which is great in its own way.

Anyway, in this case Suzune, the narrator, didn't want to stop them from chatting. Then, Suzune brought in the second

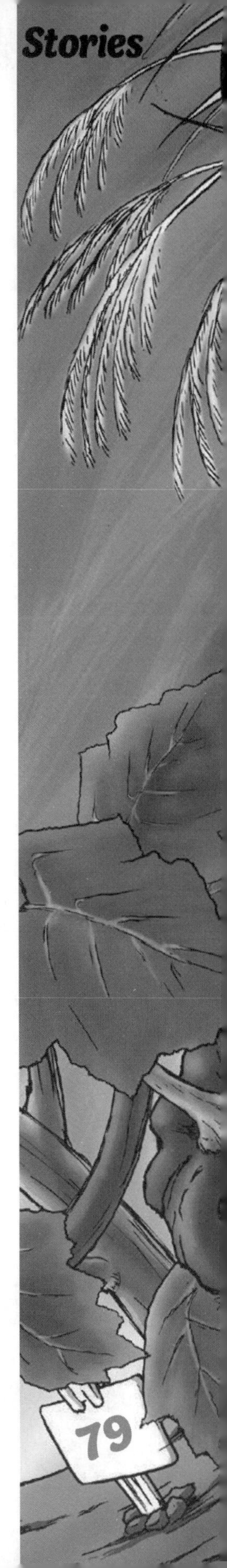

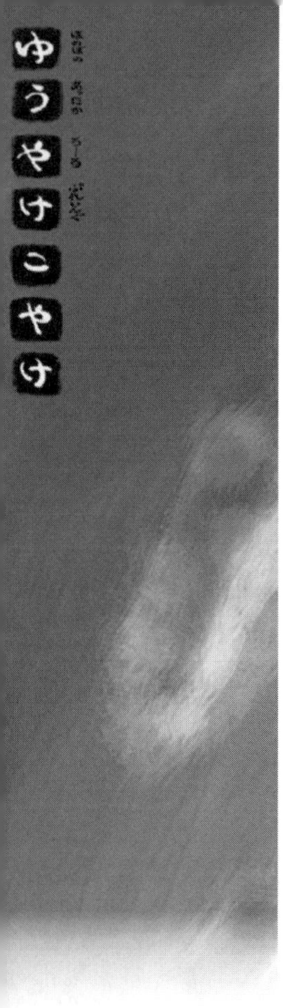

character she'd prepared to move the story forward.

Suzune: While you're doing that, you hear a girl's voice calling out, "Naoto! Where did you go?" It sounds like someone's looking for Naoto. She's slowly coming closer.

Kuromu: I'm startled, and I run away from Naoto.

Suzune: Naoto whispers, "H-Hide!"

Riko: "Huh?" I'm a little slow to figure out what's going on, you know? "But… But… Isn't that a friend of yours?" I'm a bit worried about Naoto as I try to hide.

Kuromu: I wonder who this is? It's pretty late. Maybe his older sister…?

Suzune: In any case, the panicked Naoto finds some cover to hide under.

Kuromu: I'm going to be in, like, the shadow of the fence, away from Naoto, okay?

Riko: Oh no! Now I'm all by myself! I'm flailing around, you know?

Suzune: So, the voice comes closer, and you can now hear footsteps too. Time to change scenes.

Between Scenes

During the scene new characters showed up, and time moved along, so it was time to move to bring the scene to an end. Once one scene has ended, you can use Dreams to strengthen your connections, and you can change the contents of those connections.

Suzune: Alright. I got a total of 3 Dreams from the two of you. What about you?

Riko: Umm… I have 7 points, you know?

Kuromu: I have 4 points.

Suzune: Well then, that means Riko is the only one who can strengthen a connection.

Riko: Eheheh. Then I'll use 5 points to raise the strength of my Affection for Naoto to 2.

Suzune: Alright. So you're keeping the contents as "Affection" then?

Riko: I sure am. Naoto is really cute.

Suzune: Well, well. I'd best try harder. It'll be a problem if I have too few Dreams.

Kuromu: I don't know if I can be that... flirty.

Suzune: You don't have to flirt. And Riko, if you have the Wonder to spare you should use your Carelessness power. It'll give Kuromu and me more Dreams, which will help us get you more Feelings.

Riko: Okay!

During this break between scenes, Suzune tells them about powers they should try using, and to try to get more Dreams. Naturally, she isn't required to tell them these things. However, it's important for the narrator to tell the participants about his or her intentions.

Suzune: Now, total up the strengths of the connections from yourselves to see how many points of Wonder you get, and total up your connections from others to see how many points of Feelings you get.

Riko: Let's see... Since I have a connection with Naoto, I get 6 points of Wonder, and 5 points of Feelings.

Kuromu: And I get 5 points of each.

Suzune: I'm pretty sure you have some left over from the last scene, so add those too.

Riko: I had 4 points of Wonder left, you know? So I have... 10 points of Wonder, and 5 points of Feelings.

Kuromu: I only used 1 point of Feelings, so I have 9 points of Wonder and 8 points of Feelings.

Suzune: Okay then. Your weaknesses aren't causing any problems here either. Let's move on to the next scene.

Scene Two

Suzune: Alright. You are in the same place, but it's now quite dark outside. It's now nighttime.

Riko: I sure spent a long time talking with Naoto, you know? Ahaha.

Kuromu: Should a little kid really be out this late?

Suzune: Anyhow, since the scene has changed and it's now night, Riko will have to spend more Feelings or Wonder to stay changed.

Riko: Hmmm... At night, leaving my ears and tail showing costs 2 points, right? I'll spend 2 points of Wonder to transform.

Kuromu: I'll stay as a cat.

Suzune: Very well. Just then, a tall girl comes walking along the darkened path. She looks older than Naoto. She looks to be in middle school.

Riko: I say, "Huh? Is it Naoto's big sister?" as I steadily walk closer.

Kuromu: I'll keep an eye on Riko from the shadows.

Suzune: Naoto is holding his breath. The girl is moving confidently through the dark, but she has not noticed Riko as of yet.

Riko: Okay. I'll call out to her, "It's dangerous to be out walking this late, you know? What's wrong?" Eheheh. I could really be in trouble here. It's like someone could carry me away, you know? (laughs)

Kuromu: Yeah. Great.

Suzune: Suddenly hearing a voice out of nowhere on a darkened path, the girl lets out a short shriek.

Riko: "Umm..." Oh, man. I didn't mean to scare her, but I keep Surprising people, you know?

Kuromu: Hmm... I think I'll take this opportunity to take human form and step out. That's 2 points of Wonder, right?

Suzune: Hmph. Well, since he's hiding with you, Naoto will be Surprised too. The girl is Surprised too, but she'll calm down when she figures out that she's dealing with two girls.

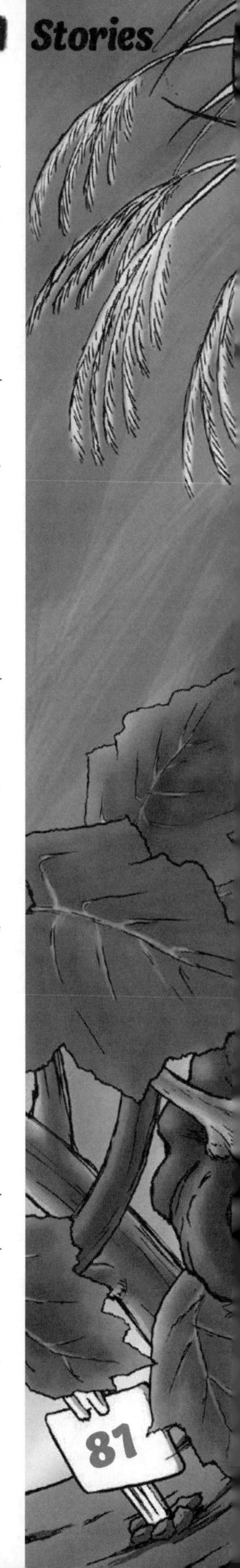

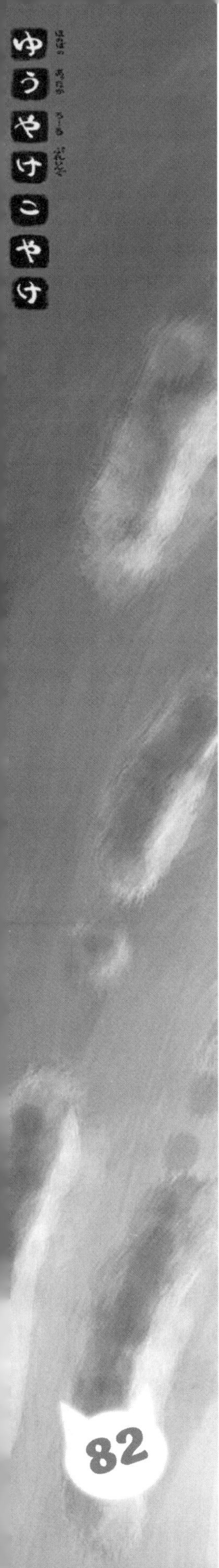

Kuromu: I calmly ask her, "What're you doing? It's pretty late."

Riko: "Oh! Hey, Kuromu!"

Suzune: "Well, I'm looking for a boy. He's about this tall." She's eyeing the two of you suspiciously.

Riko: I stand in front of Naoto. "Well, I don't know anything about Naoto."

Kuromu: "H-Hey!" I do like a spit-take without thinking about it. (bursts out laughing)

Suzune: (once she's done laughing) She looks very serious and asks Riko, "Wh-What? Have you seen Naoto?"

Riko: "Nope, Kuromu hasn't seen Naoto either, right?" I try to act casual and cheerful. (grins)

Kuromu: "Stupid..." I rub my head. (still laughing)

Suzune: She looks offended. She probably thinks you're both making fun of her.

Riko: Heeheehee. Well, since I've gotten Dreams from everyone, I'm going to use my Carelessness power, you know? So I spend 6 Wonder and everyone gets 2 Dreams.

It's up to the participant playing a given henge to decide when exactly to use his or her henge's powers.

Also, neither the narrator nor the other participants need to refuse a participant's timing decision. You don't necessarily need any powers to complete a story, but you'll likely want to try to use at least one power to participate to the fullest. If you really can't figure out a good time to use a power, ask the narrator and the other participants for suggestions.

Kuromu: Heehee. I could use those extra Dreams. Anyway, with the girl acting like that, Kuromu's stubbornness comes out, and now she doesn't want to tell her. (laughs)

Suzune: Well, well. "Look, if you know where Naoto is, please just tell me! Don't hide things from me!" she demands of Kuromu.

Kuromu: "Well, I'm not sure we can really help you." I roll my eyes, and sound a little mean.

Suzune: All right then. I think it's time for an Impression Check.

Kuromu: Woah. I think I've made a pretty bad impression though.

Riko: I'm not doing that great either.

Since the two of them have appeared in a rather mysterious manner, they'll use their Henge attributes for the check.

They have a lot of unused points of Feelings, which they use to make connections with strengths of 2 to start with. Since the two seem to be getting along well with Naoto, the connection contents on her side are Admiration.

Kuromu is still being stubborn, so her connection to the girl is a Rivalry, while Riko sees her as very responsible, and goes for Admiration.

Riko: Okay, then. I say, "B-But... I mean... We don't know anything about Naoto, and he wants to hide right now..." I'm still flailing around. Too bad I don't have enough Wonder left to use Carelessness.

Kuromu: Oh, jeez. "Stop it!" I say. I'm trying to give a retort, but I'm at a loss here. (laughs)

Suzune: The girl is dumbfounded for a moment, but then she regains her composure and shouts into the bushes, "I know you're hiding, Naoto! Come out right now!"

Riko: Oh, man. What's Naoto doing?

Kuromu: Well, I have cat eyes. Can she actually see?

Suzune: Hm. The girl is human, so she hasn't noticed yet, but you two can see Naoto. He's ducking down and trying to keep out of sight.

Kuromu: "What do we do?" I whisper to Riko.

Riko: I'm flustered and I say, "H-How did she find out?"

Kuromu: "How do you think?!"

Suzune: "Naoto! Come out right now!" She seems to be getting even angrier.

Riko: "Um… Um um… Naoto is scared right now. Maybe you could tell us what's going on?" I still have no idea why she figured things out, and I plead with her, looking like I'm going to start crying, you know?

Kuromu: "Who are you anyway?" I can't really see where this is going, so I coldly ask the girl on account of her shouting.

Suzune: "I'm just looking for him because he ran away! I've had enough of that moron!" she says, pouting.

Kuromu: "Hmm. So did you do something he'd run away from?" I ask, trying to sound mature.

Suzune: "Who knows? Maybe he was too embarrassed from being made fun of? Hmph." She turns her face away from you.

Kuromu: Now I'm getting worried about what's going on with Naoto.

Riko: Um… Uh… What should we do then?

Suzune: Well, in any case…

Here the two of them talk for a bit, but no good ideas are forthcoming.

As the narrator, Suzune was hoping they'd bring Naoto to the girl, or try to talk to the girl and get her to open her heart, but… instead they start going back and forth trying to come up with a plan, and wind up talking amongst themselves.

Suzune waits for a while, but they're not doing anything. At that point, the girl pushes the story forward. The story doesn't always have to go the way the participants want, after all. Sometimes the narrator moves the story ahead, as naturally as possible.

Suzune: "Fine. If you know where Naoto is hiding, then you can tell him he should come home. And also… he might be able to hear this right now, but… tell him Yuka isn't really mad at him." Looking at the two of you, she sounds kind of disappointed. Ah, also, you now know that the girl's name is Yuka.

Kuromu: "Hmm…" Oh man. Now what?

Suzune: Yuka slumps her shoulders and starts plodding back the way she came.

Riko: I'm worried about the girl, so I start after her, saying, "Please, wait."

Kuromu: I'm dashing off to where Naoto is.

Suzune: Very well. With each of you heading off to do different things, we'll end the scene here.

Suzune brings this scene to an end for the moment.

The three of them use their Dreams to strengthen connections, and they check if anyone wants to change the contents of any connections. Riko raises her connection to Kuromu from 2 to 3, and changes the contents from Like to Trust. ("Like" is only for connections of strength 2 or less.)

Incidentally, since Naoto didn't really do anything in this scene, they can only strengthen connections to each other and Yuka.

In the next scene, Riko and Kuromu each act separately.

Scene Three

Suzune: Alright. Let's start with Kuromu. You went to where Naoto is hiding, yes?

Kuromu: Yeah. Oh, by the way, he hasn't seen me like this before. Will it be okay?

Suzune: Hmm… Well, you do have a connection. And he saw Riko change right in front of his eyes a moment ago, so he seems to understand, more or less. Ah, and I take it you're paying the cost to transform?

Kuromu: Yeah, yeah. At night, with my ears and tail out is 2 points of Wonder.

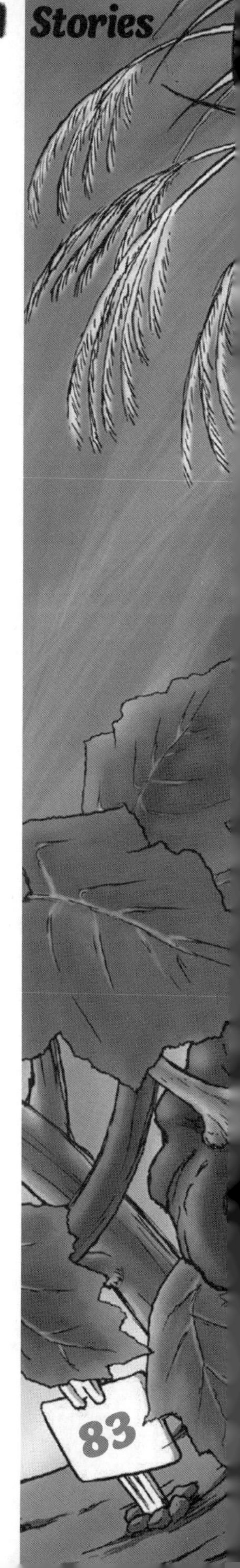

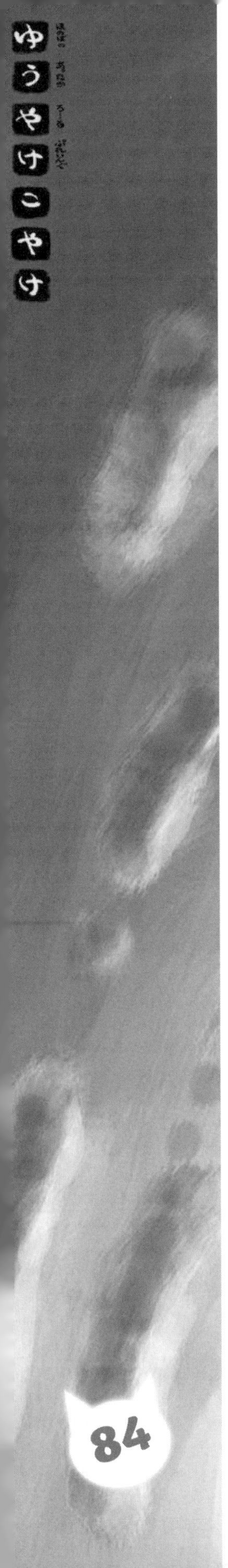

Suzune: Indeed. If you want to talk to him, do so now.

Kuromu: Okay, so, I say, "What happened?" and peer at his face with my cat eyes.

Suzune: He says, "N-Nothing!" and sounds really uncomfortable.

Kuromu: Hmm... I'm spending 6 points of Wonder to use Peek into Hearts. If Naoto is remembering what happened, I'll see.

Suzune: Well, well. In that case, you take in several things as fragments. Yuka and Naoto are the same age. They've been friends since they were little, but lately they've been seeing each other as perhaps a little more than friends.

Kuromu: So they're the same age... Well, at that age girls do get their growth spurt.

Riko: If they both start to understand, I'm sure it'll be something wonderful, you know?

Suzune: Hmm. Well, on the way back home from school today, they were holding hands, and some of their classmates made fun of them.

Kuromu: Hmm... Well it's not like they can do anything about that, right?

Suzune: They stopped holding hands and left, but one of the older people they met in the neighborhood said they looked like a big sister and little brother.

Kuromu: And he ran away because of that? (shocked)

Suzune: Indeed.

Kuromu: Naoto's got no guts.

Suzune: Well, he does fret over being so short. (harshly)

Kuromu: I say, "You didn't have to run away over something like that. Why don't you go after her and apologize? She's heading home now, you know."

Suzune: "But, even if I do apologize... I won't get taller. And she's way more responsible, and..." he says, making excuses.

Kuromu: Jeez. He's so wimpy. No wonder Yuka has to be so much more together. (annoyed)

Riko: Kuromu-san, you're good at looking out for people, you know?

Suzune: Now, let's go to Riko, shall we?

With the action split into two different places, Suzune could have split the scenes, but Yuka and Naoto are only separated by the dark, and they're close enough that Kuromu and Riko could come together at any time. Also, they can both be aware of what the other is doing.

Thus, Suzune decided to have them act separately, but without having them act in separate scenes.

Suzune: Now, Yuka is trying to go home...

Riko: "Wait!" I cling on as she drags me along.

Suzune: Yuka says, "Let go!" and stubbornly drags Riko along, trying to get away.

Riko: I say, "Are you gonna go home without Naoto? He seems lonely, you know?" as I desperately try to persuade her. (sweat)

Suzune: "Listen, Naoto—" She tries to shake you off. You need an Animal result of 2 to hold on. Otherwise you'll fall down.

Riko: Umm... In that case I'll let her shake me off. I fall down really obviously, and scrape my knees, you know?

Suzune: "Oh! I'm so sorry!" Seeing Riko like that, Yuka loses her composure, and rushes over to her as she falls down.

Riko: "Owww! That hurt!" I start crying.

Kuromu: Can I head over to where Riko is now?

Suzune: Well, Kuromu was just peeking into Naoto's heart. Very well.

Kuromu: "Oh, jeez. You..." I say, sounding pouty but worried.

From here it goes like in the story. At Kuromu's beckoning, Naoto comes out. Suzune said that to get him to come out just by beckoning, she'll need a Henge or Adult result of 4 or better. Suzune wasn't sure which would be appropriate. Kuromu used her Henge, spent some Feelings, and succeeded.

Thus, all four of them came together. At that point, Suzune once again ended the scene. Riko became closer to Yuka, and Kuromu with Naoto. Now for the next scene. This part of the story has all four of them present.

Scene Four

First, Riko and Kuromu each use some Wonder to stay in human form (at night, with ears and tails showing, it's 2 points). They might need Feelings to make checks at any time, but they don't expect to need any powers.

Suzune: So, we have Naoto and Yuka. The two of them stand apart, watching each other. Seeing them like this, you can clearly see that Yuka is a head taller than Naoto. ...Neither of them is doing anything.

Riko: Th-This is where we could make an opportunity! But, I have no idea what to do, you know? (cries)

Kuromu: Hmm... I'll slip into the shadows and undo my transformation.

Suzune: Really? You just transformed you know?

Kuromu: I'm not worried. It'll be easier to deal with this if I'm not a girl.

Suzune: Well, well. Not a bad idea.

Riko: Wow! You're amazing, Kuromu-san! Maybe I should become a raccoon dog again?

Kuromu: You can stay how you are. I'm going to use 4 points of Wonder to use my Fuzzy power on Naoto, and rub against his legs.

Suzune: Ah! I see now. An excellent idea. (I had not thought of that.)

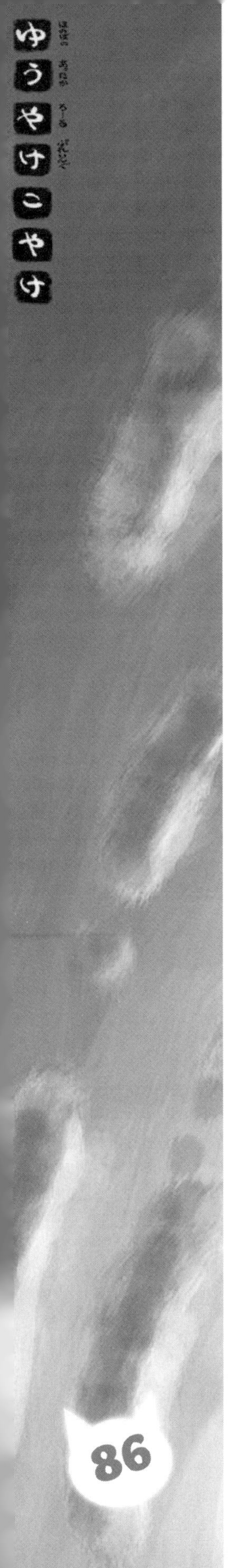

Sometimes the participants don't handle a situation as well as the narrator might've hoped. However, sometimes they come up with a far more wonderful solution than the narrator. When that happens, try to praise them. Also, don't forget that the narrator can hand out Dreams.

Kuromu: I look up at Naoto, and stay close to him.

Suzune: Naoto looks at his feet. He picks up Kuromu in his arms.

Riko: What?! A love triangle?! (blushing)

Kuromu: No way! (blushing)

Suzune: Heheheh. Sounds amusing. However, Naoto slowly steps closer to Yuka. Is Kuromu going to let him continue holding her?

Riko: What's Yuka doing? (nervous)

Suzune: Yuka is quiet as usual, watching Naoto come closer.

Kuromu: I'm content to stay in Naoto's arms. I'm a cat after all.

Suzune: "It's dark and stuff. Let's go home," Naoto says softly.

Kuromu: I'll meow from Naoto's arms, and call out to Yuka too.

Riko: I just blurt out, "You two really need to patch things up, you know?"

Suzune: Well, after a little while, Yuka nods to Naoto. He makes a quick apology.

When two of the narrator's characters are talking to each other, it's best to move things along simply. Even if the narrator can do a good dialogue all alone, it could be boring for the henge. In this case, what's important is that Yuka and Naoto patched things up, and not the exact words they used.

If as the narrator you find it embarrassing to portray characters, you can just describe the speech of all but one necessary character.

Riko: I say, "Isn't that great, Naoto?"

Kuromu: I'm still hanging out in his arms.

Suzune: Naoto says, "Yeah. Thank you, Riko."

Riko: And now, I will vanish like a dream, you know?

Kuromu: Huh? I didn't know you had a power like that.

Riko: Oh, I'm just becoming a raccoon dog again and hiding.

Suzune: Hmm. Alright. Will you make an Animal check?

Riko: Um... No need. My tail will be sticking out from the shadows and waving. And I'll use my Carelessness power!

Kuromu: Dummy... Is what I'm thinking while I receive some Dreams.

Suzune: Well, well. I see now. In that case, I get 2 Dreams each for Yuka and Naoto. Now, Yuka is bewildered by Riko's disappearance. Naoto coaxes Yuka while waving to Riko's tail.

Riko: Eheheh. I twitch my tail.

Suzune: Alright. He also sets Kuromu down.

Kuromu: Oh. I was thinking he'd take me home like that. (laughs) I'll go over to Riko, and get her tail out of sight.

Riko: Aww. But it was so cute, you know?

Suzune: In any case, Naoto and Yuka head back, occasionally glancing back at you two.

Kuromu: Are they holding hands?

Suzune: Yes, they are. Let's end the scene here. The next will be the final one.

Riko & Kuromu: Okay.

Between scenes, Riko and Kuromu strengthened their connections to each other. Suzune is unsure of what to do, but settles on strengthening Naoto's connection to Riko. At this point the story is just about over.

The Final Scene

Suzune: Alright, it's early afternoon the next day. Naoto and Yuka call out, "Hello!" as they come to the same spot as last night.

Riko: "I'm not Riko-chan at all, you know?" I say as I totter out as a raccoon dog.

Kuromu: I'm in cat form, sitting on the fence, just amazed.

Riko: I still have the band-aids from yesterday on my legs, you know? Oh, can I use Carelessness for that just now?

Suzune: Hm. You never miss a chance to use it. Well, I could use some Dreams too, so I can't complain. However, Yuka doesn't know that Riko is a raccoon dog, so she's Surprised, yes?

Riko: Oops. Well, I'll use Feelings so I don't Surprise her.

Suzune: In that case, Yuka realizes that the raccoon dog here is Riko. She takes a can of tuna, some rice balls, and tea out of her bag. The tea is in a thermos and nice and hot.

Riko: Well, since I already used some Feelings and everything, I'll go ahead and change in front of them.

Kuromu: I'll hop down from the fence, and watch from a little ways away.

Suzune: If you wish to change during the day, it will cost you 4 points if you leave your ears and tail out.

Riko: Well, it's the last scene, so I might as well use it. (She spends 4 points to transform.)

Kuromu: I like being a cat, so I'll stay that way.

Suzune: Well, Yuka is startled by Riko's sudden transformation, but she doesn't cry out or flee. She apologizes, saying, "I'm really sorry I got you hurt the other day," and offers Riko a rice ball.

The rest of the story is like in the Spring chapter.

Riko and Kuromu enjoy some food with Naoto and Yuka, who are friends once again. The story ends with the image of them eating rice balls and canned tuna and drinking tea.

Suzune: Thus, you've become good friends with Naoto and Yuka. We'll end the story here.

Riko: Okay!

Kuromu: Hm. I may have been too stingy with Wonder and Feelings.

The story has ended. Letting everyone know that is one of the narrator's important jobs. The end of the last scene is the end of the story. As the narrator, you should take care to have an appropriate ending. Specifically, you should end the story when the henge don't particularly have anything more to do. Still, they might have more to say or do. Before you end the story, let everyone know, and make sure they understand.

Now, the story is over, but there's still a little bit of work to do. This will help you remember the story. This is the cleanup at the end of the story, but also preparation for the next one.

After the Story

Suzune: Alright, we're all done… Or nearly so. We need to take care of a few things for our next story. First, let's use the Dreams from the final scene to strengthen connections.

Riko: Okay. I'll strengthen my Trust towards Kuromu, you know? I've got some leftover Dreams.

Kuromu: I'll raise my Affection for Naoto.

Suzune: Well, sadly our leftover Dreams are lost.

Riko: Too bad.

Kuromu: Well, I used all of mine.

Suzune: Next, add up the Strengths of all our connections except the one to the town.

Riko: Umm… I got 9.

Kuromu: I got kind of a late start compared to Riko. I've got 8.

Suzune: Alright. Write that number on your henge record sheets under "Memories." The connections you acquired this time become Memories.

Memories are points that you can use in place of Wonder or Feelings in later stories. In the next story, Riko and Kuromu

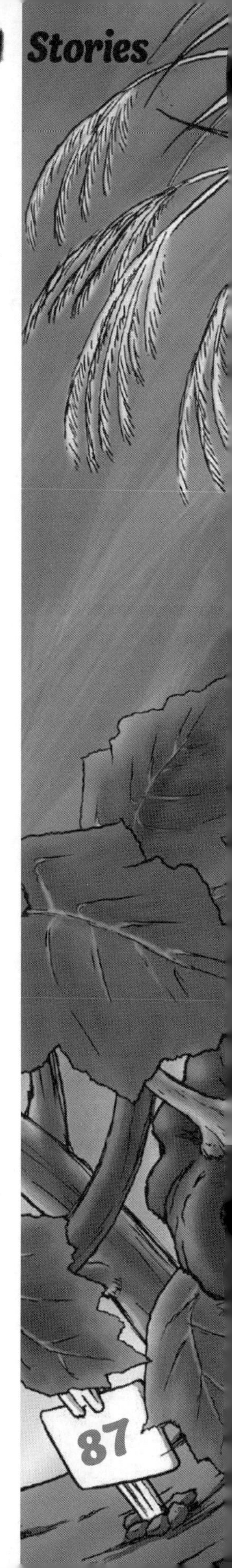

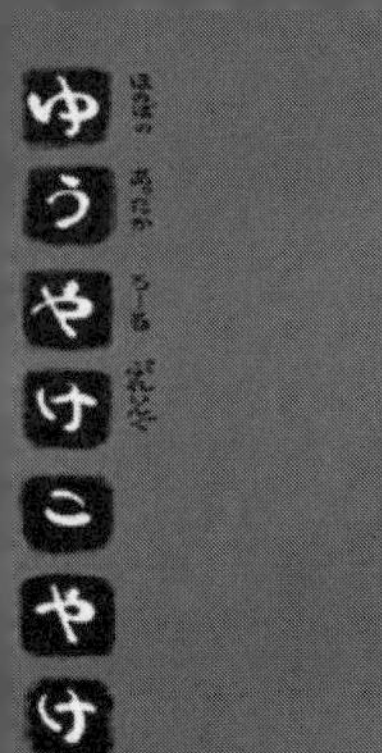

will have that much extra Wonder and Feelings to use, and they'll be able to use many powers and get high check results from the beginning.

Suzune: Once you're done writing that down, we'll move on to Threads. Copy all of your connections, except the one to the town, down as Threads.

Kuromu: All the connections except to the town would be Riko, Naoto, and Yuka, right?

Suzune: Indeed. And copy down the contents of your connections to them too.

A little later, they're done writing.

Riko: All done, you know?

Kuromu: You sure are slow at this stuff.

Suzune: In any case, we're nearly done. Next you need to erase the three connections you've made.

Riko: Woah, what? We have to erase them? (depressed)

Kuromu: So we get Memories and Threads in their place.

Suzune: Indeed.

Riko: Okay, but, today we didn't really seem to need those Memories, you know?

Kuromu: Yeah, I suppose so. We were able to get by without them.

Suzune: Then you can save them up. You'll be able to use your most impressive powers, and do things that would be impossible when you really need it.

Riko: Oh, wow!

Suzune: Also, if you want to change one of your Weaknesses, you should do it before the next story. Or if you find you have a troublesome combination, you may erase one.

Riko: I only ever used Gullible, you know?

Kuromu: And I only used Cat Tongue. They're not really limiting us right now.

Suzune: In that case, you should leave them as they are.

Kuromu: Anyway, that was a lot of fun. Good job.

Suzune: And you. Well done.

Riko: Thanks everyone!

Thus, this story is finally over.
Now do you understand better what a narrator does?
It might seem difficult and involved, but first give it a try.
If you've never been the narrator before, try playing with the introductory story, "At the Fox's Shrine."

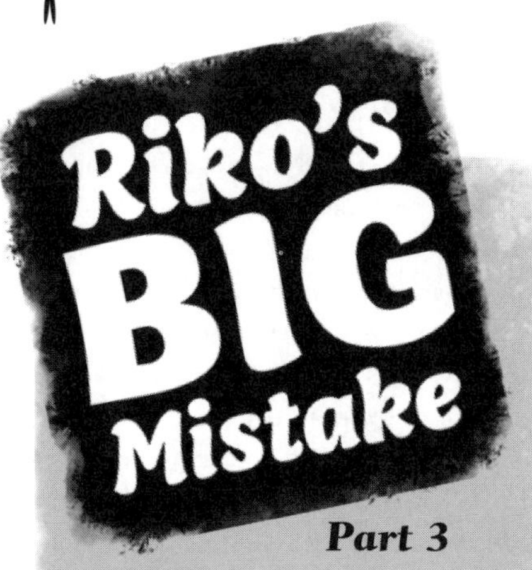

Part 3

I want to become a good narrator.

Suzune: Hello, Lady Kaminaga-hime. What does one need to be a narrator?

Kaminaga-hime: ......However many stories you weave...... you must keep gaining more experience.

Suzune: Hm. Then what should one be careful of?

Kaminaga-hime: ......There should be many ways to resolve the story...... just as I have many legs. (She flexes her eight legs.)

Suzune: I see. So, the henge should be able to resolve things however they wish?

Kaminaga-hime: Hmm...... You must also be able to see...... the thread of a solution...... when you are troubled.

Let the henge do what they want.

Suzune: But what if they don't follow the hints you give them?

Kaminaga-hime: ......Depending on the situation. If they are very clearly choosing...... badly, you may have to point them to the thread of the resolution. If they still won't follow it...... there's little to be done...... and you must tell them of the bad outcome. That's how it has to be in the end...... you see.

Suzune: Hm. I became a narrator to tell happy stories with them. I know that doesn't mean there will never be bad endings.

Kaminaga-hime: It won't be all bad..... Sometimes the outcome will be...... better than what the narrator prepared.

Suzune: When that happens, you shouldn't be particular about the ending you had in mind, correct?

Kaminaga-hime: (nods)

I want us to weave happy stories together.

Kaminaga-hime: A narrator's job is not to tell a tragic story...... even if you do trouble the henge. Have the henge make a sad story...... into a happy one. The narrator must make everyone involved in the story...... people and henge...... happy. Strive to that end. ......Weave a happy story for the depressed raccoon dog too......

Suzune: You needn't tell me that. As the narrator, I will protect Kikuna, who fears moving away, and that scatterbrained Riko! Sorry to have disturbed you. I must be going.

Kaminaga-hime: ......Don't get so keen. Fox girl...... The narrator's happiness is important too.

Story 1

At the Fox's Shrine

CHARACTERS
A Fox Henge (Narrator Character)
Participants

TIME NEEDED
2 Hours

WONDER AND FEELINGS
For this story the narrator can use 20 points of Wonder and 20 points of Feelings in each scene.

Story Summary
There is a fox henge who lives all alone in her own shrine. One day, other henge come to where she lives by herself. At first, she looks down on them. However, the more everyone gets to know each other, the more she realizes what she's been missing living alone in the shrine.

Introduction
This story is for people who are playing *Golden Sky Stories* for the first time.

In this story, the narrator only has to portray one character. The narrator will still have to handle scene changes, manage the rules, decide on target numbers, and so on, but since he or she will have lots of Wonder and Feelings to work with, he or she can use powers and take actions right at the start, which the normal participants can't.

If you're being the narrator for the first time, please try out this story. It should be very good for practicing how to portray characters. If you've already played through this story as a participant, or you want to do something more original, please look at the "Customization" section.

Narrator Preparation
For this story, the narrator only brings in one henge. There are no other narrator characters. Thus, the narrator must first make that henge. There are three requirements for this henge:

- She must be a fox. (The fox can be male or female; we're using "she" for convenience.)
- She must have the "Pride" Weakness.
- She cannot be portrayed in such a way that everyone dislikes her.

Keeping these requirements in mind, go ahead and create your fox henge. If you're really having trouble making one, you can just use Suzune Hachiman, who we've introduced in this book.

If everyone is new to the game, the narrator will have to take a look at everyone's Weaknesses. If you think you'll have a hard time keeping track of them all, you can, for example, remove all of Suzune Hachiman's weaknesses except for Pride.

For the story's setting, you can assume it's Hitotsuna Town, which is introduced in the Winter chapter. However, this is in no way a strict requirement. If you've got another town in mind that will work with this story, you can certainly use it.

Likewise, while this story doesn't take place in any particular time of year, setting it during the same season as the one everyone is experiencing in real life could help draw you all into the story more.

You will also need to learn what's written in the Spring chapter of this book, teach the participants how to enjoy the game, and have them create henge. Having one of the participants' henge be a fox would make things a little complicated for this story. Instead, have them choose from among the other five types.

Once you have the participants' henge and the narrator's fox all ready, it's time to set up the henge's connections to each other, let them have their Wonder and Feelings from those, and get the story started.

The participants' henge will not yet have connections to the narrator's fox. The fox and the henge will create connections during this story.

First Scene

LOCATION: FOX SHRINE
TIME: DAY

As the narrator, you are a fox henge. Do not forget that as you proceed. Naturally, you need to explain the situation to everyone. Read the following paragraph aloud:

> *"You all came to the Shrine Forest to play on a whim, and came across an old shrine. Beams of sunlight shine down through the trees onto this very old shrine. There is a dish for offerings, but right now it contains only fallen leaves."*

Then, try asking everyone what they're doing there. Also, since they'll all be in animal form to start with, you'll want to ask them if they want to take human form.

Start off handing out Dreams according to the henge's speech and actions. (If some of the participants are used to this, you can just match their pace.) This is especially important if the participants have never played *Golden Sky Stories* before. If people are a little lost, they'll turn to the narrator for an example to follow, so do your best.

Find out what everyone is doing. Get them to ask questions about the place and talk to each other. Of course, if you're dealing with henge who've been through many stories together, you don't have to spend as much time on having them interact.

If you're a first-time narrator and you're having trouble answering everyone's questions, just take your time. Think carefully, and calmly answer those questions. (Of course, if you're used to this, you can probably answer right away, right?) For questions about the location, keep the following points in mind, and try not to contradict yourself:

- The shrine is made of wood, and it has been damaged by wind and rain.
- There are a small dish and bottle for offerings.
- The door to the shrine is not locked.
- There is an old bell attached in front of the door to the shrine.
- There is a tattered cord attached to the bell.
- If you jostle the cord, the bell sounds. It makes a curious sound.

And so on.

Once everyone understands the location and the situation, it's time for your fox to take the stage.

The fox uses Feelings to raise her Animal attribute to 6, and stealthily appears. In order to notice, the partici-

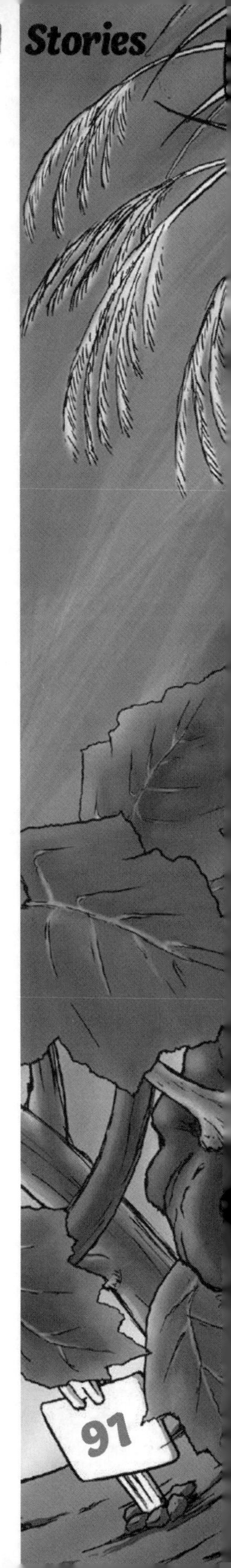

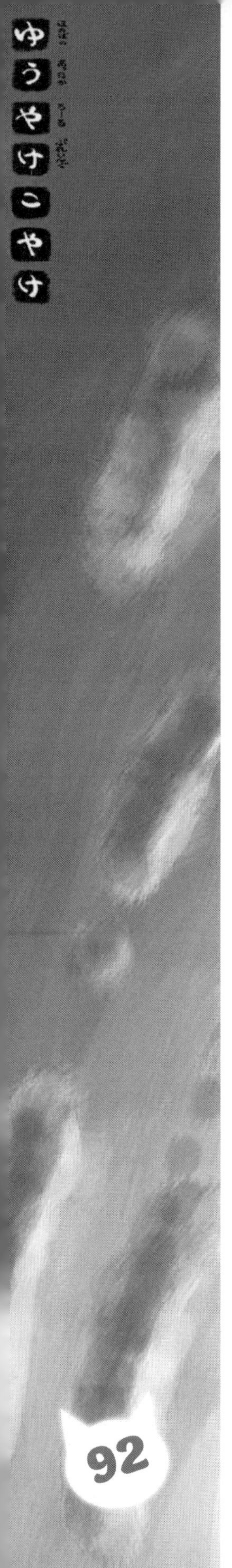

pants will have to raise their own Animal attributes to 6 as well. Tell the participants, "There's something you'll notice if you raise your Animal attribute to 6."

If someone succeeds, they will notice the fox's quiet appearance, and if they all fail then she'll suddenly call out to them. If it won't make things too difficult, you can have them subject to Surprise equal to the fox's Henge attribute.

The fox appears from inside the shrine, or perhaps from its shadow. The narrator should have plenty of points to work with. You can have the fox appear in human form if you like.

For this first part, don't forget the fox's Pride weakness. However, definitely don't push it so far that it makes everyone uncomfortable. This may be difficult to balance, but such things are what make role-playing so enjoyable.

For example, Suzune would grumpily say, "And who exactly are you? This is my shrine," as she showed herself.

Once the fox has shown herself, have her talk to the other henge. Let everyone exchange questions. The fox's questions are pretty simple:

- Who are you?
- Why are you here?

At this point, the fox will have to introduce herself. Once that's done, have everyone make Impression Checks and create connections. This scene ends when you're done creating connections.

Go ahead and take care of the stuff that goes between scenes. Once that's done, move on to the second scene.

If any of the henge are in human form, remind them that they need to pay points to maintain it. However, since the next scene is in the evening, they'd only need to pay if they want to hide their ears or tail.

Second Scene

LOCATION: FOX SHRINE
TIME: EVENING

While the henge are talking to their new fox friend, the sky gradually darkens. They can hear the sounds of crows returning to the mountains, and of the broadcast in the town square telling the children to return home.

Some of the henge may have spent most of their points on changing and such during the day. However, now they'll be able to change without spending anything at all. If no one notices, have your fox point it out.

"It seems the sun is setting. Why not take human form like me?"

If anyone isn't yet conversant in the rules, now would be a good time to explain it to them. Even those who disliked paying the cost for transforming during the day can go ahead and do so now just by saying they want to.

Once everyone has transformed, the fox can evaluate their human forms. If she has the "Strange" weakness, she'll undoubtedly make some odd comments about those who are dressed in a more current style. She might well comment that her own appearance is cuter.

If everyone happens to have taken human form during the day, the fox can ask them what they do normally. Get them to talk about their everyday lives. If it doesn't turn into much of a discussion, there's no need to force things.

Regardless, make sure the fox at least tells the other henge the following. How she goes about it is up to you.

- She has lived alone at the shrine for a long time.
- It's been a long time since it was this lively.

Also, you might have the fox show off one or more of her powers. It's up to you which one(s), but make sure you have at least 12 points of Wonder left at the end. This is so the fox can use the Fairy Rain power. However, until someone makes a successful check, the fact that the fox is using Fairy Rain should remain a secret.

After they've talked to the fox for a while, have everyone make an Adult check against the fox's Adult (you can use around 4 points of Feelings if you want). Those henge who succeed will realize the following about the fox (who will deny it if asked directly):

She is happy that everyone came.

If possible, she wants everyone to stay like this.

Now, once the discussions have passed the first stage, it becomes completely dark. Someone might suggest that they should head home. Just then, it starts to rain.

The scene ends. Tell everyone that it has started raining, and bring the scene to a close. Once you've taken care of the things that go between scenes, move on to the third scene.

Third Scene

LOCATION: FOX SHRINE

TIME: NIGHT

It is now night. Henge who want to stay in human form will have to pay points for it. The rain continues to fall. In order to maintain the rainfall, the fox spends another 12 points of Wonder on Fairy Rain. (Still a secret from everyone else, right?)

The fox recommends that they take shelter under a large tree next to the shrine. It's a very big, very old tree, and it keeps out most of the rain. Once everyone is under this shelter, the fox recommends that everyone stay here until the rain lets up.

At this point, the narrator should have everyone make a Henge check against the fox's Henge attribute (she should spend a maximum of 4 points of Feelings). If someone succeeds, tell them about the Fairy Rain fox power. When they realize this, they'll also notice that there are no clouds in the sky, and they can see the moon through the gaps in the trees. This rain is falling when the moon is out and there are no clouds.

It may happen that no one succeeds at the check. One of the henge might decide

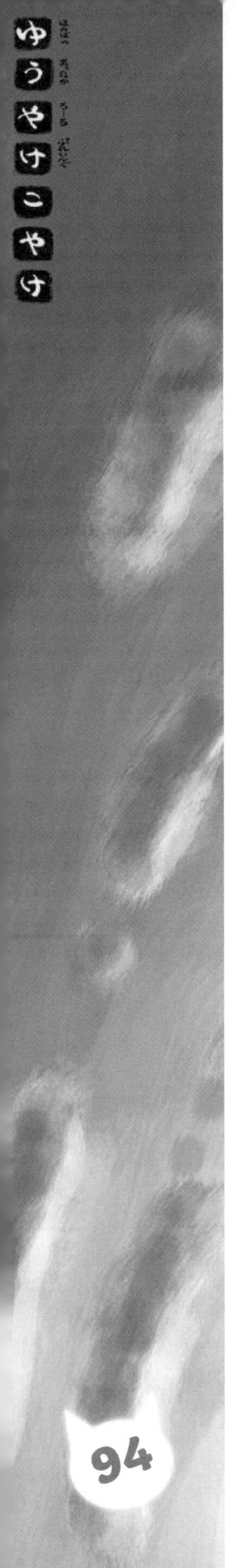

to head home despite the rain. Or someone might give some sign that the rain is a bother. If that happens, the fox will stare at the ground and explain what he or she did.

The fox wants everyone to stay, and doesn't want to be alone, which is why she did such a thing. It's up to the participants to figure out how they want to deal with this. As the narrator, think about your fox's feelings, and express them to the participants.

This dialogue might take longer than you anticipated. Or, it might not easily resolve things. What's important here is how the fox feels, and how you as the narrator express those feelings to them.

If you have an idea for how they might resolve things, offer it to the participants.

The remaining henge might spend the night at the fox's shrine, or come again the next day, which would convince the fox to stop the rain. Just make sure that it makes sense for the fox to be satisfied, and have her express that to them.

If too many of the henge decide to leave despite the rain, the fox might start crying. If they really do leave, they can't appear in the next and final scene.

When the rain stops, the fox thanks everyone. Have your fox say something to each of the other henge.

This is where the scene ends. Take care of the things you do between scenes, and move on to the final scene. It's not about what happened when the henge spent the night at the shrine or returned home late at night. For the next scene, move on to the daytime. Make sure you tell everyone that the next scene is the last one.

Final Scene

LOCATION: FOX SHRINE
TIME: DAY

It's the middle of the next day. Everyone has once again gathered at the fox's shrine, which is again lit by beams of sunlight that pass through the trees.

The fox is in human form from the start. Although she seemed very lonely the day before, she has kind of an arrogant attitude this time around. However, underneath that, this fox is very happy to see all of them, and everyone can tell.

What happens next is up to everyone to decide. If the henge aren't sure what to do next, have the fox thank them in a small voice. Their reactions to the fox's thanks should lead into more of a dialogue.

Also, let everyone know that just because a fox has the Shrine power doesn't mean that she can't leave that shrine. Furthermore, have them talk about what the fox should do or if she is going to stay there alone.

If someone suggests that they show the fox to other places, she should look troubled but still nod in reply.

And with that, the story is over. Thank everyone for participating, and do the last bit of rules stuff for the end of the story.

Customization

After you've done this story once, it would be strange to repeat it, even with a different narrator. Instead, let's think about some ways you might customize the outline of this story into something new.

If you change the story to involve someone other than a fox, and/or change the location, you can otherwise use this story more or less as-is.

The simplest change would be to use a local god. Change the location, put that place's local god in place of the fox, and you have a new story.

For example, if the henge are playing beside a river, they could meet the snake that is that river's local god. The story that follows is mostly the same, but it would feel like a new story. Naturally, the same is true if it takes place on a mountain, in a forest, or some other place. Local gods all have powers that could make it hard for henge to leave, though they may be showier than a fox's Fairy Rain power.

Changing the fox to another kind of henge, or a human, would be a little difficult, and the resulting story would be somewhat similar, but fairly different overall. It would still be a story about henge gathering around a lonely henge or human and becoming friends. They wouldn't be able to make it rain like a fox henge, but they could directly ask their new friends not to leave.

In this case, this character should recommend something during the third scene. You can end the second scene as soon as the conversation has made some significant progress.

A New Narrator

If one of the people playing this game is accustomed to it, or just has a very rich imagination, you might want to ask them to try being the narrator. Then they can lead the next story. In other words, you can become a participant with the fox henge you made for this story, and take part in the next with someone else as the narrator.

You can't always do this, but if everyone takes a turn as the narrator, you'll surely be able to enjoy the game much more than if you only played through one story.

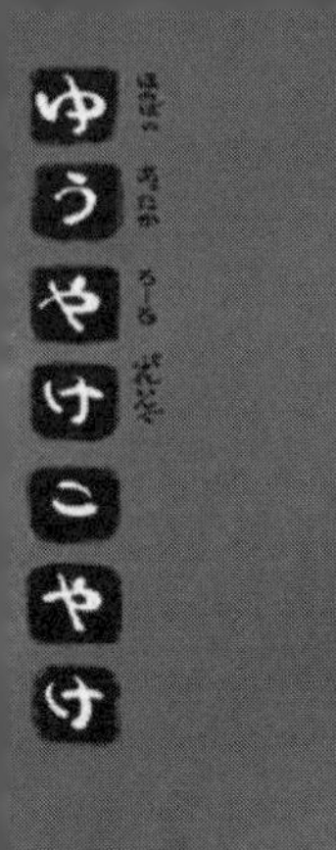

Story 2

Crying in the Night

CHARACTERS
Human Child
Puppy (Not a Henge)

TIME NEEDED
2 to 3 Hours

WONDER AND FEELINGS
For this story the narrator can use 10 points of Wonder and 10 points of Feelings in each scene.

Story Summary

One day a certain child forgot something at school. It's the autumn. After playing, he goes back to school to get what he forgot, but it's getting dark out. Then, the child meets the henge. Despite being scared, they go into the school to get the forgotten item. From somewhere in the dark school, they hear sobbing. They can hear it all the way from the front gate. But what could it be?

Introduction

This story is for people who've played *Golden Sky Stories* before. You can use it as a follow-up to "At the Fox's Shrine," though the fox doesn't appear here.

In this story, the narrator will have to role-play his or her characters being scared and surprised. Also, he or she will have to provide a detailed portrayal of the setting.

Also, with the exception of the final scene, all of the scenes in this story take place at night. Please keep in mind that henge will have to pay points to take human form. Furthermore, bird henge with the Night Blindness weakness could have a hard time here.

Narrator's Preparation

First, you will have to create the child that appears in this story. This child must be diligent enough to go all the way back to school to pick up something he forgot. You can use the "Diligent" character from the People section of the Winter chapter. Decide on the child's age and gender based on what will be easy for you to role-play.

If the henge have already met a child who would be appropriate, you can just have that child play this role in this story. Henge who've been part of several stories will surely appreciate seeing a familiar face.

Next, you need to create a puppy to finish up your preparations. Treat the puppy as a dog with an Animal attribute of 1. For more information on dogs, look at the introduction to dog henge and the attributes for dogs in the Animals section. Also, whether because of your personal tastes, or simply because you've used dogs too much in previous stories, you can substitute a kitten instead if you want.

First Scene

LOCATION: OPEN AREA IN FRONT OF THE SCHOOL
TIME: NIGHT

It is nighttime, and there is a round moon overhead. The henge have gathered in the open area in front of the school. It is full of thick grass, and they can see clearly by the light of the moon. They're not here for any particular business, just to come look at the moon and spend time together.

Try asking what the henge are talking about, and how they're passing the time.

Once you know what everyone's doing, answer any questions they might have about the location, and let the henge talk amongst themselves. If the henge have known each other for a while, giving them time for this shouldn't be a problem. When everyone is doing what they're doing to pass the time, it's time to move the story along.

In the moonlight, everyone sees a lone child haltingly making his way to the school. When he notices the presence of the henge, he fearfully calls out, asking if someone is there. One or more of the henge might want to hide at this point, but as narrator you don't need to mention the possibility. What's important here is that they meet with the child, rather than letting him slip past them.

Someone might get a bit startled along the way, but regardless here is where the child meets the henge. Have them exchange introductions, talk a bit, and make Impression Checks. Once everyone has gotten their connections, it's time to start talking about what's going on. The child's situation is as follows:

- He forgot his homework in the classroom.
- He really needs to get it, but he's scared.
- He wants the henge to come with him, because he thinks nothing bad will happen if they do.
- He also definitely doesn't want to go back home without getting what he forgot.

Once everyone heads into the school, it's time to end the scene. Take care of what goes between scenes, then move on to the second scene.

Second Scene

LOCATION: INSIDE THE SCHOOL
TIME: NIGHT

Everyone passes through the moonlit gates, and into the empty school. The light of the moon is brilliant, but the school is silent. There's no sign of people or animals. Even though it's late at night, the doors are open, and they can all enter as they please. They might want to talk a bit to distract themselves.

The interior of the school is dark, and the wooden floorboards squeak with every step, adding to everyone's fear. But, nothing is really happening. The group proceeds through the moonlit school to find whatever the child forgot.

There aren't any checks set up here. Unless the henge come up with other ideas, they'll all proceed to the classroom and get the child's forgotten item.

Now, for the trip back.

When they leave the classroom, have everyone make an Animal check. Henge who get a result of 4 or better will notice what seems like the faint sound of a sobbing child. The child with them will definitely notice, be Surprised, and cry out.

Henge who didn't notice it might well be startled by the child's cry. However, they won't be Surprised at this point. With the child Surprised, the scene ends.

Take care of the usual stuff that goes between scenes, and move on to the third scene.

Third Scene

LOCATION: FROM A HALLWAY TO THE SHOE SHELF
TIME: NIGHT

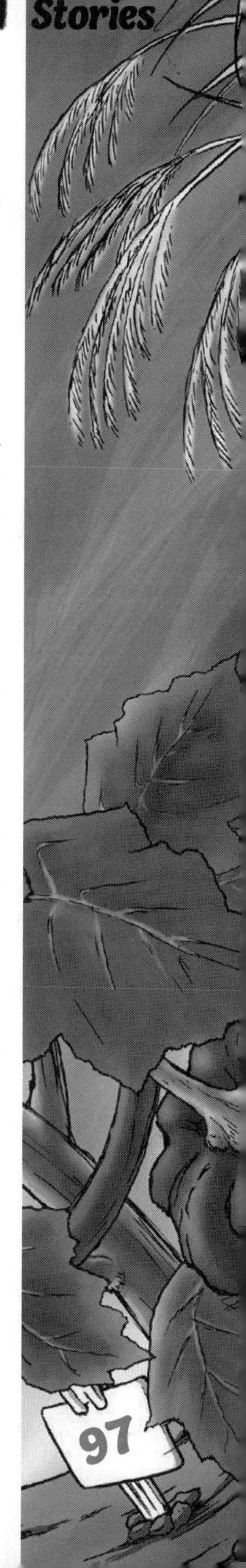

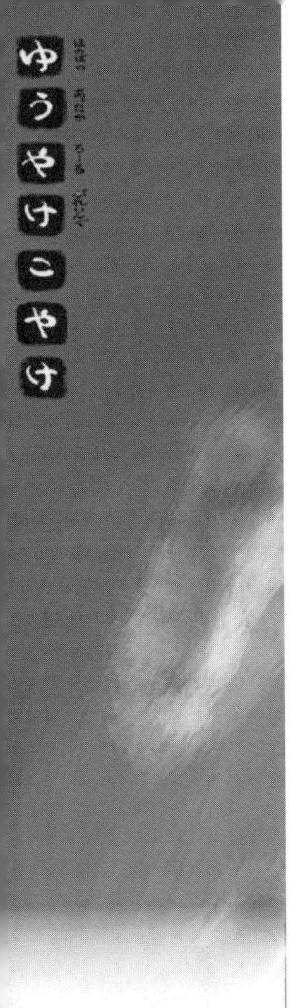

So, everyone is still in the school, heading down the hallway towards the entrance. The child is so scared that he can't even walk unless someone holds his hand. Hopefully everyone will help him get up his courage and lead him out. If they don't do a good enough job of comforting him, he'll start crying and become too scared to even head to the entrance.

Then, as they're nearing the gate…

Once again, they can hear that crying voice. It's very close now, and there's no need for anyone to make a check. It suddenly sounds as though there is a crying child right by them. At this point the child and the henge alike have to deal with a Surprise of 8. Hold back on spending Feelings so that the child doesn't brush it off. Rather he should be frozen with fear or cry out or some such.

When someone cries out or otherwise reacts, they can again hear the crying.

The crying gradually comes closer.

They can hear the voice right next to them!

And this is where the scene ends.

Take care of what goes between scenes, and move on to the fourth scene.

Fourth Scene

LOCATION: THE SCHOOL'S ENTRANCE

TIME: NIGHT

Have the henge make an Animal check. Anyone who gets a 4 or better will realize that the sound is coming from the bushes by the entrance.

Have the henge who succeeded make an Adult check. Anyone who gets a 4 or better on that will understand that it isn't actually the sound of someone crying.

The child will be so scared that he wants to run away by now. However, if someone gathers their courage and goes into the bushes, they'll find a cute little puppy there. The puppy will seem

unsure of what to do when a henge comes near it, and lacking the ability to talk it will start barking. That will reveal to everyone very clearly that they're dealing with a puppy. When the child realizes that it was just a puppy all along, he'll feel ashamed after clinging to someone in terror for so long.

If someone pets the puppy, it will very quickly take to them. When that happens, let them make Impression Checks to form connections with the puppy. Also, if there happens to be a dog henge in the group, he or she will be able to tell that the puppy is hungry and cold.

No doubt everyone will take pity on a puppy all alone in the night. Let the child and the henge talk about what to do for the little puppy.

Once that's decided, the child will return home. Of course, the puppy might go home with him. As the narrator, you should help decide whether the puppy can go home with the child, or the henge will have to look after it. If there's a dog henge in the group, he or she surely couldn't ignore the situation.

Once they've decided what to do with the puppy, it's time to end this scene.

Once you've taken care of the items that go between scenes, tell everyone that you're moving on to the final scene.

Final Scene

LOCATION: ?
TIME: EVENING OF THE FOLLOWING DAY

What happened with the puppy at the end of the previous scene? Where this scene takes place depends on how that turned out. In the evening of the following day, everyone gathers wherever the puppy ended up.

We've provided several possible resolutions. However, these are ultimately just examples. If the child and the henge come up with a solution not listed here, you as the narrator should respect that.

THE CHILD KEEPS THE PUPPY

In this case, the next day the henge and the child head to the child's house after school. Let them talk as they walk down the road. When they arrive at the house, the puppy greets them, far happier than the day before. They can play with the puppy for a while, and then the story ends.

FIND THE PUPPY A HOME

The child found someone who could take care of the puppy at school. A "Princess" (see the People section) could be a good choice. Or, if the henge have met someone appropriate in a previous story, you can have them play this role in the story.

This person who appears at the end will surely become good friends with the henge.

If they're meeting for the first time, have them make Impression Checks and create connections.

This new person discusses the puppy with the child, everyone talks some, and then the story ends.

THE HENGE LOOK AFTER THE PUPPY

In the evening of the following day, after school is over, the child comes to the open area in front of the school. The henge and the puppy are playing. The child is sorry that he can't keep the puppy at his own house, but he saved some of his lunch for the puppy to eat.

If the henge suggest looking for someone to take care of the puppy, he might well find someone the next day.

The story ends with the child and the henge discussing what to do with the puppy, and playing together.

Now, the story is finished. Thank everyone for taking part, and take care of the things that come after the story is over.

However, there might well be more scenes after this. Also, the narrator can customize the details of this story in many different ways.

Create your very own story, and add new things to it.

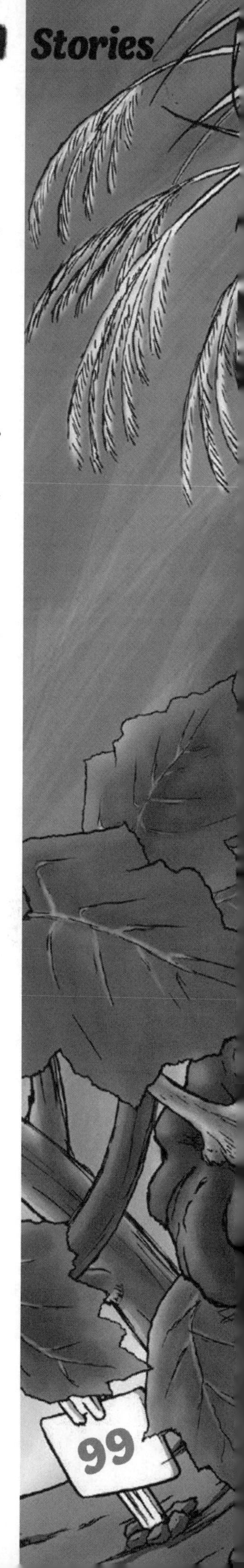

About the Countryside

This article originally appeared in Tsugihagi Tayori Vol. 1 *under the title* Inaka Iroiro. *It was written by South (さうす) of Majo no Kai, the current publisher of* Witch Quest. *Although originally aimed at Japanese readers, it has some invaluable insights on the Japanese countryside that can help enrich your stories.*

If you happen to be able to read Japanese (or are willing to be sufficiently tenacious with an online translation tool), you might also get some further insight from this countryside FAQ:

http://www5.ocn.ne.jp/~shimoxx/faq/index.htm

Countryside Stories

There are two main kinds of everyday magic stories. There are those that have wondrous beings residing in cities with many people, and those that take place in the sparsely-populated countryside. For the purposes of *Golden Sky Stories* we will take a look at the latter. It would not be an exaggeration to say that *Golden Sky Stories'* countryside setting, a town called Hitotsuna Town that seems like it could very well be real, is an important part of its appeal.

This book contains enough information on the setting to play the game, but for people who haven't ventured into the Japanese countryside, playing a game set there may seem daunting. Thus, I have put together some things to keep in mind as you put together scenarios for stories taking place in the countryside.

Images of the Countryside

I probably don't need to present my credentials here, but I'm from Noto, and currently live in Kanazawa. I'm pretty clearly a country bumpkin, and I'm more attached to the countryside than the city.

That isn't to say that I hate the city. Kanazawa, where I'm currently living, is a city after all, or at least feels that way. For someone from the countryside the city is like a daydream of some fantastical place, and for people from the city, the countryside must be every bit as wondrous.

On the other hand, someone from the city who has little direct experience with the countryside might see it through fantastical images. They imagine nature everywhere, students walking across open fields to get to school, local festivals and local customs in bloom, young and old living together in peace, that kind of thing.

Well, that's not a lie or anything. Taking a detour returning home from elementary school could take you to a harbor, fields, or mountain trails. I did that plenty myself.

However, people raised in the countryside know that there are some unhappy realities. People are not always as kind as you might think, farmers often have to take part-time jobs to make ends meet, and (although it's rare) there have been cases of criminals driving in from the city to do their wicked deeds.

But, setting aside the fact that keeping up on geeky hobbies takes a lot of work and participating in events means a lot of travel expenses, it's really not that bad.

The Countryside in RPGs

For everyday magic stories, it's better to set aside a lot of the bad stuff rather than trying to convey the "true" countryside. Sometimes the reality can be a considerable hindrance.

We have no way of knowing whether you or your friends are from the city or if you've lived in the country. It's hard to divine the experiences of the people at the gaming table. In other words, there's no need to make scenarios dependent on knowledge of the countryside.

An RPG scenario isn't a simulation of the countryside, so it's safer to go for portraying a "fantasy countryside."

Different Kinds of Countryside

There's another important thing to keep in mind about the countryside. A certain pattern emerged in online discussions. Many people assumed that areas with a given population would all be the same.

Some people seemed to think of the countryside as being all commuter towns, and even some people who live in the countryside think that way. Most of the people living in my hometown were employed locally, and there really weren't any cities within commuting distance. The Hitotsuna Town described in this book was in fact designed as a commuter town with some through traffic.

Still, the countryside is quite varied from one place to another, and the people who live there are generally aware of this. That means that you can create your fantasy countryside without worrying too much about the fine details.

Making a Fantasy Countryside

So, what can you do to better portray the countryside in RPGs? Put simply, it's a matter of showing off the differences between the country and the city. Of course, you're surely wondering what those differences actually are. Let's see if we can give you something useful.

Rules-Related Factors

Hitotsuna Town is very much an archetypal countryside setting with everything you'd expect it to have. If you're not used to working with this kind of setting, making use of an existing one is likely easier than trying to create one from scratch on your own.

The rules themselves also provide you with plenty of things to make use of. The "Acceptance" connection from the town is a perfect example. In the countryside there is a very pronounced sense of "in-group" and "out-group."

Being accepted by the town means that you're not an outsider, but a part of the community. Make good use of this feeling of acceptance and the comfort it provides.

"In Town" and "Everything Else"

Even in Hitotsuna Town there is a sense that "in town" is the main shopping area, and what lies beyond that is "everything else." "In town" is relatively open to "strangers," but the places where the mysterious happens, the everyday magic, are trickier. Use places for different purposes depending on who people meet and when. The center of town is surprisingly good for events taking place at night. Once the sun sets, the shops all close up and the whole place seems to go to sleep.

(Well, truth be told, there are places in the country with 24-hour convenience stores, but let's ignore those, shall we?)

Effective Use of People's Notice

This might come as a surprise, but in the countryside there are more watchful eyes than in the city. Or rather, there are more people who are interested in

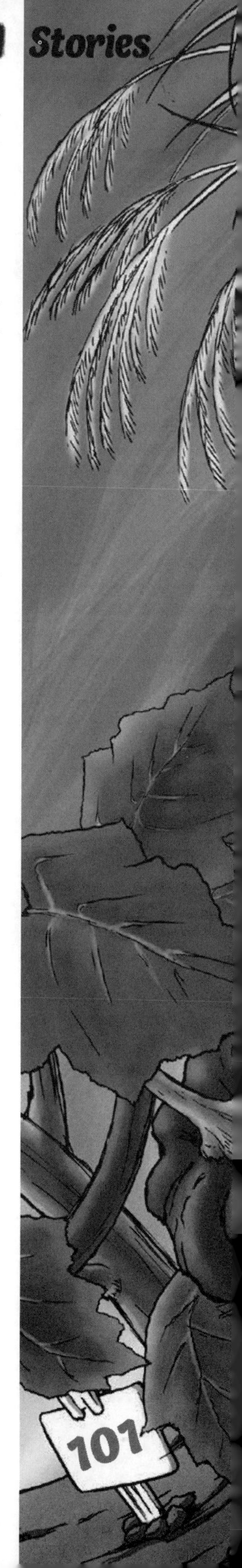

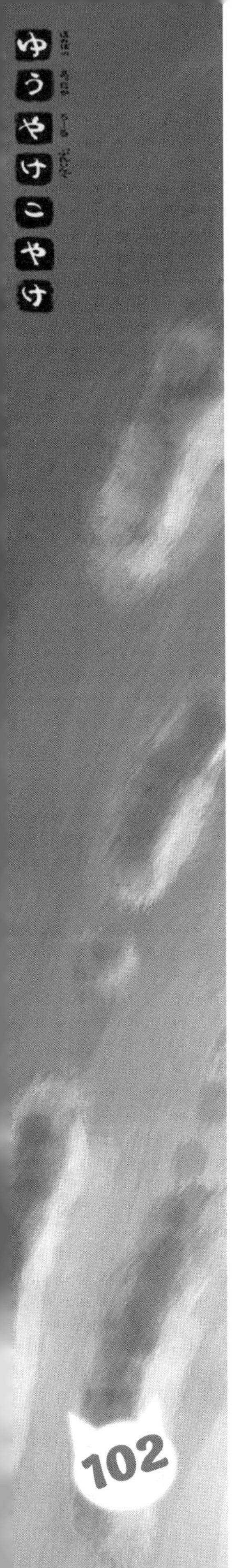

what's going on around them. An unfamiliar face, even just hanging around, will definitely attract attention. Whose house they went into, who they talked to, and what they had for lunch could all be spread around the town by the next day.

You'd think that the fields and rice paddies would be vacant in fair weather, but that's just when the farm workers will be out in force, all with their watchful eyes. Compared to the city, cars are a rare sight on the roads and on the paths between rice paddies, so they stand out to the people on foot.

It's not the same as the distinction between "in town" and "everything else," but things do still draw attention from all around. It all depends on the situation in the scenario.

Effective Use of Time

Even in such places, the people all but disappear in the evening and twilight, and that's interesting. Once the sun goes down, it becomes too dark to see what you're doing, so outdoor work like agriculture and forestry becomes nearly impossible. When that happens, people go back to their homes in twos and threes, and sharp-eyed henge can do as they please in the darkness.

In the middle of the night it becomes very dark outside of the center of town and peoples' homes. Behind a shrine or on a mountain road, the only relief from the deep darkness is the round moon and the beautiful stars. This isn't a problem for henge, but any children with them could be pretty scared.

However, given how dark and quiet the surroundings are, it definitely stands out when children make light or raise their voices. This could attract the attention of whoever's on fire patrol[1] or anyone who happens to live nearby.

Visiting Neighbors' Homes

Unlike in the city, people have no problem leaving their windows and doors unlocked. (Lately there have been problems with burglars coming from the cities, but let's ignore that.)

It's much easier to slip in and out of someone's house unnoticed at night, but normally you're supposed to call out their name at the entrance, lest you be mistaken for a thief. Children often have their rooms separated from where their parents sleep, so they can sneak out of their houses much more easily, whether to go out somewhere or just use the toilet.

Lots of Things Are Missing

In the countryside it's not at all unusual for people to have to take a car or train to go to a larger town to buy things that go beyond basic necessities. (And needless to say, kids and henge alike can't drive.)

In some places there are no government offices or banks nearby. In some places you could easily have to take a fairly long drive if you want to go shopping at night. Arcades? Movie theaters? There's nothing like that.

The countryside is lacking in certain things to the point where it's often perfectly reasonable to just say, "There isn't one," or "You'd have to go to the next town on the other side of the mountain." If you're not used to this kind of thing, you can pretty much assume that anything not in the description of the town in the rulebook just isn't in the town.

On the other hand, once you're more accustomed to this kind of setting, it might be interesting to build scenarios around things that the countryside has but cities don't.

---

[1] *Small towns can have* "hi no youjin," *people who check for fires and crime at night, and carry wooden clappers to alert people if something happens. They are usually young men, but children sometimes fill this role too. Needless to say, they could well become friends with the henge.*

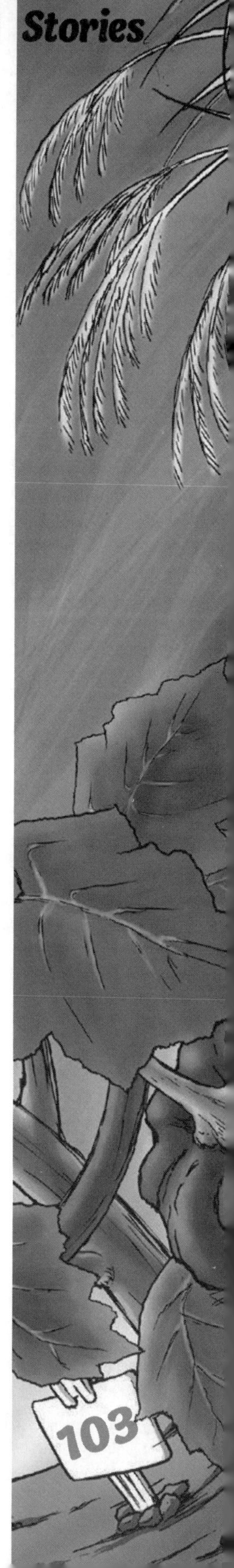

Bring Other Things in As Necessary

Don't get too carried away with the fine details. There are plenty of things about the countryside that you can use, like how people are more religious, or the eldest son is highly regarded, or people are called by their trades as well as their names, or how there's no cell phone reception in the mountains, but try to use them a bit at a time as inspiration for your scenarios.

Stepping Away From the Town

Up until now, we've been concentrating on using Hitotsuna Town as the backdrop for your game, but you could well use an original countryside area, or move to somewhere else connected via train or roads.

This is just for reference (and merely my own biased views), but here are some different archetypal varieties of country towns. There may well be others, but you can at least use this as a starting point.

PROVINCIAL CITY/COMMUTER TOWN

The area where I'm living now is very much like this. It is a rural area full of rice paddies and fields, and in the middle of that is a residential area, all near the mountains. It's near a city, and there's public transportation for commuters, so while you can get access to most anything you want with only a little effort, the area is still rich in nature, and there have always been lots of farmers around.

This is the kind of place where you don't see fireflies anymore.

TOWN WITH THROUGH TRAFFIC

Hitotsuna Town is like this. There are trains and roads that go through it that some people use to commute to work or school, and mountains, coastline, or rivers cut the town off from its immediate surroundings. Although it's relatively isolated, a fair number of people still go to and from the city.

Here you can find fireflies around clean, pure water as long as you're not in the middle of town.

THE MIDDLE OF NOWHERE

My hometown was like this. These are towns on peninsulas or surrounded by mountains that have little through traffic, so public transportation will likely have been operating in the red for a long time, or may even have stopped service entirely. There are also places where a thriving nearby town has pulled away the population, or an industry that formed the heart of the local economy like coal mining has declined. Many places are troubled by depopulation.

In a place like this, there are necessities like clinics and post offices, but options for entertainment are rather limited. There are of course fireflies.

ISOLATED VILLAGES, ISLANDS

These areas will have one or two single-lane roads (which might not even be paved), and way back when used to have maybe one phone in the larger houses, while in some cases there's neither telephone lines nor electricity.

Streetlamps are also few in number, and there are no traffic signals at intersections. Houses are hundreds of meters apart. Schools combine elementary and middle school under one roof, or in some cases due to school closures they may be on the other side of a mountain, requiring a commute of an hour or more.

There might be a single bus per day, there's a shrine to the local deity in the forest, and the festival only needs a single booth to sell toys. The only grocery in the village closed up shop because of depopulation, but there are still traces of the ancient sign and vending machine.

In the case of an island, coming and going, as well as deliveries of goods, is limited to once or twice a week, so moving around is very difficult.

In the summer you can see countless fireflies near the rice paddies and irrigation channels.

MOUNTAINS, DESERTED ISLANDS, GHOST TOWNS

Perhaps there never were any people, or perhaps they're all gone. At this point we've gone past the category of "countryside."

A Final Note

I've written a few countryside scenarios for *Witch Quest*. Scenario Guide 1, "The Summer Vacation that Disappeared into a Picture Diary" is about a boy who came from the city to the countryside to play and meets a girl, and Scenario Guide 4, "Railroad Memories" is about local people and a discontinued rail line. Scenario Guide 3, "Trampled Cat Waltz," is more of a tale of ruins in the mountains than of the countryside, but it too was influenced by my upbringing in the countryside.

The raw materials of the countryside feel are nostalgia for a simpler time and a warm pleasant feeling. The word "countryside" in the game should invoke the same feeling that "hometown" would, because the Japanese word *"inaka"* contains both meanings.

Through playing this game, you can find a hometown for your heart.

Winter is the season of endings,
The season when fertility and life hide themselves,
The season when everything seems to stand still.

Here you will find various kinds of information for Golden Sky Stories.
A town where stories can take place. People who live in the town. Animals of the town.
And, the mysterious local gods.

These things are written here.
Please, use them to tell your very own stories.

冬 Winter

Animals

There are many ordinary animals who are not henge, the kind we all know well, living in the town.

Humans can't talk to them, and for the most part henge can't either. Furthermore, most living things don't really have time to think about anything besides living their lives with everything they've got.

Henge can speak to animals of the same types as themselves. Those animals will tend to be absorbed in their own affairs and thus unable to really be all that helpful, but it's probably a good idea to at least say hello.

Finally, encountering an injured or lost animal could be the beginning of a story.

FOXES

HENGE: 1 **ANIMAL:** 2
ADULT: 1 **CHILD:** 0

Foxes live deep in the forests and mountains, and seldom show themselves before humans. However, when people hang persimmons, foxes will sneak up and eat them sometimes. Foxes generally fear people and other animals, but when they have friends, they will play pleasantly together.

For more information on foxes, see the introduction to fox henge.

RACCOON DOGS

HENGE: 1 **ANIMAL:** 2
ADULT: 0 **CHILD:** 1

Raccoon dogs are laid-back animals that take life at an easy pace. They live in forests and mountains, but they do sometimes show up in villages or fields. They're timid, yet inquisitive, so they may approach henge of other animal types.

For more information on raccoon dogs, see the introduction to raccoon dog henge.

CATS

HENGE: 1 **ANIMAL:** 2
ADULT: 0 **CHILD:** 1

Cats all live according to their whims. Sometimes they stick close to people, and sometimes they wander off without a second thought. They're so whimsical that sometimes they'll leave the town

entirely. Cats know all of the hidden paths through town, and they'll deliberately come in contact with henge.

For more information on cats, see the introduction to cat henge.

DOGS

HENGE: 1 **ANIMAL:** 0-2
ADULT: 0 **CHILD:** 0-2

There are many kinds of dogs. There are cute little puppies, which can seem like completely different animals from the big dogs that people train. Even the biggest dogs can be gentle and friendly to people. Dogs are known for their perseverance, and they follow what their owner or leader tells them to do.

For more information on dogs, see the introduction to dog henge.

RABBITS

HENGE: 0 **ANIMAL:** 3
ADULT: 0 **CHILD:** 0

In the town there are not only rabbits kept as pets, but many wild rabbits. Rabbits are timid animals, but their curiosity leads them to go into places with people again and again. It is not easy for a normal person to catch a rabbit that is running and jumping as it flees. Even for henge, this would be a difficult task.

For more information on rabbits, see the introduction to rabbit henge.

BIRDS

HENGE: 0 **ANIMAL:** 4
ADULT: 0 **CHILD:** 0

There are many different kinds of birds in town. If you go into the forest or mountains, you will find even more birds. There are migratory birds that are only around during certain seasons. The attribute numbers listed here are for a typical bird that can fly. If a bird is hurt and unable to fly, all of its attributes become 0. Such a bird will not be able to survive unless someone helps out.

For more information on birds, see the introduction to bird henge.

BEARS

HENGE: 0 **ANIMAL:** 6
ADULT: 0 **CHILD:** 0

Bears are the strongest of the animals in the town, and very big as well. If a bear stands up, he is much taller than a person (2 meters or more), with sharp claws and exceptional strength. No other animal can match a bear for sheer strength.

Bears mostly live in the mountains, and seldom come down into human settlements. However, a hungry young bear searching for food might well pursue henge and hurt them.

Bears are good at climbing trees and swimming, and despite being so big, they're surprisingly quiet when they walk. Henge and people alike shouldn't get too close to a bear without a good reason.

In the winter, bears will hibernate in a hole. When a bear awakes from hibernation, whether normally or because his sleep was interrupted, he will be very hungry. Also, many bears become local gods of mountains. Bears tend to be moody and shy, so they'll throw their strength around when only slightly startled. They're generally very mild, easygoing animals, but they're so strong that they're not good at holding back.

Some areas don't have bears. If bears aren't appropriate to the setting, the narrator can decide that there aren't any.

BEE SWARM

HENGE: 0 **ANIMAL:** 3-4
ADULT: 0 **CHILD:** 0

The most dangerous of all the animals in the town are actually the tiny bees. They build hives in the most unexpected places, so it's entirely too easy to stumble across a beehive and get attacked. They construct their hives in thickets, under overhangs of roofs, and anywhere with

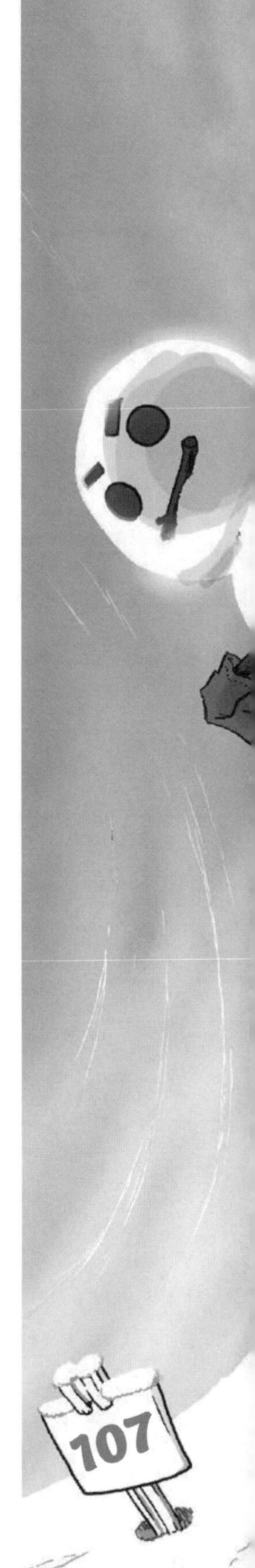

some shelter, and if you get too close they'll attack with their small poisonous stingers. Bees can fly through the air very quickly, and once angered, they do not forgive. If a swarm is after you, you'll have to flee indoors or underwater to have any hope of escape.

Bee stings are not only painful, but can cause swelling and fevers. While individual bees are weak, they can display incredible power as a swarm.

Bees do not become henge or local gods. Even henge and local gods should not recklessly go near their hives either. One sting should be enough to teach anyone that they should stay away from bees.

You can find different varieties of bees in different places, but they're everywhere. If angered, they're more dangerous than poisonous snakes. Please be careful.

BOARS

HENGE: 0 **ANIMAL:** 5
ADULT: 0 **CHILD:** 0

Boars are the sturdiest of the animals that come down to the town. They have sharp tusks, and they're far stronger than their mild looks might suggest. Boars tend to charge when they're startled, angrily stabbing with their tusks, but they won't do more than chase away whoever is right in front of them. They won't chase after people or henge just for being next to them. If you have children with you, it's probably best to make sure they don't wander off, but otherwise you'll be fine around a boar as long as you're careful. However, when food becomes scarce in the mountains, they sometimes come down into town. When that happens, they may charge at people without thinking.

Child boars are cute animals with a striped pattern on them. They will get along with other animals in the mountains such as rabbits and raccoon dogs, and even play together. Boar parents also get along with other animals. For animals that live in the mountains, a boar resting in the shade of a tree is a common sight. Many boars become local gods, and these are among the more easy-going local gods.

Also, boars prefer mild climates, so they don't live up north. If the setting isn't appropriate for boars, the narrator may say that there aren't any around the town.

CHICKENS

HENGE: 0 **ANIMAL:** 1
ADULT: 0 **CHILD:** 0

These are flightless birds that may be kept at the local school. Chickens can't fly, but they can run better than your typical bird. Also, chickens that are used to being outside can flap their wings to jump higher, or to hop from tree to tree. They have a very distinctive, loud call, which you no doubt know well. In a small town, it can seem like there are chickens calling from every nook and cranny.

In towns where people are raising lots of chickens, an escape can cause quite a ruckus as people try to catch them again. Chickens aren't troublemakers or anything, but they sometimes get restless from being cooped up so much.

Chickens are domesticated birds, and every morning they let out lively calls, but for the most part, they do not become henge. Even when chickens do become henge, they don't care much for people. Let's just try to be grateful to chickens for the eggs they give us.

You can find chickens wherever there are people raising them. People usually keep them in cages or pens, but in the mountains, people will let them graze.

COWS

HENGE: 0 **ANIMAL:** 4
ADULT: 0 **CHILD:** 0

Cows are animals that people keep in pastures or barns. They're bigger than boars and quite strong, but they prefer not to move around. They also have a calm temperament. If someone gets them excited, they will break into a powerful run, but normally they just walk around at an easy pace.

They do have horns on their heads, but except on certain cows used for labor, they aren't dangerous. Most cows have people to protect them, and they're big enough that most animals won't trouble them.

No matter what the situation, cows think and move at a leisurely pace. They're not interested in anything other than eating grass and raising children. Cows never become local gods, and never become henge. Whether they will be around depends on whether there is someone who wants to raise cattle. Pastures and barns are often in the mountains, so it's not unusual for them to get to know the animals that live up there.

DEER

HENGE: ○ **ANIMAL:** 4
ADULT: ○ **CHILD:** ○

Deer are docile animals that live in mountains and forests. The males have large antlers. In the summer, they grow a white-flecked pattern on their bodies, and they run around among the mountains and trees. Deer are normally docile, but when they're taking care of their children, they won't go near people or other animals. Deer can run very fast, and they're incredible jumpers. They can easily clear small fences.

Deer live in large families or herds, never alone. If you encounter deer, you'll meet several of them at once.

Older deer sometimes become local gods. Deer become calm, quiet local gods, but they do not desire contact with people. They prefer a calm, quiet lifestyle. They dislike engaging in violence themselves, so if a problem arises, they'll likely ask henge for help finding a peaceful solution. They're usually good friends with rabbit, raccoon dog, and bird henge.

Deer tend to live in one particular area. Depending on the region, this may be in the heart of the forest or the mountains, but they will not go near where people live. They eat grass and wild fruit, so they have no need to go near people. Thus, in most places you will never see deer near where people live.

FISH

HENGE: ○ **ANIMAL:** ○ (3 IN WATER)
ADULT: ○ **CHILD:** ○

In ponds, rivers, and seas, fish play the leading role. Killifish, loach, carp, catfish… countless different kinds of fish live in the water. The world of water where the fish live seldom has any contact with the land. Fish are powerless on land, but in the water, no other living thing can compare to them. Just as birds are unmatched in the air, fish are unmatched in the water.

Since fish dominate the water, they often become local gods of ponds or rivers. Many fish also become henge that never come on land. They like living under the water. When they do wind up on land, it's because a fisherman has dropped something strange into the water, or has been catching too many fish. Even then, they try to resolve things as quickly as possible. They often ask other henge for help. Fish who become henge or local gods tend to be long-lived, and acquainted with the foxes.

Fish can be found anywhere. Every town has some water, and it only takes a little bit of water for fish to have a place to live. In a coastal town, the fish will likely have no choice but to deal with the town from time to time.

MICE/RATS

HENGE: ○ **ANIMAL:** 2
ADULT: ○ **CHILD:** ○

In the town there are mice and rats, on the plains there are field mice, and people keep hamsters as pets. These

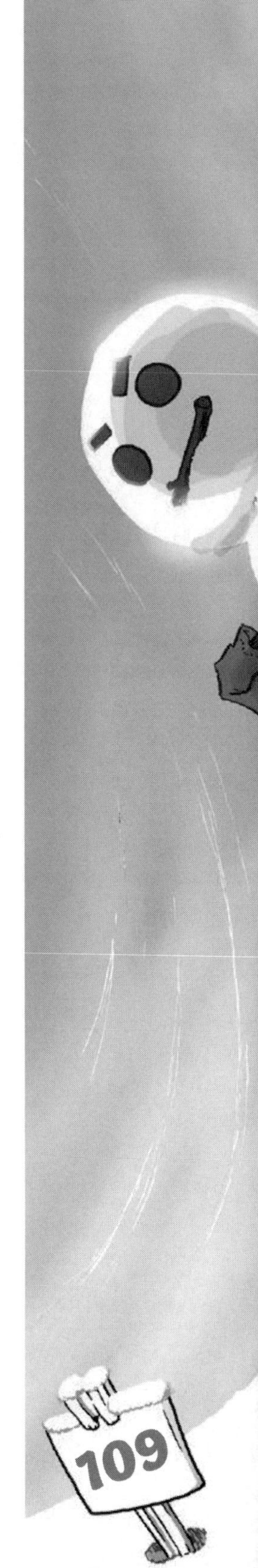

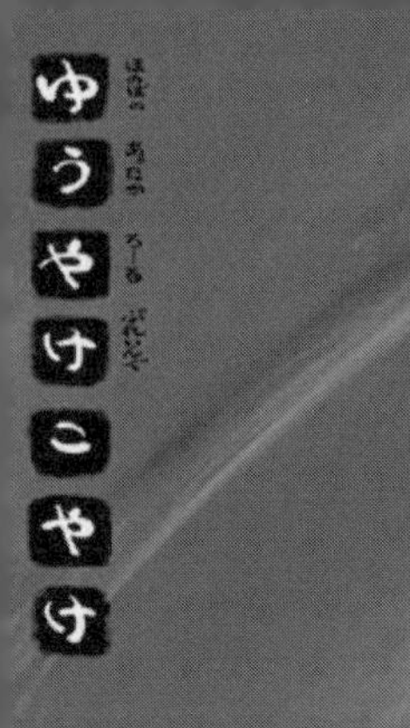

nimble little creatures are not strong animals, but they make up for it with sheer numbers. Mice can live in the smallest cracks and many other places you wouldn't expect.

There are mouse henge with strange powers. They're small but smart animals, who think of themselves and their families first.

Mice will naturally take anything interesting or pretty that they find back home with them. They're also known for using their sharp teeth to gnaw on houses or trees until they've ruined them.

Mice seldom become local gods, but there are mice with strange powers who make trouble and become a burden on the town. They tend not to get along with cats or foxes. However, they can become good friends with lonely rabbits.

Mice live most everywhere. You can find mice anywhere where people live, and there are mice who live in the mountains or near the water.

MONKEYS

HENGE: 0	**ANIMAL:** 2
ADULT: 0	**CHILD:** 1

Monkeys are smart, dexterous, fairly strong animals that live in the mountains and forests. They always live in groups, and freely run around the tops of trees, sometimes even chasing bears away. Although clever, monkeys love picking on others. If a person or henge is carrying something that looks interesting, monkeys will be quick to try to take it. The bonds between them are very strong, and they specialize in teamwork. For that reason, if you see one monkey, chances are there are plenty of others nearby. They're quick to inform their fellows of food or danger, and the whole group can gather very quickly.

Monkeys frequently spill from their mountain or forest homes into human settlements. Given their penchant for harassment, these monkeys will spell trouble for people and animals alike. When this happens, it's possible to get the boss monkey to have them return home, but this requires a henge or local god. However, while some monkeys rise above the rest to become a leader, they do not become local gods.

Monkeys live all over the place, but there are regions without any. If the narrator thinks that monkeys aren't appropriate to the setting, he or she may decide that it has none.

SNAKES

HENGE: 1	**ANIMAL:** 2
ADULT: 0	**CHILD:** 0

Snakes live on plains, in fields, watersides, forests, under the overhangs of roofs, and so on. There are many varieties of snakes. In Japan a big snake is about a meter long, but most of the ones you might encounter aren't that big (though there could well be even bigger ones around). Snakes don't do anything particularly bad, but people tend to hate them. Contrary to how they might look, snakes do not bite for no reason.

However, there are adders, vipers, and other poisonous snakes. These snakes will bite anyone who threatens them. Poisonous snakes are about as dangerous as bears, so please be careful.

Also, it's not unusual for older snakes to transform and become local gods or henge. Many have been around for a long time, and such snakes are likely acquainted with nearby fox henge. Snakes with the power to transform are usually very large, and some of them are 5 or more meters long.

Because snakes are cold-blooded, they do not live in cold areas. Furthermore, they hibernate in the winter, so one would not meet any snakes at that time of year.

WEASELS

HENGE: 1	**ANIMAL:** 3
ADULT: 0	**CHILD:** 0

Weasels have long bodies, slim legs, and move around quickly. They're only about 30 centimeters long, but they're known, along with cats, as some of the shrewdest animals in town. They're incredible jumpers, and they can leap further and higher than the lengths of their own bodies. They can climb trees, swim, and dig holes, so you can find them in the most unexpected places. In snow country, they dig tunnels through the snow, and you can never be sure where one will appear. Furthermore, they can spray a foul smell from behind when they're being chased or scared[1].

Many weasels become henge. However, they're even more whimsical than cats, and tend to stay away from people. They can get along with other henge reasonably well, but they're too willing to wander around to become local gods.

Weasels can basically live anywhere. Among their relatives are martens that live deep in the mountains, and sea otters that live in the water. From north to south, from coastline to mountains, you can find weasels and their relations.

Other Animals

Bats fly around in the evening. Flying squirrels come out at night. Squirrels and wildcats live in the forests. Moles live underground. Frogs croak before it rains. Turtles swim in the pond. Raccoons come from outside to the waterside.

There are many other kinds of animals in the town. Depending on the area, there could be countless others.

People and henge alike seldom see these animals, so we haven't provided introductions to them here. However, they might show up unexpectedly. Furthermore, henge might meet them in the form of a local god. The narrator can put together attributes for these kinds of animals from those of similar animals and his or her own impressions.

Abilities of Animals

The animals that live in the town and aren't henge still have special abilities. These aren't mysterious or magical abilities, but are special abilities nonetheless.

Fish can swim in the water, snakes and bees have poison, and weasels have their spray. We'll leave special abilities like this up to the narrator's judgment. We might well add rules for such animals in the future, but for now we'll leave it all up to the narrator.

Likewise, you can treat the animals that can become henge but haven't been covered in the rules (mice, weasels, etc.) as simply "animals capable of human speech." If you think they should be able to use powers from other animals, feel free to let them do so. For example, a bat could surely use a bird's "Wings" power.

Animals in Stories

If the narrator brings animals into the story, they'll likely have something to ask of or tell to the participants' henge. On the other hand, they could just help paint a picture of what it's like to go deep into the mountains.

When you want to tell stories that involve meeting animals, think carefully about where those animals should be living.

Furthermore, please remember that henge cannot talk to animals of a different type from themselves. If a bear wandered into town, the henge would have to find some means other than words to persuade him to head back into the mountains.

For ideas on how to include different kinds of animals, read through their respective descriptions.

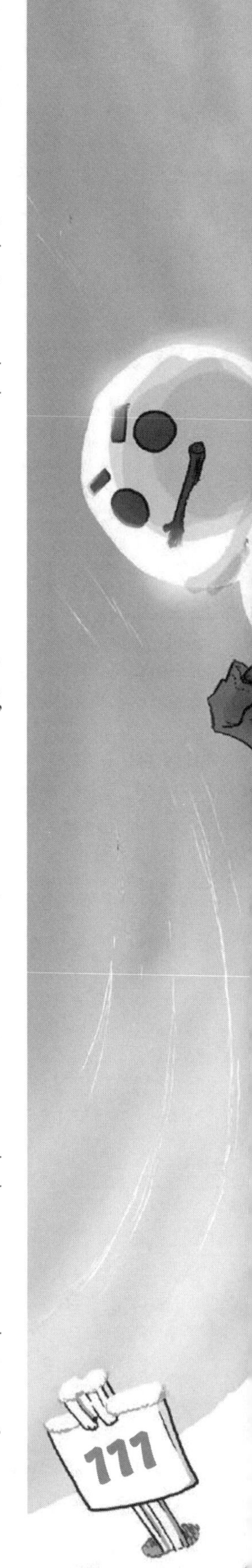

[1] *Weasels are related to skunks, and have a similar natural defense.*

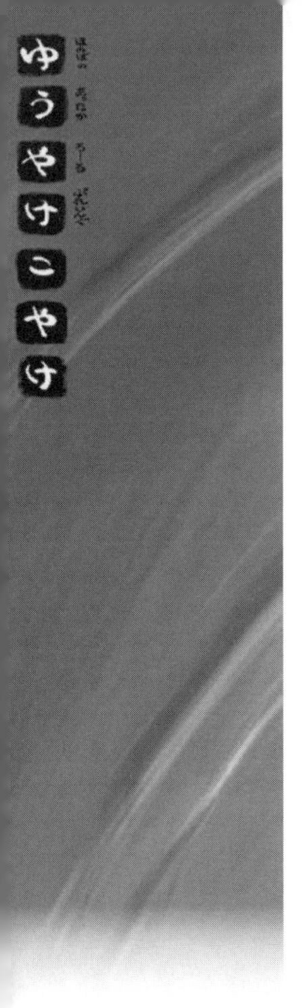

Participating as Animals

If you've played *Golden Sky Stories* many times already, and tried your hand at being a narrator as well, you can participate as an animal if the narrator allows. However, unlike people and henge, animals can't talk. They can only express themselves through body language and calling out.

For example, if someone is participating as a monkey, he or she could tug on sleeves or screech to grab people's attention, but that's about it. This is a real challenge, and you'll need to be both expressive and imaginative. Still, if you've become experienced with the game and playing the normal way is getting a little boring, go ahead and try it out.

However, if you're playing with someone who's new to the game, you'd best not participate as an animal. This is basically a special rule to add something interesting to the game for people who are well-accustomed to it.

You create animals in the same way as henge, but they cannot take human form and don't have any powers. Make your character's attributes the same as that type of animal normally has. For example, if you're participating as a bear, you'd have Animal at 6 (the usual limit of 4 doesn't apply here). Naturally, if you want to play as a particularly young or old bear, you could have different attributes with the narrator's permission.

The narrator should give these animals some difficult Weaknesses to deal with, and there are some animals (like fish or bees) that just aren't that good for someone to play. If you're thinking about participating as an animal, go over the whole thing with the narrator thoroughly before you play.

People

Many people live in the town. These people are all doing their best to live each day. They all have their own worries, and they have their own joys. Henge can meet people, talk to them about different things, help them out… and the days will continue on.

People are another potentially important part of a story. Each meeting with a person can be a story. Meeting someone for the first time, exchanging words, and getting to know each other is also a story.

Now, let's take a look at what kinds of people live in the town. Then, let's find out what might be troubling them.

LONELY

HENGE: 0	**ANIMAL:** 1
ADULT: 2	**CHILD:** 2

This person is introverted, but doesn't like being alone. He tries his best to show a cheerful face, to get someone to take care of him. There are people like this everywhere.

He's always worried about things where no one is at fault. He's suffering alone to make sure he doesn't trouble others. He actually could do all kinds of things, could come to like all kinds of people, but somehow he can't.

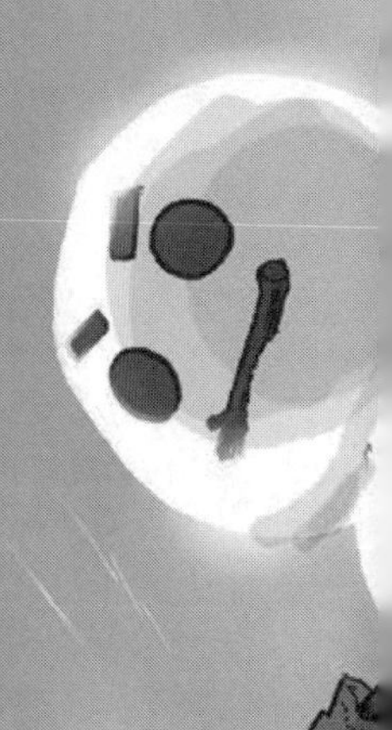

JAPANESE NAMES FOR PEOPLE

You might not be sufficiently familiar with Japanese names to come up with them for the people in your stories. There are other resources you can turn to, but here is a quick guide. Just pick out names that you think sound nice.

Female Given Names: Aiko, Akane, Akira, Aoi, Arisa, Asagi, Asuna, Ayumu, Chiaki, Chihiro, Emi, Ena, Fuuka, Haruka, Haruko, Haruna, Hikari, Himeko, Hoshi, Kagami, Kana, Kasumi, Kaori, Kazumi, Kumiko, Kurumi, Makie, Michiru, Mika, Minako, Misa, Misora, Miura, Miyako, Nanami, Nodoka, Sae, Sakurako, Satsuki, Setsuna, Tomo, Yotsuba, Yue, Yui, Yuka, Yukari, Yuki, Yuko, Yuna, Yuno

Male Given Names: Akihiko, Akio, Akira, Akito, Asuma, Ataru, Fuyuki, Gen, Harunobu, Hayate, Hideki, Hiro, Hiroyuki, Hitoshi, Isao, Jinpachi, Kanji, Kaoru, Kazuto, Ken, Kenta, Kiichi, Kosuke, Kyo, Kyusaku, Makoto, Manabu, Masaharu, Mitsunori, Nagisa, Natsuki, Nenji, Shigeo, Shinji, Shu, Shutaro, Souichiro, Sunao, Takahiro, Takashi, Takayuki, Takeo, Takeru, Takuma, Takumi, Tomokazu, Toraji, Yuichi, Yuji, Yukito

Family Names: Asakura, Ayase, Hasegawa, Hayasaka, Hayashi, Inoue, Ito, Izumi, Kagura, Kagurazaka, Kakizaki, Kasuga, Kimura, Kitagawa, Kobayashi, Koiwai, Komatsu, Kurosawa, Mihama, Minami, Miyakawa, Miyamoto, Miyata, Miyazaki, Mizuhara, Momose, Sakurazaki, Saotome, Sasaki, Sato, Serizawa, Shiina, Shiraishi, Suzuki, Tachibana, Takara, Takeda, Takino, Tanaka, Tanizaki, Tominaga, Ueda, Uehara, Yamada

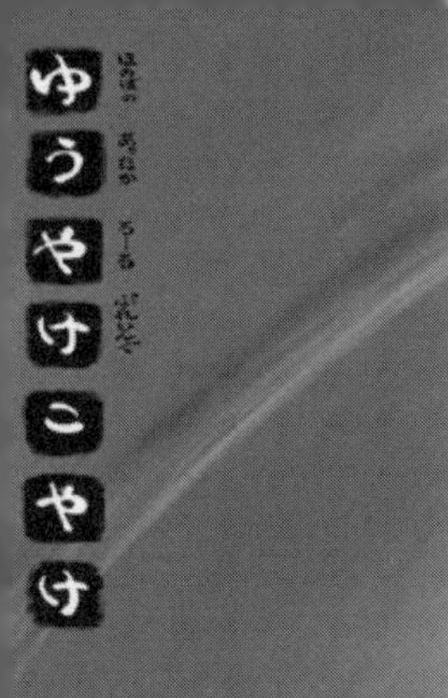

When henge find someone like this, they feel the need to become friends with them. Lonely people like this don't always realize just how lonely they really are. When others do become friends with them, such people will still be restrained without really knowing why.

Slowly, gently, show them warmth and caring. A lonely person is a friend, once that loneliness is gone.

STORY FRAGMENTS:
He might be troubled because he can't show his true self at school or at home. He might not be able to say what he wants to for fear of being hated. He might just sit in his room, reading books and sighing. If he sees something magical, perhaps he winds up crying because no one believes him. Being so shy, he can't make any friends, and he goes home alone. Perhaps when he gets home, his parents are still working and he's all alone.

TOP BRAT

HENGE: 0	**ANIMAL:** 2
ADULT: 1	**CHILD:** 2

This kid is a leader of sorts to other kids and an instigator of mischief.

Kids who fill this role are usually healthy and big, but any kid with charisma and guts can do it.

It doesn't take much for the leadership to shift to another kid either. A formerly timid child might pull his courage together. The children may stop following a leader who's too violent, and they sometimes drop their support after even a small failure.

The leader has to be ready to take the initiative for anything and everything, so it's not that easy of a position.

When henge run into children, a child like this will invariably be the first to speak up.

STORY FRAGMENTS:
He may have set the kids on a bit of mischief that is going too far, and now he can't stop it. He might have thoughtlessly quarreled with friends or family, leaving him troubled. He might have clumsily fallen in love with someone, leaving him totally lost as to what to do. He had planned to pull a simple little prank, but it got out of control and now he's really worried. He might get depressed if a pleasant day looked like it was going to be ruined by rain. He could feel lonely if he caught a cold and no one paid him a visit.

DILIGENT

HENGE: 0	**ANIMAL:** 1
ADULT: 3	**CHILD:** 1

This is an honors student and a very diligent child. He's always watching what's around him, and always getting the short end of the stick, but he still tries very hard every day. Having decided on his own position and value, he's always worrying and suffering.

Let's help him loosen up. Let's help him feel comfortable. It might seem like he'll just keep being stiff and diligent and nothing will change, but if you show him another point of view, he'll surely discover that there is more.

He's very dedicated, and while he's not always the most tactful kid around, he's definitely not a bad person. Just a little clumsy.

STORY FRAGMENTS:
He might be troubled when he accidentally drops or forgets something. He could get really depressed over some tiny little mistake. He might paint himself into a corner by pretending to know what he's doing. He might want to cry, want to complain, and be unable to express himself. Even if he falls in love with someone, he might not want to admit it even to himself. He might act too stiffly and be left out.

PRINCESS

HENGE: 0 **ANIMAL:** 1
ADULT: 3 **CHILD:** 3

Even in a town surrounded by nature, there are rich, well-to-do families. A "princess" from such a family is a little different from the other kids. She can get all kinds of things from her family, but there are all sorts of intangible things that it takes from her.

To a princess, the outside world is dazzling, and even just meeting some henge and talking to them a little bit could become a precious memory to her.

A princess always has a direct path right in front of her. This path is safer and freer of worry than anyone else's. However, sometimes she'll want to go a little astray, to see what lies beyond the path laid out for her. Henge will surely call to her from the side of the road. We can only hope they'll somehow become friends.

STORY FRAGMENTS:
She might be tired of her family's restrictive customs. Even if she falls in love with someone, she might not be able to tell her family. She might want to play in the hills or by the river like the other children. She might have a strange encounter with a henge taking a nap. Caught out in a downpour and soaking wet, she might start crying as she tries to find shelter somewhere. She might raise flowers with some henge. She might not realize that someone else is in love with her.

MISMATCHED COUPLE

HENGE: 0 **ANIMAL:** 1
ADULT: 2 **CHILD:** 2

These two are lovers who aren't quite meshing right at the moment.

These kids aren't quite confident that they're really lovers. Or maybe they're still young enough that they don't quite understand love. Or perhaps the love is actually one-sided. The two lovers could be very stubborn. Or one of them might not be confident that they really belong together. Whatever the case, their young love is at turns dangerous, amusing, and irritating. When you see them together, you can't help but want to meddle.

It wouldn't take much for true love to blossom. But somehow, things never quite seem to come together. Just seeing them, not only henge but other people want to get involved. Meddling leads to more meddling, one misunderstanding leads another, and somewhere in there you could have a story on your hands.

STORY FRAGMENTS:
They might have a little bit of a quarrel, and not forgive each other even though they want to. They might be stubborn and unable to be honest with each other. With people making fun of them, they might say the opposite of what they're really feeling. One of them might be holding back to be tactful, and be unable to express how he or she really feels. Someone might have a one-sided love for a henge, or there might be someone for whom a henge could have his or her own one-sided love.

SIBLINGS

HENGE: 0 **ANIMAL:** 1
ADULT: 1 **CHILD:** 2

These kids have been together their entire lives, and they have a very strong bond. They are connected by blood, a bond they couldn't break even if they wanted to. A bond they couldn't forget, even if they wanted to. The bond between them is strong enough that they'll quickly bounce back after any quarrel.

However, that bond doesn't mean they can be together all the time. That's why sometimes the henge need to cut in between them. Sometimes they need help to patch things up too. Step inside their world. It will teach them that there are things you can't understand alone,

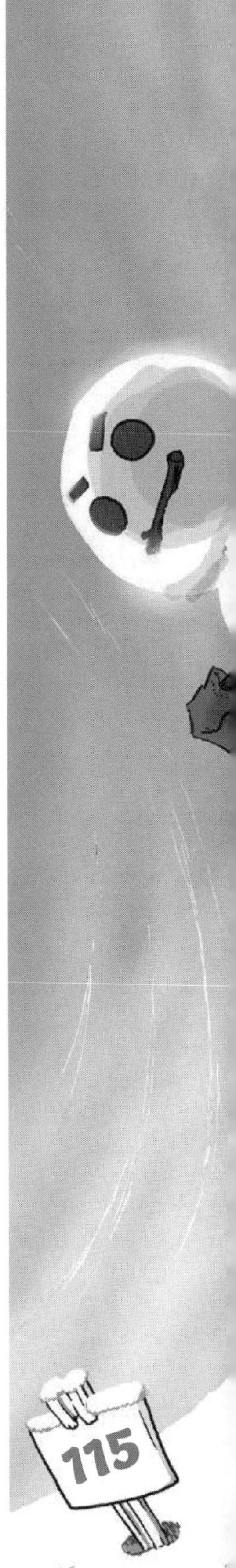

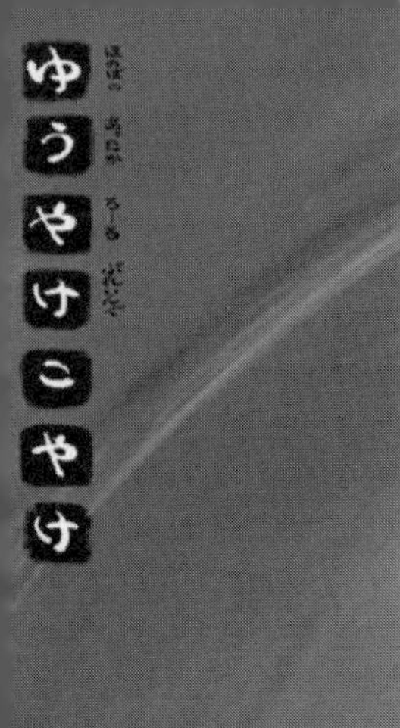

and things you can't accomplish alone. You should be able to teach them.

This is a bond that you can find anywhere, among most anyone, but coming together is very significant. Also, a henge's brother or sister might show up one day too.

STORY FRAGMENTS:
An older sibling might say something unreasonable to a younger sibling. A younger sibling might say something selfish to an older sibling. If a quarrel goes too far, the younger sibling might start crying. Twins might change places to play some mischief. An older sibling might be stubborn about something when he or she really shouldn't. Siblings might get along a little too well, so that the older one starts spoiling the younger one. Henge can also have brothers and sisters.

FARMER

HENGE: 0	**ANIMAL:** 2
ADULT: 2	**CHILD:** 1

This is a person who makes a living in fields or rice paddies, raising vegetables, fruits, or rice. If your town is near the sea, you can treat fishermen the same way.

Farmers sell their crops, but even if there's no problem with the taste, they'll have trouble selling produce that doesn't look good. They usually take all the produce that doesn't look good enough to sell, and give it to people who live nearby. Everything is tasty when it's just been harvested, and henge whom they consider friends can also get such gifts.

There are lots of farmers in the town, and they can make all different kinds of things using terraced fields in the mountains, regular fields, rice paddies, irrigation, reservoirs, and even home gardens. Towns are usually self-sufficient for food.

STORY FRAGMENTS:
They might let the henge have some of their fruit or other crops. Henge might get a reward for helping work in the fields. A car or bicycle someone is using to go along the roads between rice paddies might fall in. Henge might be asked to do something about monkeys that are devastating a farmer's fields. A playing child might fall into a rice paddy or irrigation canal. Someone might dig something very old out from a field. The thing they dug up might be something significant to a fox or local god.

CITY PERSON

HENGE: 0	**ANIMAL:** 1
ADULT: 4	**CHILD:** 0

This is a transfer student, or maybe a teacher who's relocated, or an adult on a business trip, who's come from the city. Such people are from a big, bustling city, very different from the small town.

These people lead busy lives, with little time to spare to experience the mysterious. For that reason, they won't believe in henge or other mysterious things at first. When a city person is Surprised, treat her attribute as being 2 less than normal. They'll be really startled by such things.

In the countryside there are skies full of stars, fireflies that fly about the rivers, crows that caw before the rain, and the sound of cicadas filling the air. The city lacks these things, and upon encountering them, at first a city person will have trouble accepting such mysterious things.

Still, one day they too should be able to become friends with henge.

STORY FRAGMENTS:
A city person might become lost in the unfamiliar countryside. Guided by the common sense of the city, she might not be able to accept henge. Even after meeting someone, she might still stay in a locked house and refuse to come and play together. She might have trouble adjusting to a new lifestyle and become sick. Unfamiliar

with nature, he or she might get injured. She might have trouble making friends, and feel lonely. She might be bewildered at the sight of unfamiliar animals.

BABY

HENGE: 0 **ANIMAL:** 0
ADULT: 0 **CHILD:** 3

This is a tiny little baby that someone in the town is taking care of. Henge will likely have many opportunities to play with babies who laugh and cry.

It takes a lot of work to take care of a baby, but a baby's smiling face can make up for any hardship. Normally it's the mother and father that look after a baby, but it doesn't take much for henge and other residents of the town to wind up lending a hand.

When the mother's body is weak, especially after giving birth, she'll have to see the doctor a lot. When that happens, she'll really need the help of family, neighbors, and perhaps even henge.

STORY FRAGMENTS:
A baby might wander off while the mother is looking away for just a little bit. Something might happen while someone is babysitting. A mother might ask some henge to look after her baby while she goes to take care of something. With the mother away, the father might have a really hard time taking care of the baby.

GRUMPY OLD MAN

HENGE: 0 **ANIMAL:** 1
ADULT: 2 **CHILD:** 0

This is an old man who often yells at and lectures kids who are up to mischief. A teacher who often scolds the kids is basically the same.

Although he's a short-tempered curmudgeon, he doesn't hate children, and he certainly doesn't want to hurt them. He gets so angry because he worries about the kids, and he gets mad, even though he'd prefer it if they liked him.

Among adults, the old man definitely isn't a bad person. If he doesn't know about henge, he might angrily yell at them the same way he does the children. Henge with a high Adult attribute should be able to figure out how he really feels.

STORY FRAGMENTS:
He might be troubled because he unintentionally got a little too mad and made some kids cry. He might get drunk and start crying as he tells the henge about the past. Even if he does know about henge, he might still keep yelling at them. A child who he yelled at might ask the henge to go see the old man in his place. If someone properly apologizes, the old man might give them a treat.

SENSEI

HENGE: 0 **ANIMAL:** 1
ADULT: 3 **CHILD:** 3

"Sensei" is a Japanese word that people use as a term of respect for not only teachers but people of many different learned professions. This includes novelists, potters, painters, doctors, scholars, and school principals. A sensei is someone people respect. Some days he can be very busy, while other days he'll be quite bored. A sensei can become quite good friends with children. If they should meet, he can become friends with henge too.

A sensei is an adult, but at the same time they are very childish in certain ways. That's why everyone likes and respects him. A sensei knows about all kinds of things, but can still play with children and animals. He also knows all kinds of different ways to play. Also, he can teach children, henge, and animals many things.

STORY FRAGMENTS:
A sensei won't be able to play when he's busy. When that happens, he might get angry and yell, then apologize later. A

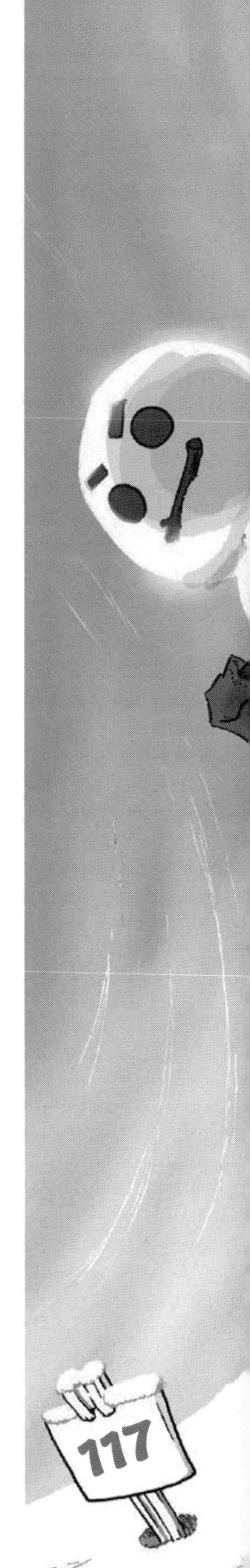

sensei might have many visitors coming and going from the city, so the henge might run into all sorts of people. While playing with the sensei outside, the henge might discover something unexpected. The henge might meet a dog or a cat at the sensei's house.

LADY FROM THE GENERAL STORE

HENGE: 0		**ANIMAL:** 1	
ADULT: 1		**CHILD:** 2	

This is the (old?) lady who runs the general store—which doubles as the town's only candy shop—by herself.

She loves children, and she's always giving sweets to the henge. A fox might pay with money from her shrine's offering box, or the lady from the store might let them help out at the shop instead, but she tends to just give treats to cats and birds. Since henge always stay as children, she has some inkling of the fact that they're not human, but rather than shutting them out, she welcomes them.

The store stocks traditional sweets and toys, and items for everyday life. It sells ordinary food, medicine, books, and newspapers. The town may have many stores like this, and there's usually a dedicated bookstore and candy store.

For both the henge and the people of the town—not just the children—her store is indispensable.

STORY FRAGMENTS:
If she has a cold or some business to attend to, she might ask some henge to mind the store. An older henge might have been friends with her for a long time. If someone helps her out a little bit around the house, she might give them some candy. If someone falls asleep while eating candy at the store, she might let them sleep on a futon. She might give away some old products that she hasn't been able to sell.

BUDDHIST PRIEST

HENGE: 1	**ANIMAL:** 1
ADULT: 2+	**CHILD:** 1

This is the priest of the town's Buddhist temple.

We're calling this a Buddhist priest, but you can treat him as a *kan'nushi* (Shinto priest) or even a Christian priest (if there happens to be one). In a town with so many mysteries, he is the one with the most opportunities to become acquainted with them.

As such, the priest is unlikely to be surprised by thoughtless actions. He knows about both the henge and the local gods. His attribute goes up by 4 (no need to spend Feelings) for Surprise.

The priest is always in his own temple, shrine, or church. If henge should go there to play, he'll welcome them warmly. When people are troubled, he could be a good person to go to for advice. His wisdom might well be of use for other things too.

STORY FRAGMENTS:
The priest might get mad at children or henge who play around graves. He might mistake mischief around the temple for the work of the henge. He might ask henge to help out with a ceremony or festival. If someone comes to the temple seeking shelter from the rain, he might invite them inside.

SHRINE MAIDEN

HENGE: 1	**ANIMAL:** 1
ADULT: 1+	**CHILD:** 2

This girl is a daughter of the family that runs the Shinto shrine, and is working as a shrine maiden, or *miko*. She wears a white kimono shirt and red *hakama* (split skirt), and has long, black hair. You often see her cleaning up the grounds of the shrine.

If a fox with a shrine is nearby, they'll likely have been friends since she was little. She probably knows about the henge and the local gods. Such a miko's attribute goes up by 2 (no need to spend Feelings) when making a check for Surprise.

She cleans, makes offerings, and lives every day the same way at a leisurely pace. For both the henge and the children who come to the shrine to play, she can be a good friend to talk to.

STORY FRAGMENTS:

A normal girl might start to idolize her. Her strict home life might mean she can't play when she wants to. She might have made a promise to a local god or henge when she was very young. Not being very athletic, she might try to ask her fox friend to make it rain on the day of the athletics festival. She might blame her own failure on a fox, and later apologize. She might get in an argument with a fox over something small. In the fall or winter she might make a bonfire with the fallen leaves she's swept up, and roast sweet potatoes and such.

LEAVING TOWN

HENGE: 0		**ANIMAL:** 1	
ADULT: 1+		**CHILD:** 1+	

This is someone who will be leaving the town soon. They will be going somewhere far away—It could be because of something going on with their family, it might be for their dreams… or it could be something they want to avoid. This person is going to a different town. They might even… Well, they might even be going somewhere far from this world.

Whatever the case, this person will be gone soon. They won't be showing up anymore after this story ends. If they do come around again, it'll be many years later, if at all. In a story about someone who is leaving, the last scene is their parting. Have everyone see them off. Please, don't forget.

STORY FRAGMENTS:

They might have something important they want to say to people they love, people they hold dear, friends, teachers, everyone. They might have not told everyone that they're moving away. They might have made an unexpected promise. There might be something they really need to apologize for. They might want to tell someone that they love them. And that someone might be a henge instead of another person.

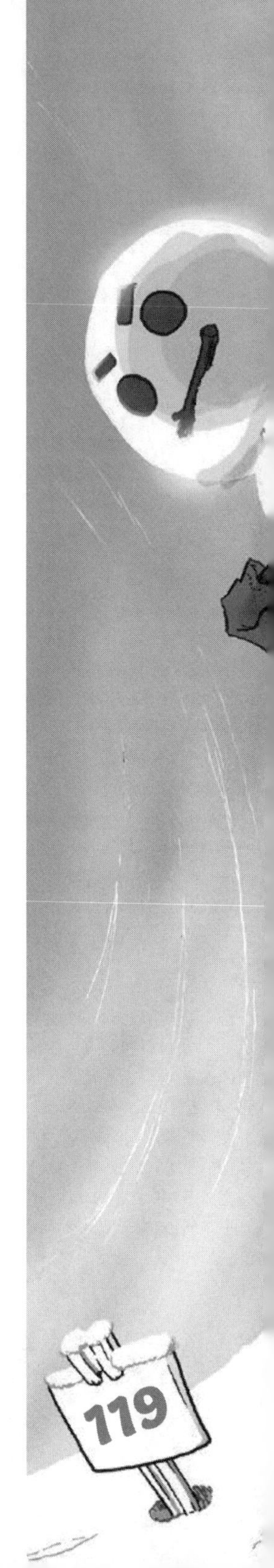

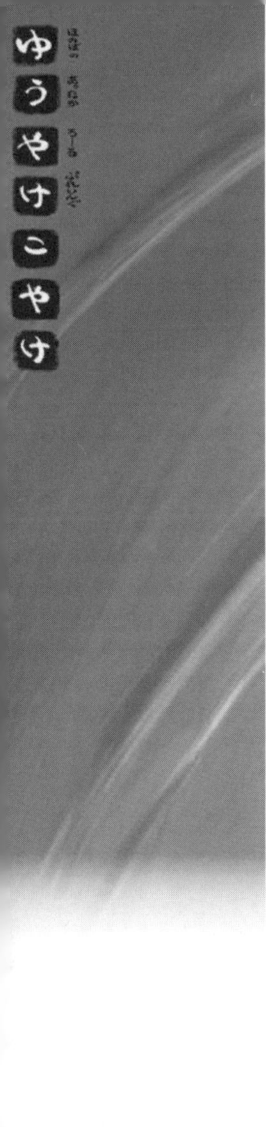

People in Stories

People have no mysterious powers. They can only use Feelings.

Thus, people can't do anything by themselves. If there isn't someone else who has "feelings" for them, people can't become strong. Unless the description specifically says otherwise, people don't have any powers to speak of.

The people that henge meet in the course of stories will have some small problem that can become the seed of a story. Through henge discovering these problems and helping resolve them, the story can grow.

However, please remember, for this game you don't need a plot or an incident to unravel. There needs to be encounters, contact.

Participating as People

If you've played Golden Sky Stories many times and become used to participating in stories, and if the narrator gives you permission, you can participate in a story as a person.

However, people are not as free as henge or animals. Children don't have the freedom to stay out all night, and they can't stay home when they have school. This means that depending on the story, it could be hard on a participant, and there could be a lot of scenes where his or her person couldn't appear. Still, if you're well-accustomed to the rules and you're a little bored with participating normally, go ahead and give this a try.

However, if it's your first story, or if someone is joining you who's never played before, it's not the time to participate as a person instead of a henge. This rule is just so you can add something a little different when you're playing with a regular group.

You create people the same way as henge, but people can't transform or use powers. They don't have any Weaknesses either. Look at the attributes of a similar type of person, and use those scores. For example, if you want to participate as a Princess, you'll have Animal 1, Adult 3, and Child 3. Also, people can only have Henge and Animal at 2 or lower, though in exchange they can have Adult as high as 5.

In any case, if you're participating as a person, please discuss the matter thoroughly with the narrator first.

JAPANESE RELIGION

Golden Sky Stories is not a religious game, or even a game about religion, but Japanese religion and mythology definitely inform its sensibilities. However, religious characters are ultimately in the game as potential friends to the henge, just like everyone else. That means that if you want to have a Buddhist priest appear in a story, what you really need to know is that he's a wise and kind man in a black robe, and he lives in a temple that has a big bell and a graveyard in the back. That's much more important than knowing which sect of Buddhism he comes from or how he sits when he meditates.

Religion in Japan is a curious thing, and doesn't at all conform to Western ideas about what religion is and isn't. Very few Japanese people consider themselves religious, but everyone goes to a Shinto shrine on New Year's Day. Japanese religion is about ideas and rituals that inform people's daily lives. For Japanese people, religion is a way to celebrate life in this world.

Shinto is Japan's animistic native religion, and it's all about the worship of the kami. People often translate kami as "gods," but that's not quite right. Kami are the spirits that reside in all things, and they're not transcendentally different from people the way gods or angels are. The local gods that appear in Golden Sky Stories are greater in stature than people or even henge, but they're still beings you can talk to and become friends with. While Shinto does have greater kami that are more like a pantheon of gods, people tend to offer worship to whichever kami is most qualified to help them. That means that people often turn to smaller, local kami, who are better suited to smaller, local requests.

A Shinto shrine is a symbolic dwelling for a kami. It is shaped like a house, and contains an object such as a mirror or a sword that represents the kami. There are great shrines that are national monuments and tiny, forgotten ones in the wilderness. Priests (kan'nushi) and/or shrine maidens (miko) preside over an active shrine, performing purification rituals, making offerings to the kami, offering protective amulets (omamori) and other good luck charms to people, and performing ritual dances.

Buddhism was very important in Japanese history, and developed differently from other countries. Traditional Buddhism encourages its followers to lead a solitary, ascetic lifestyle apart from the rest of the world, but Japanese Buddhism has long been intertwined with regular society. In particular, most funerals in Japan are Buddhist ceremonies, and consequently, people tend to think of Buddhism as the religion of the dead. This is one of the things that makes Japanese Buddhism a bit different from Buddhism in other countries, but it also means that Buddhist priests are an important part of the community, even if they're important for one of the sadder parts of life.

In the present day Japanese people do not take religion all that seriously, but people still commonly engage in celebrations with religious origins that help them feel connected to the world and the community. These include traditional Japanese holidays like Hina Matsuri and Tanabata, Buddhist ones like Obon and Higan, and even Western celebrations like Christmas. Just as Christmas, Thanksgiving, birthdays, and so on help us feel more connected to our friends, families, and communities, these celebrations can bring your henge and the other inhabitants of the town closer together.

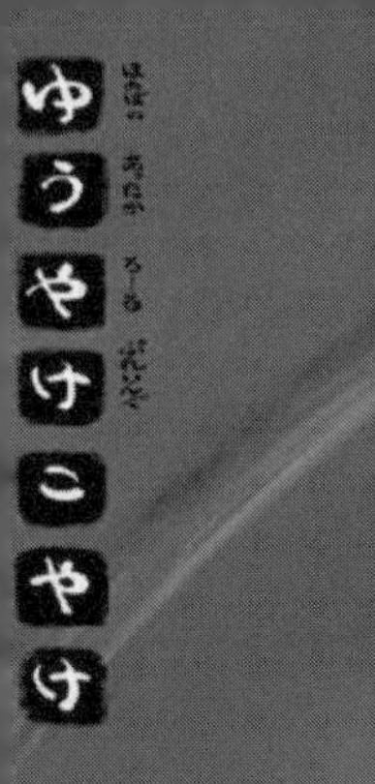

Local Gods

What Are Local Gods?

Henge deal with people in their everyday lives. However, there are beings within the town that have little to do with people. They are not merely living things, but beings that seldom concern themselves with humans and that possess mysterious powers. These are called the local gods (*tochi kami-sama*), or sometimes the *nushi*[1].

Each local god protects his or her own territory. Or to put it another way, a local god cares only for his or her territory and those that live within it (including henge). For better or for worse, they ignore everything that falls outside of that area.

Local gods are not unlike henge, but they have very powerful abilities, and wield all sorts of powers. However, these are all for the god's own territory. For a local god who's left his or her own territory, even taking human form takes a lot of effort.

There are local gods all through the different bits of land around town. These are not regions created by people; they must be areas of land formed by nature.

A local god's power is directly determined by the size of his or her territory. For example, a local god that watches over an entire mountain is more powerful than a local god who protects a single pond. Local gods seldom associate with anyone who doesn't have a strong tie to their own territory. If there is something that needs to be done, they're more likely to ask henge or animals for help.

Powers of Local Gods

Local gods possess the special powers described below. All local gods have these powers regardless of what kind of land they protect.

Speak to Animals (○)

Local gods can speak with animals that live in their own territory whenever they want. Unless the local god has somehow harmed them, animals that live in a local god's territory will never hurt them. However, this power does not work on animals that might wander in from outside.

Guardian (○)

A local god can know everything that has happened and is happening in his or her territory. If a single tiny button has fallen to the bottom of a lake, a local god who watches over that area can see where it is without searching. As long as it's within their territory, local gods can know of anything that happened, no matter how long ago.

Change (?)

A local god's normal form is that of an animal. However, particularly for local gods who are giant spiders or centipedes, it's best not to carelessly show their true forms in front of people. Thus, they can take human form by spending Wonder and/or Feelings depending on the time and desired form, just like henge.

---

[1] "Nushi" *is a Japanese word that can mean, amongst other things, a person who's lived in a particular area for a long time, or an animal with spiritual powers that rules a certain place.*

Vanish (3)

A local god can vanish into his or her territory at any time. Local gods who are using this power give no sign of their presence, and no one can see them. However, once they've disappeared this way, local gods can't do anything except subtly communicate what they want. They can reappear at any time just by wanting to do so. This effect lasts until the scene changes.

Carry Out (5)

If something is within a local god's territory, he or she can quickly get it out. This power carries whatever the local god chooses to expel right to the border of his or her territory. This power works regardless of how big or heavy something might be, but it can't remove that which doesn't want to move, much less the land itself.

Assorted Local Gods

POND GOD

HENGE:	4	**ANIMAL:**	2
ADULT:	3	**CHILD:**	1

ANIMALS: Turtle, Fish, Snake, Shellfish, Frog

Pond gods protect ponds deep in the mountains, or that were created long ago. A pond is a quiet, stable place, and the local gods who watch over them tend to be calm. As they're close to people, they're on good terms with the people and henge of the town. A pond god might get angry if people do too much fishing or throw trash in his pond. On the other hand, if you happen to drop something in the pond by accident, much less fall in yourself, he'll be glad to help. They are seldom scary, and there will sometimes be small shrine on the edge of the pond.

Pond gods are surely the local gods people most often meet.

Power: Water-Strider (5)

The pond god can make anything float in water, no matter how heavy or damp it might be. This power will let people and animals walk on the surface of the water. This effect lasts until the scene changes.

STORY FRAGMENTS:

Someone might need the pond god's help to get something that fell into the pond. Someone might fall into the pond and call for help. If no rain falls for a long time, a local god might come to ask a fox to make it rain. If children's mischief gets out of hand, the pond god might ask some henge to do something about it.

RIVER GOD

HENGE:	6	**ANIMAL:**	3
ADULT:	1	**CHILD:**	3

ANIMALS: Fish, Snake, Giant Centipede, Otter

River gods can watch over the tiny river that flows from the mountains, a basin of a large river, or similar. Rivers are ever-flowing, and they sometimes rise up to wash things away. The local gods who watch over them are similarly whimsical. Even so, once they do decide on something, they'll stubbornly stick to it, and they can be a bit selfish and self-centered.

Perhaps because human habitation too often dirties the water, river gods don't care much for people. They will listen to what henge have to say, but they'll get angry if people do bad things at the river. Among the things that can get a river god angry are overfishing and throwing trash into the river. If people make a river god too angry, she might cause a flood. Please, be careful how you treat rivers.

Power: Soak (8)

A river god can cause a bucket's worth of water to fall down wherever she wants. If she drops the water on a person's head, they'll be completely soaked, of course. If someone wants to avoid getting wet,

they'll have to get an Animal result better than the river god's Henge result. This water doesn't have any special powers in it, but if a person or henge gets suddenly hit with water, they'll suffer a Surprise equal to the river god's Henge plus 3. Furthermore, depending on the season this might cause you to catch a cold.

STORY FRAGMENTS:

Kids from the town might get the river god really mad with a little bit of mischief. She might mistake something accidentally dropped into the river for garbage, and get angry. The river god might use her Soak power on a child, and then be worried when the kid catches a cold. Such a moody local god might fall in love with a human.

FOREST GOD

HENGE: 5 **ANIMAL:** 1
ADULT: 1 **CHILD:** 4

ANIMALS: Fox, Deer, Bird, Raccoon Dog, Giant Spider, Large Tree

This is a local god that has watched over a forest since ancient times. Even a small forest will normally have a local god. A particularly large forest could have several different local gods.

Local gods of the forests can be laid-back, and take things at a leisurely pace. They are kind to people and henge alike, and at times they will interact with those who venture into the heart of their forest. However, there is one small problem. Forest gods tend to be lonely, and they have their own peculiar way of thinking about time, so if they like someone, they might not let them leave. If you clearly refuse, they won't press the matter, but when you're dealing with a gentle and lonely local god, it can be hard to do that.

POWER: LOST IN THE WOODS (6)

This causes others to get lost on forest paths, and become unable to leave the forest. This power can affect several people at once, but the forest god must pay for it again for each victim. While they're lost, they can't get out of the forest, even if they just keep heading straight ahead. This lasts until the local god cancels it, or the scene ends.

POWER: DARKNESS (12)

The forest suddenly becomes as dark as night. While this lasts, treat the time of day as night. Also, in this darkness people with a Child attribute of 3 or higher (except henge, who aren't affected) have all of their other attributes at zero. This effect lasts until the end of the scene.

STORY FRAGMENTS:

A local god might not let children who came to play leave the forest. The local god might worry about raccoon dogs, foxes, rabbits, and so on who left the forest and go looking for them. When a local god asks henge to bring someone to her, they might take her into town instead. If a local god falls in love with a person or henge, she might try to keep them from leaving the forest.

MOUNTAIN GOD

HENGE: 4 **ANIMAL:** 7
ADULT: 3 **CHILD:** 3

ANIMALS: Bear, Boar, Snake, Fox, Giant Spider, Giant Centipede

These are respected local gods who each watch over one mountain. Because mountains include forests, the sources of rivers, and so on, mountain gods inevitably find themselves serving as mediators for other local gods. Also, because they have many responsibilities, they naturally tend to have very responsible personalities.

Mountain gods decide on rules for their own mountains, and the animals and the other local gods of those mountains abide by those rules. As such, one cannot say that mountain gods will all be kind or strict when it comes to people.

Mountains are profound things that seem to exist eternally, and they convey profound emotions just by being there. When you're visiting a mountain, it's best to find out about that mountain's local god first.

Power: In the Mist (16)

The mountain god wraps her entire mountain in a thick mist. This mist is so dense that you can't even see your own hand in front of your face, and for the most part one must be a henge or animal to be able to move freely through it. The mountain god can lead those who are in this mist in whichever direction she wishes. If you want to go your own way instead, you'll have to make a check and exceed her Henge attribute. This effect won't disappear until the scene changes.

Power: Rain Shower (20)

A mountain god can cause a sudden downpour to fall on her mountain like a waterfall. The sky suddenly becomes overcast, and then this rain begins to fall. This rain doesn't have any special effect on those it hits, but it will make you cold and wet. On the other hand, if you take even one step out of the mountain, the rain will seem to stop as though it never was. This effect continues until the scene changes.

STORY FRAGMENTS:

If the mountain god distrusts people, she might not let people come to her mountain, no matter what the reason. A mountain god who is kinder to people might invite children to come and play. When there are landslides or falling rocks, a mountain god might use this as a rather destructive way to chase off people or henge. A child might get lost deep in the mountains and fall asleep. The mountain god, not knowing where the child lives, could ask some henge to take the child home.

FIELD GOD

HENGE: 2 **ANIMAL:** 2
ADULT: 0 **CHILD:** 6

ANIMALS: Bird, Fox, Rabbit, Deer, Snake

There are small fields all around the town. However, there are much larger fields on the outskirts. Spring, summer, and autumn each bring their own kinds of flowers to these fields, and they are always warmed by sunshine during the day. The local gods who watch over such fields tend to be naïve and innocent, like younger siblings to the local gods and henge around them. They're very curious, and often leave their territory to visit other local gods and even the town. When that happens, field gods can be rather vulnerable, and others will have to protect them. Field gods are more childish than most actual children, and they're quick to befriend any children who might come to play.

Power: Sunny Day (16)

Regardless of rain or strong wind, a field god can suddenly call up a clear, sunny sky. The sky becomes refreshing and invigorating, and it gives 4 points of Dreams to everyone in the field other than the field god. This effect continues until the scene changes.

STORY FRAGMENTS:

Henge might accompany a field god on her way into town to play to make sure she doesn't get lost. A field god might get too attached to children or henge she's become friends with and not want to go home. A field god who ventured into town might be unable to get back to her own field. A field god might start crying because of some small thing children or henge did.

OCEAN GOD

HENGE: 6 **ANIMAL:** 4
ADULT: 0 **CHILD:** 2

ANIMALS: Fish, Giant Turtle, Snake, Octopus, Crab

This is a local god of the ocean... or rather, of the seashore. The local gods of the sea are too distant from the human world, and you're very unlikely to meet one. However, the local gods who watch

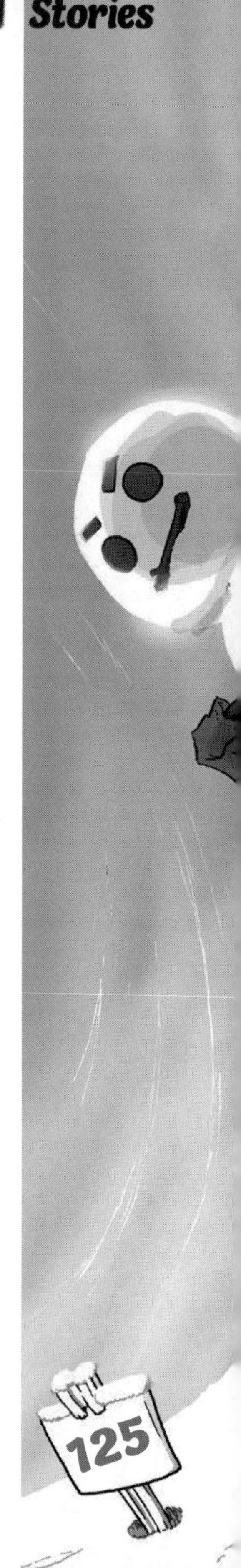

over the seashores have a low opinion of humans, much like river gods. Not only that, but a lot of them are just indifferent to people. Even when it comes to henge, they tend to only have dealings with the bird henge that tell them of distant places. Because of that, they seldom leave their own stretch of seashore, and if they need something from the outside world, they'll probably ask henge for help.

Power: Sea God (8)

An ocean god can cause great waves to crash down on the beach, or calm the waves. Until the end of the scene, the local god can control the waves however he wants. He can make things floating on the water wash up on the beach, or use the waves to wash things out to the open sea. However, this power can't move things that are particularly big or heavy.

Story Fragments:

If someone has lost something in the sea, they might have to ask an ocean god for help getting it back. If something strange washes up on the beach, an ocean god might try to find someone to help him figure out what to do with it. If people are dirtying the beach (even if it's actually a misunderstanding), an ocean god might get mad and send waves at them.

Local Gods in Stories

Local gods possess powers far more potent than those of henge. They understand things that henge don't, and they can easily go places where henge can't. However, all of that only applies to the local god's own territory. Outside of his or her own territory, a local god is actually less powerful than an ordinary henge.

Local gods give henge advice and sometimes ask favors of them. They are definitely not enemies to fight, but neither are they allies who will always help. A local god only protects his or her land and its inhabitants.

Incidentally, participants cannot participate in stories as local gods. The local gods fundamentally must protect their own territory, and the range of things they can do is vague yet much too broad. Also, unlike henge, human common sense doesn't work with them. Local gods are definitely for the narrator to use. If you really want to portray one, try being the narrator.

Hitotsuna Town

This is one town that can serve as a backdrop for your stories. It's also where the stories in this book take place, and the home of the six example henge. It's called **Hitotsuna Town**. *Hitotsuna* is Japanese for "one name," though few remember its original significance.

The Towa River stretches from one end to the other of a certain prefecture, and this is one of the towns that sit along its length. The river divides the north and south parts of the town, and there is only one bridge that crosses it. People used to use ferryboats to cross the river, but they've fallen out of use since the completion of the bridge. Also, since there's now a train station on the north side, that side has become the center of town.

It's not as though the residents of the north and south sides of town don't get along. It's just that the south side lacks the train station and school, so it's less convenient. Because there's plenty of land and low, wide buildings are simpler than tall ones, there are no buildings over three stories tall. The only three-story buildings are the school and the hospital.

The town is rich with thickets and meadows full of vegetation. There are many fields and rice paddies, countless creeks, and many irrigation channels. There are places in the mountains where power lines don't reach, and cell phones only work at the train station and part of the town hall. All of the houses in the town have running water, but it wasn't so long ago that there were still a lot of places where people got their water from wells. There's no sewer system either.

This is Hitotsuna Town.

Now, let's take a look at the important places around town.

Hitotsuna Station

This is a rural train station that sits right along the train tracks that follow the path of the Towa River. The station has only one platform, and people wait in the same place regardless of which direction they're traveling. Not many trains come through.

There is only one station attendant, and the ticket window is only open in the morning and evening. It's a local line, so there are only local trains of two to four cars, and no express trains at all. Trains basically come once an hour. In the morning and evening, when there are lots of people going to work, and high schoolers going to neighboring towns, there are two trains per hour.

Because the line travels through the mountains, train service will sometimes halt because of landslides or fallen trees.

Train Station Shops

Here you'll find the general store, vegetable store, butcher's shop, pharmacy, liquor store, barbershop, appliance store, and so on. The town's one bank and single post office are also here.

This area is all shops for people who are coming and going, so there are no book shops, cafes, or anything like that. The train station shops are at the heart

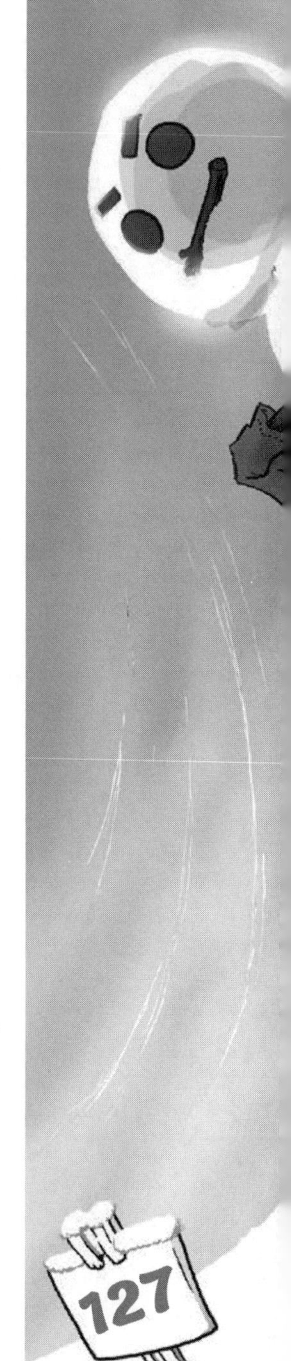

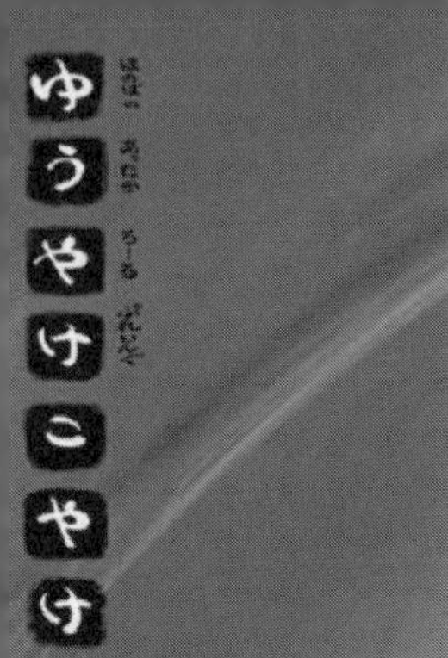

of people's lives, so it's always thriving during the day. Most of the shops double as homes, so the people at a given shop will live on the second floor or in the back.

Misuzu Farm

This farm sits on a hill, and the people there raise cows and chickens and such.

To be precise, it's more of a collection of several small livestock farms, and there's no single owner. The cows spend most of their time in a barn, but the farmers periodically let them out to graze.

Rabbits and boars frequently take the cows' food.

Hitotsuna Town Hall

This two-story town hall has stood since the Taisho Era[1].

All kinds of people, young and old, come and go from the town hall, and it has a small library and community hall. The library's collection comes from what the townspeople have gathered, so the selection is a bit "mixed," or "personal" if you prefer. It feels less like a library and more like a used book shop, and the librarian seems to have a tough time organizing the books.

People use the community hall to prepare for festivals, and for movie showings and local performances.

Hitotsuna School

This school is a combination elementary school and middle school.

It doesn't include a nursery school, but since there are only so many kids in town, the elementary and middle school students together only number about a hundred. Each classroom handles students of two grades, and there are around five teachers.

The older students often help the younger ones study and play together. With kids of different ages all together, the school is boisterous and always lively. However, even in this noisy atmosphere there's a lot to learn. None of the students seem dissatisfied with this school.

Misuzu Hachiman Shrine

On the north side of the river, atop a long stone staircase, is a shrine dedicated to Misuzu Hachiman.

This is a relatively new shrine, but it has become the main shrine of the town. In the forest behind this shrine, there is a much smaller shrine, where the fox named Suzune Hachiman lives.

Hitotsuna-Nushi Shrine

This is an old shrine to the south side of the river.

The shrine is dedicated to the local god of the Hitotsuna River, Hitotsuna-Nushi. There are also shrines to other local gods from the area, and shrines to local gods of the south side of the river. There may also be shrines to foxes and other henge who live in the mountains.

Mt. Kaminaga is right behind this shrine. Mt. Kaminaga provides natural protection for the shrine.

Amao Temple

The temple itself is small, but it has large grounds for Buddhist events like Obon and Higan[2]. The temple hall has a large bell, and children sometimes find it fun to come and ring it. Every child in Hitotsuna Town rings the bell hanging from its long cord at least once.

There are rows of graves behind the temple, and children often go there for tests of courage. The priest won't mind kids ringing the bell during the day or evening, but he hates it when they play around the graves or ring the bell at night, so please be careful.

Haunted House

This very old Western-style house sits on the outskirts of town.

---

[1] *The Japanese arrange history into eras named for emperors. Taisho was from 1912 to 1926.*

[2] *Obon is a festival to honor the departed, while Higan is a memorial festival held at the equinoxes in the spring and fall.*

If you ask a fox or local god, they'll tell you it's from around the Meiji[1] or Taisho eras. There are rumors of ghosts, and the children and even adults rarely go near the place.

Since no one is here, henge probably won't come here either. We'll leave it up to the narrator to think about whether there's something here, and the state of the house's interior.

Reservoir Ponds

All around town, especially around the fields and rice paddies, there are many small reservoirs.

Some keep extra water for water-filled rice paddies, while others are ponds for raising lotus flowers. There are also some that people use for fishing. Some of the reservoir ponds are large, old ponds, where fish, turtle, or snake local gods live.

Towa River

This is a large river that flows through the town from east to west.

It's not normally that way, but if it rains long enough, the river will overflow its banks and become a great raging flow of water.

Normally, you often see people fishing or walking their dogs along the riverbank. Also, in the summer not a few children go swimming in the river.

A different local god handles each basin of this great river. The river is so big and long that no one local god could watch over all of it.

Hebiko Island

Everyone calls this long, narrow sandbank in the middle of the Towa River, "Snake Island."

There's a rather unreliable bridge that leads to the island, and it's home to a shrine dedicated to a snake god named Towa Gozen, who watches over the Towa River basin. No one else lives there, however. The island is small, and the water level can rise high enough to mostly submerge it.

There are many snakes on the island, and people say that if you pester the snakes there you'll be punished.

Mt. Misuzu

This mountain lies on the north side of town.

The terrain is relatively open, but there is a road that goes over the mountain anyway. Foxes and raccoon dogs have been known to live here since ancient times, and there are many shrines to foxes deep in the mountains.

There are many tiered fruit fields in the mountains, so farmers from town often travel up and down.

Apparently in olden times when people went to the mountains, foxes would ring bells and get the people lost, hence the name Misuzu, or "deep bells."

Mt. Kaminaga

This is a steep mountain on the south side of town.

Very little of the terrain is open, and the plants are very dense. The only paths are those made by animals.

A giant spider goddess called Kaminaga-hime[2] governs the mountain, and people seldom venture there. Kaminaga-hime dislikes people, and when someone she doesn't like comes to her mountain, she chases them off with mist and rain. This local god is kind to henge, animals, and certain children she's come to like, but the requests of people she's just met will usually fall on deaf ears.

They say that long ago, Kaminaga-hime had a human husband though…

Suzunari River

This is a brook that gushes out from Mt. Misuzu.

It starts as a tiny stream by the mountain, but before it joins with the Towa

---

[1] *The Meiji Era was from 1868 to 1912, and marked the beginning of major Westernization in Japan.*

[2] *Kaminaga-hime literally means "long-haired princess."*

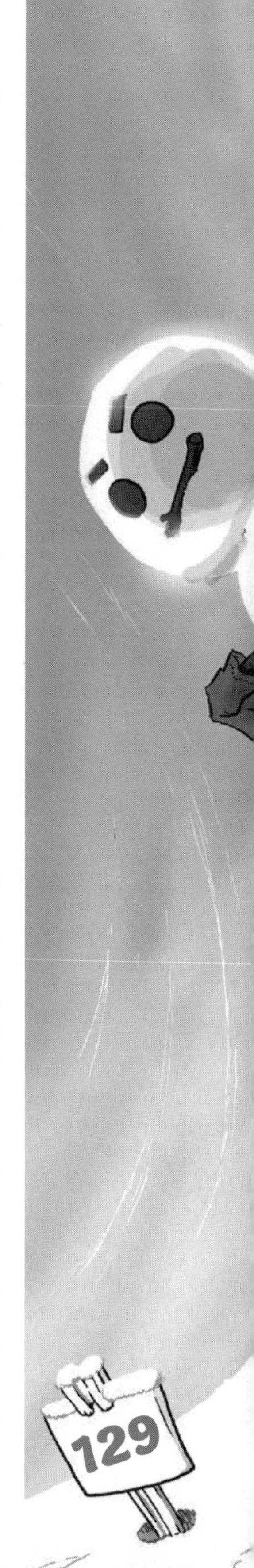

River it becomes enough of a stream to merit a small bridge. Many river crabs, crayfish, and small fish live here, and children often come here to play during the summer.

Miko River

This small river flows from the hills that are home to a farm and a shrine. It's not nearly as wide as the Towa River it intersects with, but everyone knows it well because it flows right through the middle of town. Where it goes into town, people mostly use it for irrigation, but there's a small shrine near the bridge, and even today people venerate the local god of the Miko River.[1]

Gokou River

This small river gushes out from Mt. Kaminaga, flowing down through many small waterfalls and streamlets.

A giant centipede goddess called Gokou-hime[2] lives here, and they say she will punish anyone who dirties even the lower reaches of her river. Gokou-hime is fairly friendly to people and henge, but she will not tolerate anyone polluting her river.

Hitotsuna Bridge

This bridge connects the northern and southern sides of town that the Towa River splits apart.

It used to be that every time a typhoon came through, the wooden bridge would be washed away, but about 20 years ago they built a sturdier bridge that has stood ever since. The bridge is divided into lanes for cars and pedestrians (which is very unusual for Hitotsuna Town), and it's one of the very few examples of modern construction in town.

This bridge is very long, but without it the northern and southern halves of the town would be cut off from each other.

---

[1] *In this case "Miko" does not mean "shrine maiden." It's written with the characters for "deep" and "old."*

[2] *Her name comes from the Chinese characters for centipede.* Mukade *(centipede) can be written as* 蜈蚣*, and by taking out the* 虫 (mushi/*insect) part, you get* 呉公 (Gokou)*, plus* hime/*princess is her name.*

Creating Your Own Town

When all is said and done, Hitotsuna Town is just an example. If you happen to live in a town by the sea, or in the far north or south, this town might not be so appropriate for you.

In order to make a town to use for your stories, you need to decide on the places that the henge will use. Places like police stations, banks, and hospitals are very important for people, but not necessarily for henge. Also, it should be very unusual for this game to include stories that depend on having a police station or bank in the first place.

If the town is by the sea, it will have a beach, a harbor, and perhaps some small islands in the open sea. If the town is up north, it will sometimes be covered with snow. Think about such things.

Henge don't fight bad guys or uncover corruption. Please remember what we talked about at the very beginning of this book as you try to create a town of your very own.

Even in the Hitotsuna Town that we've just finished explaining, there should be plenty more mysterious places, plenty more fun places to see. When you're first starting out, try changing and adding some places to it. That way, after telling many stories you will have many memories that belong only to you and your friends. Then, even if you still call it "Hitotsuna Town," it will still be your own town.

Hitotsuna Town
NORTH
MT. KAMINAGA
HITOTSUNA NUSHI SHRINE
TOWA RIVER
HITOTSUNA STATION
GOKOU RIVER
HAUNTED HOUSE
HITOTSUNA BRIDGE
HEBIKO ISLAND

MT. MISUZU
SUZUNARI RIVER
MISUZU FARM
HITOTSUNA SCHOOL
MISUZU HACHIMAN SHRINE
MIKO RIVER
BANK
TRAIN STATION SHOPS
HITOTSUNA TOWN HALL
AMAO TEMPLE

Riko's BIG Mistake

Part 4

They couldn't stop the move, but...

Kuromu: So in the end, Kikuna had to move.
Riko: Yeah...
Kuromu: You seem pretty happy though. Why's that?

We parted ways, but we didn't!

Riko: I asked Kikuna why she didn't want to move, you know? It turned out she didn't want to be away from Hiroko, her doubles tennis partner.
Kuromu: Huh. Then what?
Riko: Then the morning of the move Hiroko came to Kikuna's house. And she said, rather than teammates, they'd have to become rivals!
Kuromu: Hmm...
Riko: So they promised to do their best so they could meet again at the national tournament. So they became even better friends than before, you know? Weird, huh?
Kuromu: I see. (avoiding her gaze)

True Friendship

Riko: Oh, by the way, I'm pretty sure I saw Hiroko-chan waving to you, so, like, are you guys friends?
Kuromu: Not really. It's nothing.
Riko: It seemed like she was saying thank you or something, you know?
Kuromu: Huh. I don't know anything

about that. Are you sure you're not imagining things? (still avoiding Riko's eyes)

And on to the next story…

Suzune: Well, well. Just when I was starting to worry about them, it seems they seem to have found their way again.
Koro: Woof! Riko and Kuromu did their best for their friends! They're great! They deserve so many treats!
Sarah: Someone said, no matter how far apart you are, there are still threads that connect you. I forgot, but it's important.
Amami: It's good to have friends. I wanted to be friends with them too…
Suzune: In that case, you should take part in the next story, Amami. Every time we tell stories, we accrue more threads.
Koro: Woof! I'll do that too!
Amami: Anyway, everyone remember to take good care of me, okay?
Sarah: Huh? What was I talking about…? I forgot. But I think it was a warm story.

Let's create a town together.

Suzune: Hm. The more stories we tell, the more threads will form between people, and we'll create more priceless stories that belong to us.
Koro: And then we can learn more and more about our town! My master takes me for walks, so I know!
Suzune: This is our own irreplaceable town. And for that, the narrator must be prepared…
Sarah: The narrator makes information about the town. But, everyone in the story helps it come to life.
Suzune: Yes. Now, it's getting dark. I must return to my shrine.

All of this is so you can tell your very own stories. May the light of the setting sun always wrap your henge in its warmth.

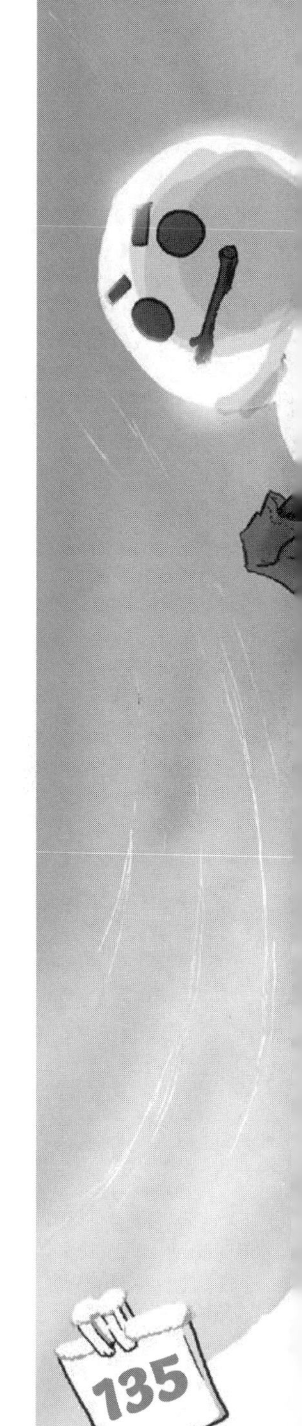

Translator's Afterword

By Ewen Cluney

This is a strange and wonderful place to be, publishing another Japanese RPG, and *Golden Sky Stories* of all things. Doing *Maid RPG* in English was an incredible experience for everyone involved. Not always incredible in a good way—the rush to be ready for Gen Con was painful—but incredible nonetheless. I didn't have a rational reason for wanting to release *Maid RPG* at all, much less doing so before *Golden Sky Stories,* but in the end I'm glad we did. The random slapstick game about maids gave us some experience that I think we needed to do *Golden Sky Stories* justice, so I have yet another reason to be grateful to all of the people who helped make *Maid RPG* such a success.

Needless to say, I consider this to be a really exceptional game. Well before publishing it became a real possibility, it managed to become an important part of my life. Along with *Maid RPG* it has had an incalculable influence on how I look at RPGs, and I even did a partial translation of it as my graduate thesis at San Francisco State University. And that's to say nothing of what happened when I actually played it.

There are all kinds of amazing RPGs from Japan, and ordinarily I'd feel a little guilty about disproportionately representing a relatively obscure designer (Two Ryo Kamiya games, but only one from Jun'ichi Inoue[1], and no Gin'ichiro Suzuki[2] at all?!). The thing is, I find Ryo Kamiya's games amazing, and *Golden Sky Stories* is perhaps his best so far. It isn't quite like anything else out there. It isn't the game that'll make you throw out all of your other RPGs, but it's a game you can turn to every now and then to get together with some friends and go somewhere warm and safe, something I think we all could use sometimes. It might seem odd that the designer of *Maid RPG* came up with a game like this, but if there is a common thread among all his games (even that adults-only one we're never, ever going to publish), it's that they're unabashedly about being fun to play. *Golden Sky Stories'* heartwarming role-playing approach isn't completely novel (there's this other much older Japanese RPG called *Witch Quest*, for one), but it's highly unusual and, in my estimation, quite welcome.

For *Maid RPG*, we rushed to put out a volume containing nearly all of the published Japanese material. This was partly because the 32-page core rulebook felt a bit lacking by itself, and partly because we had no idea whether we'd get the chance to publish more. *Golden Sky Stories* has a total of three supplements in Japanese, which add a total of ten new character types between them. However, a book encompassing the core rules and all of those would've been more than twice the size of this one, and thus even more unwieldy of a project than the comprehensive *Maid RPG* book turned out to be. Luckily, the original Japanese version is eminently complete with just its 120-page core rulebook. I'm very excited at the prospect of being able to bring you the rules for mononoke, Elder Henge, and so forth, but I wanted this book to be just right, because I think *Golden Sky Stories* deserves nothing less.

While our task of preparing and offering this book is done, a role-playing game is a conversation that keeps going long after you've finished reading the last page. If you haven't played this game yet, I implore you to talk to your friends about it, because *Golden Sky Stories'* real beauty emerges when people gather and enjoy it together. Whatever your experiences with it are, please feel free to talk to us about it, be it online, in person, or wherever you might find us. Not every game designer or publisher says such things so plainly, but it bears

[1] *Designer of* Tenra Bansho Zero, *as well as a prolific number of other games from Japanese RPG publisher* F.E.A.R.

[2] *Venerable Japanese game designer, best known for launching the* Monster Maker *franchise.*

mentioning that games are for playing and sharing, and we love hearing that the games we've worked so hard on have helped people have fun together.

THANKS

Thanks to Kamiya-sensei for creating another incredible game and for answering many little questions.

I translated the first two chapters of this book for my graduate thesis, and as such I am deeply in debt to my graduate adviser, Professor McKeon of San Francisco State University, for her patience and support. Professor Minami and Anita Axt also provided valuable assistance.

Thanks to Andy Kitkowski for being generally awesome and helping make things happen.

Editor's Afterword

By Mike Stevens

"How can a non-violent game be compelling?"

That's the most common question I've gotten when I've talked about this game online and at anime conventions. I never consider it a dismissive comment on the game itself, and honestly it's a fair question that game designers all over the world have been asking themselves for quite some time. Any game, or any story for that matter, needs to have some kind of challenge or problem. The easiest type of conflict that can be represented and handled with game mechanics is violence in some fashion. Don't get me wrong, I love some of those games—they've helped me through many a bad day—but as they say, if you just have a hammer, you're going to see everything as a nail.

One of my favorite play tests of *Golden Sky Stories*, which highlighted this very issue, was at A-Kon 2010, where I met a young anime fan who had scrimped and saved to attend her very first convention with her mother in tow. Neither of them had ever played any kind of role-playing game, but they were kind enough to give me and a fellow RPG veteran their time. In about 15 minutes everyone knew the rules and were well on their way to making a character. The girl played a fox, while her mother played a cat, and the other player was a rabbit. While the rabbit was oblivious to wanting to hang out with his friends, and the cat wanted attention, the fox felt threatened by the cat, and acted bossy around her. While this was going on they were helping out a child who was being pestered by a spirit who was full of itself. When it came to the scene where they confronted the spirit, the fox was ready to just use her fox fire to blast it like Team Rocket.

I simply replied that it would work for the short term, but it would eventually come back to trouble the child. The situation called for a more creative solution. The girl looked at me, kind of confused. You're supposed to blast the antagonist in most stories, right? After a short discussion, they came up with a clever mix of powers and discussion of respecting others, all while we were rewarding our favorite moments of this finale with Dream points. Most of the problems were resolved in a satisfying way, everyone liked how the game worked out, and most amusingly, the girl and her mother both were surprised at how two hours passed by so quickly.

I knew before that this game was pretty unique with its "good samaritan" style of play, but right then I recognized the bit of magic *Golden Sky Stories* has: It got a group of people of different age groups and experience levels to tell an exciting, clever story in a couple of hours within the game rules. But don't just take my word for it. If you're still a bit skeptical, give it a try with some new or old friends and see for yourself. You might be surprised how compelling a non-violent game can be.

THANKS

My family for supporting me on this project, Jennifer Jennings, Casey Mysilwy, Mori McLamb, Meghan McGrath, Jennifer Noelle, Kai Tave, Alishia Larsen, and all the fa/tg/uys and ca/tg/irls out there.

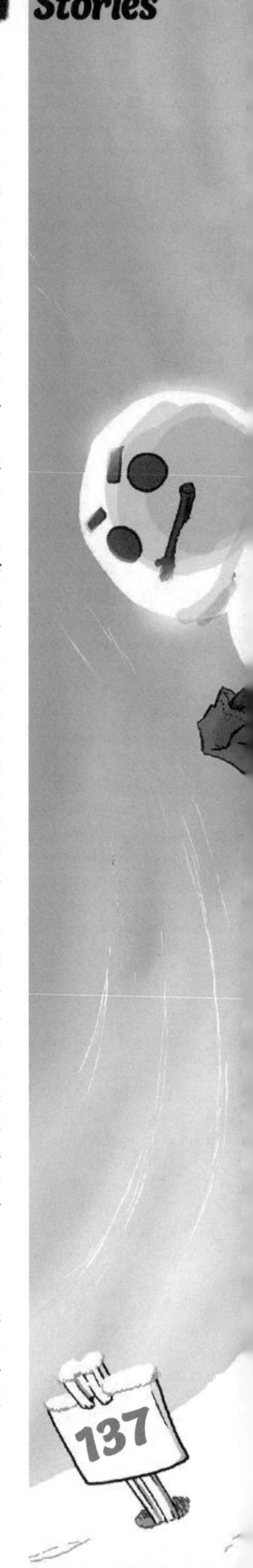

KICKSTARTER BACKERS

In April and May of 2013 we held a Kickstarter to fund the initial publication of Golden Sky Stories. We were confident that we could reach our modest goal of $7,000 and go a bit over. Instead we succeeded beyond our wildest dreams, and when it ended we had 2,350 backers and had raised about $85,000. Along with everything else it was extremely gratifying to see so many people give a heartwarming, non-violent RPG a chance. This is a list of our backers, and we're deeply thankful to all of them.

Venerable Local Gods

Carl Rigney, Martin Kjærvoll, Sam

Respected Local Gods

Alex Stocker, Arcane Snowman, Jonathan Thiele, Joshua "Cielchocobo" Jordan, Joshua T. Johnston, Kitagawa Anjin, Patrick Burke, Paul Hachmann, Stephan Szabo, Timothy Moncivaiz

Local Gods

Allie Kat Kartzoff, Anton K, Austin "Hiro" Jimenez, Benton Wilson, Bryce Undy, CyberLeo, Daniel Chang, Dr. Andrew J. Nowak, Eric Esquibel, George O'Dell, Greg Matyola, Ian McFarlin, J. Quincy, Jacques DuRand, Jairain, Jake Baker, James Marsters, Jason Italiano, Jeremy Land, Karsing Fung, Keith Preston, Mark Lambe, Marley Griffin, Michael "Tatch" Acevedo, Miss Conduct, Nam Nix, Nicholas Laune, Pierre Chaloux, Rufei, Sascha "Wolf" Rück, Sean Aliff, Shiden Nakajima, Simon Ward, Stephen Slaby, Thomas Delicourt

The General Store

+1 Gaming, Atlantis Games & Comics, Bridgeport Comics and Games, Cape Fear Games, Commodore Campbell, Elaine Powell, Game on comics, james spinner, Matthew Morgan, Sphärenmeisters Spiele, Sunken Treasures Games, Tim Morgan, Tyche's Games

Mononoke

Aaron J. Schrader, Adam "WhirlwindMonk" Bednarek, Aleesha Lowry, Alexis Cole, Alphonse Du, Amonchakai, Andreas Rugård Klæsøe, Andrew Lloyd, Andrew Park, Antoine "Illyan", Benjamin L. Liew, Björn Schneider, Bradford Cone, Brendan Flaherty, Brook Hubbard, Bruno Alves Marques, Bryon Yamada, Calvin D. Jim, Chris Vincent, Christopher Gunning, Cooper Lushbaugh, Corinna Howard, Dan Wilson, Daniel Wewasson, David Lucardie, Dominique del Mer, Elegant Fugue, Elijah Kautzman, Erin Hermanson, Extraordinerdy, FannishMinded, Francis Helie, Grant Chen, Gremlin Legions, Guerric Samples, Harry Salzman, Hector R. Mojica, Hilton Cao, Hsile Amune, Hunter W., Iain MacPhee, jacugo, James Dawsey, Jamie Yakeleya, Jeff Zitomer, Jeffery Murphy, Jeffrey Speer, Jeffrey Wong, Jere Manninen, Joe Iglesias, Joshua Thompson, Joshua Wolfe, Jussi Myllyluoma, Kirby Bridges, Knuckles1388, Kong Ja Yu, Lanir, Lester Ward, Lord Nightwinter, Lukas Myhan, Magus, Marc Poirier, Marcus Arena, Mark Wolff, Martin Friedrichs, Matias Duarte, Matthew Coverdale, Matthew Sullivan-Barrett, MC3, Michael Scott Smith, Morgan Weeks, Niall Paton, Omer Ahmed, Paulo Rafael Guariglia Escanhoela, R. James Bradshaw, Revis Dumas, Ricky Dang, Robert "Jefepato" Dall, Robert H. Mitchell Jr., Ryan Poss, S_T, Sam, Sam Garamy, Sam Gibbins, Samma Fagan, Scott F., Scygnus, shameimaruaya25@gmail.com, Shawn Heezen, Sir Nicholas Del Guercio, Socratics101, Stephen Ho, Steve van Weelij, Steven Siddall, Sydney Bridges, Sylvain "OgGy Tanguy, Teddy Kirwan, The Walkers Four, Thomas "Turey" Hall, Thomas Trutch, TJ Mathews-Nack, ToastCrust, Troy C. Collins, USRPG, Warren P Nelson, Wataru Mori, William R. Edgington

Artistic Kamiya Fan

Aldaroc, Alex Rawlins, Andrew Brumer, Andrew M. Crawford, Andy & Liz, Anthony H, April and David Perlowski, Ashleigh Hughes, Bradley Eng-Kohn, Brady Licht, Brice "bakadevil" Lavigne, Charles Petty, ChiHime / sokeang lor, Chris Trinh, Don Shaffer, Drew "Industrial Scribe" Scarr, Eduardo Guimaraes, Einar Fagerdal Karlsen, Endre Enyedy, Epistolary Richard, Eric Schmid, Garret Blue, J. A. Aczel, James Bruce, James Keener, Jarod Cain, John Rutherford, Jose Alva Jr, Joseph G. LaCasse, Joshua Genrich, Josias Gomez, Justin D Coleman, K. David Ladage, Kassidy Helfant, Justin Purcell, Kevin Tyler, Lonoxmont, Lord Fuzzeth, M.R., Michelle Haward, Nicholas DeMauro, Nicole Mezzasalma, Pep Sun, Pixelberry Studios, Posthumus Smith, Ryan Garringer, S. Modarressi, Sati Stewart Singleton, ScenicRoute, SilentGeek, Simon Do, Steve Hudson, Stras "Cat Henge" Acimovic, Teemu S. Salo, Xavier Robledo, Zajan Decuir

Artistic Sociable Henge

Aaron Burkett, Aaron Lopez, Alexis & Jeremy, Ami Silberman, Andreas "Kargha" Persson, Daniel S. Luces, David Semenick, Dylan Enloe, John "Z" Zeitler, Jory, Streamjumper, Tony Lower-Basch

Kamiya Fans

A Boy Named Sue, Aaron Lingenfelder, Aaron Nowack, Aaron Tiffner, Aaron Wong, Adam Hegemier, Adam Koebel, Adam Plant, Adam Szpakowski, Alessandro La Valle, alexbarker116, Alexis B. Edminster, Alexis Perron, Allison & Kory Kaese, Mystic Station Designs, LLC, AML, Andre Braghini, Andrew "B.T. McGee" Sier, Andrew Byers, ANTHoNY J.J.JoNES, Anthony R. Evans,

Antoine Boegli, Aurynn Shaw, Austin "crab henge?" Loomis, Axebeard McBeardaxe, Baek Koung Nak, Barak Finney, Barbara Krumbach, Barry Scot Morgan, Ben Spurlock, Bill West, Bradley Rogers, Bram & Bresniv, Brandon Doxtater, Brian Allred, Brian Nguyen, Bruce Novakwoski, Bryan Patrick Girard, C Burgess, C.S. McKinney, Charles Parker, Chase Wassenar, Chris, Chris Bernhardi, Chris Fazio, Christopher Cansler, Christopher Trapp, Ciro M. Guerra IV, Cody and Allena, Conan Brasher, Conrad "Lynx" Wong, Coonie and Matthew Malone, Cris Frank, Curtis 'Wolfson' Lyon, D. Lacheny, Dale "RandomSelekt" Fassoth, Dan Dubinsky, Daniel HP Campbell, Daniel Yankowsky, Darcy Ross, Dave Tomczyk, David, David Ginsburg, David Henion, David J Blair, David Tran, Devin Breaux, Devin Fitzgerald, Dio Goldengate, Dj Roberts, Donovan Breth, Duane Moore, Dustin Jay Williams, Dusty Robertsn, Dylan Gwin, E Whitten, Earl S., Ed Moretti, Ed Oviedo, EdM, Edward Karuna, Eldersprig, Emily Grindberg, Emma Allen, Emma Laslett, Eric & Stephanie Franklin, Eric Tirrell (Troll), Eric Yamanuha, Esaotuler Almbakaarn, Esker, Euan Reid, Felipe Shingo, Fr. Adrian Milik, Franck VIDAL, Frankie Mundens, Franklin Hamilton, Gabrielle Menard & Jennifer Nuñez, Garry Frankowski, Gary A, Gilberto Leon, Gino Rodrigo, Gold Star Anime & Games! in Edinboro, PA, Graham MacLean, Graphite Scribble, Hussain Ahmadi, Iain Milligan, Ian "Coyote" Woolley, Ian Johnson, Ian MacRae, Ian Petrunia, Ian Raymond, Ignatius Montenegro, Ingo "The Duck" Arendt, J Brad Woodfin, J. S. Brown, James Dugdale, James Flaagan, James Graham, James W. Wood, Janus, Jarrod Holst, Jason K Averill, Jason Leinen, Jason Miller, Javier Alexander Hinojos, Jeff Painter, Jennifer Fuss, Jeremy Budds, Jesse Morgan, Jesse Smith, JinHwan Hwang, Joe Giguere, John Gaskell, John M. Trivilino, John NM Wilson, John Plunkett, Jonathan Abbott, Jonathan Marshall, Jonna Hind, Josh and Zach P., Josh McDonald, JP "Kooma-Kooma" Manzana, Julie L Spradley, Justin Triplett, Justin Xavier, K Liu, Kai Zhao, Karl Theller, Keith D. Evans, Kendrew Starr, Kevin Martin, Kirk Tolleshaug, Kitsune Heart, Koda, Konstantin Gorelyy, Konstantinos "Yo! Master" Rentas, Krister Sundelin, Laura F Bosche, Lawrence Huang, Leslie "Moyashimaru" Furlong, Liam Murray, Lisa Black, Lloyd Rasmussen, Loo Choo Khong, Lotyrin, Louis C. Martin, Lucas Cooperberg, Lucas Wells, Lucas Yew, Lukáš "denzil" Frolka, Luthorne, maldar, Malpraktis, Marcelão E. A. Faria, Margaret Norris, Mark van Esch, Markus Viklund, Matt Dunn, Matthew L Johnson, Matthew Ladd Anderson, Matthew Swetnam, Maximilian Wolfgang Niver, Md. Muazzam B. Sham Khiruddin, Megan Ortiz (RBMidknight), Micah Wolfe, Michael J Kruckvich, Michael Lord, Michael Thomas Landreth, Michal E. Cross, Mike "Ski" Thomas, Miles McPea, Minje Lee, Mitchi, Moah, Morbus Iff, Nathan Johndro, Nathan Latty, Nei "Morrighan" Crawford, Nick Colucci, Nick Robertson, Nicolaj Klitbo, Nikolas Eissinger, Omar Mukhtar Bin Ambok, Owen Nicholson, P. R. T., Patrick O'Shea, Patrick Sarmiento, Pavel Hinev, Pável Ojeda, Peter Isaiah Browning, Peter Norraba, Pia Pol, pinvendor, Legendary Merchant of Pins, Pumchu, Rachel Gollub, Rax, Richard Allred, Rick Neal, Ritz, robert Wood, Sabi and Hiyo, Samuel Brana-Soto, Samuel David Bailey, Scott Whipkey, Sean Huguenard, Sean K.I.W. Steele/Arcane, Shadizar, Shawn Ingram, Shay Stringer, Sheila Davis, Shelby Mehl, Simon Gough, Sky Reid-Mills, Stephen, Stephen Harvey, Stephen Honea, Sterling Brucks, Steve "Slipperboy" Donohue, Steve Lord, Steven Stadnicki, StevieP, T. Stevens, Tak Suyu, Tannyx et Miettinator, The Bhoo, Thiago Gonçalves, Thomas Willoughby, Timothy Bell, Timothy Martin, Tiphanie Gammon, Tobias Schewe, toffeeyak, Tom Kellett, Tom Klein, Tracy Cruz, Travis Rich, Triddek, Tristan Franco, Tucker McKinnon, Vincent "Balrog" Genna, Vincent Ecuyer, Vit Kozusky, Vitamancer, wadledo, Xavier Wolfs, Yumeko, Zaachary Erfman, Zabuni, Zachary T Cross

Sociable Henge

Abel, Alex Gwilt-cox, Alex Stone-Tharp, Alexander Gusev, Andrew Glasscock and Catherine Hughes, Andy Hauge, Andy Powell, Blue Door Comics & Games, Brent P. Newhall, Cédryck Mimault et Laura Iseut Lafrance St-Martin, Charles Hsu , Christoph Laurer, Chuck Childers, Corey Brin, Crispin Wilson, Cory Leugemors, Daniel Huckabone USMC, Daniel Luce, Daniel Westheide, Danielle Wayts, Davey Constas, David Drake, Donald Tyo, Drew & Geordie, Erica "Vulpin the ponyfox" Schmitt, F. Wesley Schneider, gamefiend, Gil Yolo, Gunnar "VVolfsong" Kulleseid, Hans Holm, Idle Red Hands Podcast, James Allen, James & Julie Kilbride, Jared Ritter, Jim Gogal & Jeanie Rabatsky, John F. Kadolph, John H. Reiher, Jr, Jonathan Rush, Jürgen Duvendack, Katy Okamoto, Keaan Mason The Sociable Henge, Kelley "Iron Bond" Vanda, Maeve McCartan, Mahtias Crestborn, Mark Snyder, Mark Woodhouse, masamunemaniac, Mondbuchstaben, Nancy Feldman, Narrenspiel+kia+dx1, Nocturama, Norbert Westenberg, Patrick Braasch, Patrick J Steiden, Patrick Pautler, Peter Ellvåg, PJ Schnyder, R Brubaker, Rasmus Durban Jahr, S L Schneebeli, Samael the Butterdragon, Sandy Moose, Shan Shan Li, Shawn Ang, Shawn Cooper, Shawn Hagen, Speccy, Steven Martindale, Tim Bugler, Zee!, Zoë Shafer

Elder Henge

Al Gordon, Albert Andersen, Andi Carrison, Andrew Lemos, Antoine Chauvet, bakumaru, Bardic Kitty, Ben White, Benjamin Juang, Beron the Grey, Brian Ngov, Brian Wu, Bryne Oliver, Caitlin Eckert, Cameron Sery, Chad Seiichi Fujioka, Choi Won, Chris Chambers, Christopher Challice, Clement Chow, Craig Judd, Crix, Daniel Adinolfi, David Breithaupt IV, David Headquist, David Kim, David Male, David Terhune, Derek Guder, Dmitry Kolobov, dsiewert, Edouard Contesse, Edward MacGregor, Elizabeth Sawyer, Fireside, For Sophia LeBel, Garrett Holmstrom, Gibbs B. Moore, Grant Edwards, Guy Builta, Hampton Pleshe, Hans Christian Andersen V, Harrison Barber, @IcarusMustBurn, Jake Richmond, Jarrett Perry, Jason Schindler, Jennifer & Tyler Turk, Jerry E Ozbun, JJangSung, Jose Pecina, Julia B. Ellingboe, Jung Seok Hyun, Kane McDonald, Keary Read, Konstantin Koptev, Kyle Lisk, Kyle W, Kyodachi, Lee Deppen, Leonardo Fonseca, Lim Ye Ping, Liralen, Malcolm Ross, Mark Rutledge, Michael Stevens, Michael T Mc Donnell, Minheack Choi, Mr. Mick Liverwitz Steins Kraus the 3rd, MysticTemplar, "N8Dogg5k" Nathan Barlow, Paul Thompson, Petter Wäss, PMBQ, Ric Wagner, Richard Fawcett, Rob Townsend, Robert Musser, Robert S., Sam Stickwood-Hanink, Scott K. Johnson, Sheena Mensinger, Sorin, Stefan Feltmann, Steven Fujisaka, Stuart Chaplin, Subhan Michael Tindall, Sushma J. Chandran, The Woods Family, Timothy Leong, Timothy Miller, Topi Törnroos, Vytautas Juodis, William "Shadowjack" Spencer, Wizbang The Mighty, You-Keun Kim

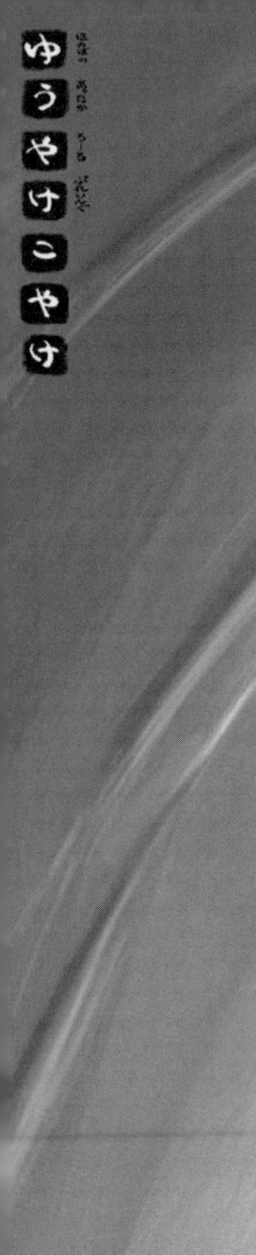

Henge

#orz, :P, A 'Woulf' Fink, A. Friend, A. Simpkins, Aaron Gordon, Aaron Klein, Aaron Mailloux, Aaron Rhoads, Aaron Smith, AB Thomas, Abbott, Abe Letter, Adam Benedict Canning, Adam Coleman, Adam J. Piskel, Adam Rajski, Adam Robichaud, Adam Singer, Adam Surber, Adam Vajcovec, Adam Waggenspack, Adrasteae, Adrian M Cheng, Adrian Maddocks, Ajoxer, Alan Chang, Alan Phillips, Albert Nakano, Alec Bates, Alex, Alex Bareham, Alex Hunter, Alex Lapin, Alex Loret de Mola, Alex Osecky, Alex Tigwell, Alexander J Draper, Alexander Newman, Alexander Wilkinson, Alexandra Hebda, Alexandre "Magnamagister" Joly, Alexis "poetfox" Long, Alexis Middleton, Alexis Siemon, Alice Fairfield, Alicia Allardyce, Alina Pete, Amanda & Jeff Thomas, Amanda V., Amelie Harms, Amie C. Lin, Amy Gunther, Amy Sutedja, Andrea Martinelli, André Bougie, Andrés Mpodozis, Andrew "Codemaster" Kane, Andrew Armstrong, Andrew Finn, Andrew Kelman, Andrew Portner, Andrew Saunders, Andy Hopp, Andy Winham, Andy Zeiner, Angel Baker, Angelo Pileggi, Angus Abranson, Anna and Elias Davis, Anne Moore, Anne Schmid, Annerire Il Fuoco, Annisa Jones, AnnMarie Russell, Anopheles, Anorak of the Darklight, anotherc, Ansel Wong, Anthony Berry Duquette, Antoine Fournier, Anton Heyder, Aphrae Lovelace, Ara, Aragorn Weinberger, Arik ten Broeke, Arikail D'Marco, Ash Brown, Ashley Stevens, Astra Downer, Auden Reiter, Aurelia Wyler, Aurora & Horatio Butler-Schilling, Austin Miner, Austin Sirkin, Axis Sunsoar, B. English, babus, Backer, Bastian Diedrich, Beatrix Root, Ben and Jess Feehan, Ben Barrow, Ben Hale, Ben Leftwich, Ben Mandall, Ben Reddersen, Ben Timmins, Bencent Crump, Benjamin Levy, Benjamin Travis, Benoit Devost, Biagio Cephalus, Billy Fuss, Blair Limcangco, Blake Hutchins, Bo Saxon, Bobby Skeens, BorgKitten, Brad Hinkel, Brad Luyster, Brad Morgan, Brandon Coleman, Brandon Kleinschmidt, Brandon Landry, brazil808, Brendan Harder, Brendan O'Donnell, Brent Dorsey, Brent Evans, Brent Wolke, Bret Gillan, Brett A. Bell, Brian Cooksey, Brian Horn, Brian Munro, brian peters, Brian S. Stephan, Brightfires, Bryan A Campbell, Bryan Hunt, Bryan Lee Davidson, Bryan Rosander, Bryant Durrell, Bully Pulpit Games, Caias Ward, Cairnryan Mower, Calvin Chou, Cameron Youngs, Can Gemicioğlu, Cara Melvin, Carly Ho, Caroline Choong, Casey DeWitt, Casey M., Cayen, Cédric Jeanneret, Celadon J., César "Kimble" Luz, Chamonkee, Chad Myles, Chance T., Chaosfiredragoon, Charles E Miller, Charles Schley, Charles Starrett, Charlie Payne, Chase Wong, Chaz Straney, Chester B Barrington, Chiaki Hirai, Chloe Anya Mirzayi, Choark - Barbarian Ninja, Chris "Grimtooth" Colborn, Chris & Candi Norwood, Chris Bisanar, Chris Caldwell & Jennifer Pullen, Chris Chinn, Chris Elledge, Chris Hartford, Chris J. Jeffery, Chris Longhurst, Chris McEligot, Chris Mortika, Chris Powell, Chris Prestwich, Chris Slazinski, Chris Solis, Chris Volcheck, Christian A. Nord, Christian Lajoie, Christian Melancon, Christopher, Christopher Brandl, Christopher C. Jones, Christopher Dade, Christopher E. Gerber, Christopher Haas, Christopher Pease, Christopher Wilmoth, Chyna 'Bug' Farrell, Claes Florvik, Clayton Odom, Clément Prévoteau, Clyde L. Rhoer the 3rd, cobaltflares, Cody Marbach, Cody Semer, Colin M Matter, Colin Souva, Colin Urbina, Corrina & Lila Voytek, Coureton Dalton, Craig Hargraves, Curt Meyer, Curtis Hay, Cyfnos Blaidd, Cyra, Damien Swallow, Dan Bidwa, Dan Harms, Dan Maruschak, Dan Noland, Dan Pierz, Dan Winterlin, Dana Bayer, Dana Russo, Danakir, Daneward T. Locke, IV, Daniel "DM" Martins, Daniel Chick, Daniel Condaxis, Daniel Garcia, Daniel H Boling, Daniel H. Levine, Daniel J. Owsen, Daniel Joseph Tavares Moore, Daniel Lewis, Daniel M. Kane, Daniel Norton, Danilo Alexandre Soares Takano, Darren Miguez, Darwin Bell, Dave Luza, Dave Peterson, David Buswell-Wible, David Devaty, David Emler, David Farnell, David Hawkins, David Isaac Frohman, David Lupo, David J Prokopetz, David Millians, David Paul, David Weaver, Delbert Thompson, Dennis Rude, Dhanyel, Diogo Tristão, Docteur Half, Don C., Don Frazier, Don White, Douglas "Strange Quark" Reed, Douglas Snyder, Drew Childers, Drew Wendorf, DrGambit, Duncan A. Doherty, Duncan Mann, Dustin Cooper, Dustin Dunaway, Dustin Flowers, Dutiful Reed, Dylan Carey, Dylan Green, Dylan Hollinden, E Graham, Ed Kowalczewski, Ed McW, Eddie Sells, Edgar Gonzalez, Eeshwar Rajagopalan, el Miko, Elisabeth Espiritu, Elise Roberts, Elizabeth Eldridge, Elizabeth Kelly, Elizabeth Roach, Elliott Freeman, Emeraude, Emily Kintanar, Emmanuel Greene, Eric, Eric Johnson, Eric M Jackson, Eric Michael Montoya, Eric P Tryon, Eric S., Eric Steinbrenner, Eric Zylstra, Erik Hedqvist, Erik Kristiansen, Erik Lagerstedt, Erik Ottosen, Erik Sieurin, Erin "taichara" Bisson, Erin Bournival, Ernesto Pérez, Esther Shanks, Eusebi Vazquez, Eva Schiffer, Evan Silberman, Evelyn McNaughton, Evelynn Frost, Fabrice Dorantes, Fagner Lima, Fallenseraph75, fanguad, "filkertom" Tom Smith, Forrest D. Johnson, Fox McGregor, Foxears Jackson Tegu, Frank Hall, Frederic Fleury, Gail Terman, Gareth "SongCoyote" Storm, Garrett Pearson, Garry Gross, Gary Lau, Gavin, riffin, and Emma Miller, Gavran, George Breden, Gilbert Milner, Giulia Cursi "Nenhiril", GMGerrymander, Graham Starfelt, Granieri "Walking-Pat" Patrice, Grant Thompson Jr., Greg Walters, Gregory Allyn Lipscomb, Guillaume "Nocker", Guillaume "yume" Boutigny, Guillaume Vidal, Guy Shalev, Gwiffon, Ha Family, Hal Mangold, Halen McMahan, Hali and Miya Shin, Heath White, Hendrik Little, Henry Wong, Hillary Brannon, Hippy Joe, Ho Wee Siong, HunTurkey, Ian Auger-Juul, Ian Cunningham, Ian Homeyard, Ian Z., Indi Latrani, Innergnome, Ira, Irven "Myrkwell" Keppen, Isaac J. Karth, Isabel M., Ishai Barnoy, Ivan A Jones, Ivan Finch, Ivan V.A.N. Slipper, J. A. Lauritzen, J. Black (G_Q), J. Glenn Snyder, J. Hayden Pretzman, J. Robert Anderson, Jack Gulick, Jack Waitkus, JacLyn S. Jones, Jacob Randolph, Jacob Saurer, Jaime Herazo, Jake Irving, James "Ven'Tatsu" Morgan, James Barry, James Hagan, James John, James Lee Sanford, James Ritter, James Stuart, Jamie Lackey, Jane C., Janne Vaateri, Jason and Sylvia Wodicka, Jason Corley, Jason Feldman, Jason Lescalleet, Jason R Krook, Jason Ramsey, Jason Scott Timmerman, Jason Storey, Jason Thompson, Jason Tseng, Jay Estrada, Jay V. Schindler, Jayson Cooper, JDC Burnhil, JDnD, Jean Pierre Pietza, Jeff Kahrs, Jeff Troutman, Jeffrey Craft, Jeffrey Wu, Jenny Lin, Jer "OmniJerBear" Flores, Jeremy, Jeremy Butler, Jeremy Douglass, Jeremy Kostiew, Jerome Isnard, Jerry D. Grayson, Jesse R, Jessica Chai, Jessica Kiffmeyer, Jessica Sywyk, Jim Heath, Jim Jacobson, Jim Long, Jim McKinley, Jiseob Kim, Joe Mcdaldno, John "Shadowcat" Ickes, John & Amber Dickens, John Daly, John F. Zmrotchek, John Fiala, John Fred Obedoza, John Krulick, John Lafin, John Latona Jr., John Mehrholz, John Melton, John Moran, John Simutis, John Taber, Johnathan Chand, Johnson Ow, Jon Maness, Jon Niehof, Jon Robertson, Jon Rosebaugh, Jon Scott Edwards, Jonathan "BonBon" Bonilla, Jonathan Gibbs, Jonathan McCulley, Jonathan Walton, Jonathan Young, Jordan K., Jordan Klinefelter, José Manuel Palacios Rodrigo, Josema "Yrdin" Romeo, Joseph "UserClone" Le May, Joseph Johnston, Joseph Kogin, Joseph Moore, Josh Crowe, Josh Cupp, Josh Inman, Josh Peters, Josh Rensch, Josh S, Josh T Jordan, Joshua, Joshua Baum, Joshua C. Varrone, Joshua De Santo, joshua everman, Joshua James Gervais, Joshua Jones, Joshua Minol, Joshua Ramsey, JP Luscombe, Juan Martinez, Juan-David Vega (Ender of Sekrit Club), Judd Karlman, Judd M. Goswick, Julian J. Kuleck, Juliusz Doboszewski, Justin Dorsey, Justin Fritts, Justin Lee Jackson, Justin Mcdaniel, Justin Tolmar White, K J Miller, K. Glenn, Kaiaa, Kanryu Golden, Karl Deckard, Karl Hauber, Kathy Daniels, Katie Gamblin, Katie Nuyda, Katt Owens, Kawaii Kawaii Panda, Kayla Bayens, Kelly Brown, Ken B., Ken Finlayson, Kenny "Krivvin" Bailey, Keto, Kevin "Kaos" Peña, Kevin "Norumu" Casper, Kevin & Jessi, Kevin A Swartz, MD, Kevin Ascott, Kevin Leach, Kevin Portland, Khalifa K., Kimberly Wrane, Kit Fowley, Kitka, Klawzie, Knox & Logen, KotetsuTheO, Kryptovidicus, Kumiko Yamazaki, Kurisu Titor, Kurt Collins, Kurt T. Runkle, Kwyndig, Kyle Silverthorn, L. E. Larsen, Laiel Shepherd, Larry Ngo, Laura R. Osborn, Lauren Williams, Laurence J Sinclair, Lawrence Parks, Lawrence Srutkowski, Lee Torres, Lena Erickson, Level 99 Games, Liam Fisher, Lily Tenebrae, Linda Clem, Lindsey Wilson, Lior =^_^=, Lisa B & Brian M, Liz Sander & Brian Crucitti, Logan Powers, Long Viet Le, Lorelei Nguyen, Lorien, Louie, Louis B Schoener, Louis the Great, LS Kuro, Luis Cerdas, Luke Bailey, Luke Gaul, M. Justin, M.W. II, Maggie and Josie Horneff, Mainjari Friedland, makkura, Malik Amoura, Mario Meo, Mark Andrew Wilson, Mark Argent, mark balbuena, Mark Diaz Truman and Marissa Kelly, Magpie Games, Mark Foley Jr., Mark Hanna, Mark Harrop, Mark Horne, Mark Knewstubb, Mark Mohrfield, Mark Richardson, Mark Woodside, Martin Bourque, Martin Greening, Martin Severin Jensen, Mary Frances Harrison, MasterMulle <3, Mathias "Kaga" Radtke, Mathias Lechner, Matrixvingian, Matt Appuhn, Matt Baning, Matt Herron, Matt Jett, Matt Logan, Matt Pinkerton, Matt Sanchez, Matt Shoemaker, Matt Steen, Matt Widmann,

Matthew Campbell, Matthew Christodoulou, Matthew Cramsie, Matthew Edwards, Matthew Ericksen, Matthew 'Gairne' Mole, Matthew Gray, Matthew Hartwell, Matthew Karabache, Matthew Lind, Matthew McDonnell, Matthew Newell, Matthew Nielsen, Matthew Ostapchuk, Matthew Rai Terwilliger, Matthew Watkin, Matthias Light, Maya and Harvey Hudson, Meg Keen, Megan Greathouse, Megan McFerren, Megann OlyWA, Mejiro, Mel Hall, Mendel Schmiedekamp, Mendez, Michael "G-Nitro" Camacho, Michael "Maikeruu" Pierno, Michael & Ashley Grenon, Michael A.C. Stevens, Michael Beck, Michael Carini, Michael Davis, Michael Feldhusen, Michael Fowler, Michael Hill, Michael Hopcroft, Michael 'Jinrai' Biggers, Michael Knowles, Michael L. Kerr, Michael Lawrence, Michael Maroon, Michael McDowell, Michael Ostrokol, Michael Sands, Michael T. Pureka, Michael Tree, Michele Gelli, Mika "Deva" Halttunen, Mike, Mike Brand, Mike Cameron, Mike 'Carlson' & Christopher W. Davis, Mike Kelley, Mike McArtor, Mike Welker, Miles Foxx, Mister Fiend, Moe moe Jeff-tan, Monica R. Medina, Morgan Hazel, Most Refined Whale-chan, Myaan, Nadia Cerezo, Nat "woodelf" Barmore, Nate "EmCeeKhan" Baumbach, Nate Robinson, Nateal "Kalylia" Erickson, Nathan M Huss, Nathan Mooney, Nathan Reed, Nathaniel Cole, Nathaniel W Jordan, Neal Cooper, Neal Kaplan, Neal Tanner, Nespress, Nicholas "Anthony" Arroyo, Nicholas Barabach, Nicholas Decker, Nick Bate, Nick Keyuravong, Nick Larocco, Nicky Hunt, Nikolai C., Nikolainn H., NinjaDebugger, Noah "Teegan" Hinz, Nolan "Kitsunora" Antonio, none, Norah Bryant, Nufar & Joye, Octavio Arango, Oliver Vulliamy, Ottergame, Otto lam, PandaDad, Pat Harrison, Patrick Ley, Patrick Vaughan, Patty Kirsch, Paul, Paul Belemjian, Paul Bendall, Paul Dobson, Paul E. Olson, Paul Echeverri, Paul Sangho Kim, Paul Sudlow, Paul Vogt - The Hopeless Gamer, Paul Watson, Peregrinus, Persona, Pete Hurley, Peter Aronson, Peter Dommermuth, Peter O'Hanley, Peter Paulsen, PHAN DANG Kim-alexandre, PHGamer, Phil Hanley, Philature, Phill winters, Phillip and Amanda Skaggs, Phillip and Traci Humphrey, Phillip Wong, Pilar Leber, Pontus Ilbring, Preston Coutts, Prof. Redwood, ProxyFox, Puppy <3s Kitty, Quinn Heath, Quinn Wilson, Quote, Rachael and Seth Blevins, Rachel E.S. Walton, Rachel Pfefferle, Rachel Saling, Raechel Coon, Rafael Rocha, Rain Donaldson, Randall Zimmerman, Randel N. Evans II, Raphael Montero, Rasamune, Ray Harris, Rebecca Rraze, Rene Hernandez, Rev. Keith Johnson, Rice Honeywell, Richard J. Rogers, Richard T. Balsley, Rick Sorgdrager, Rigo family, Rob Heinsoo, Robert, Robert Anderson, Robert H. Oates III, Robert ruckman, Robert W, Roberto Quintans, Robin Lee Sanford, Rodney Thompson, RodolfoF.M., Roger N. Dominick, ron beck, Ronald Conner, Rook, Ross A. Isaacs, Ross Bowman, Rowan, RowanYote, Roy Killington, Rushyo, Ryan & Shayna Gobel, Ryan Latta, Ryan Shelton, Ryan Wells, Ryon Levitt, Sabastian Wilkinson, Salvador Melo, Sam "Tzenes" Rossoff, Sam Tlustos, Samuel Esposito, Samuel Munilla, Samuel-Louis Gardiner, Sara Peters :3, Sara Sestak, Sarah E. B. Grimsley, Satu Nikander, Sean Harvey, Sean M. Dunstan, Sean M. P. Kennedy, Sean O'Leary, Sean Pelkey, Sean Swanwick, Sebastien Julien, Seth Brodbeck, Shal Loraine, Shameless, Shane Williamson, Shane Zeagman, Shard73, Shayne Olson, Sheila Thomas, Shelton Brown, Shervyn, Simon Davis, Simon To, Sixten Zeis, Skwiziks, Skyesby, Skylor Cox, SL, Sonja Viljamaa, Soren Ludwig, Spencer E Lathrop, Stan Yamane, Stan!, Starry Sky, stephan corniuk, Stephane Drouin-Moreland, Stephanie Bryant, Stephen G Matthews, Steve Jakoubovitch, Steve Johnson, Steve Laubner, Steve Rubin, Steve Sensiba, Steven Swanger, Steven Thesken, Steven Wyman, Strange MD, Sulgi, Supa Hamsta, Surprenant, Sushu Xia, Sword'n'Board, T.S. Luikart, Tamara Wharton, Tamiki, Tania Joyce, Taren J. Teague, Ted Kaplanis, Tem White, Terry Varga III, Tessa, Thayne Blake, The Bradley-Ryder Family, The Burning Wheel, The Daughters of Verona, The Family Houle, Theodore Jay Miller, Theodore T. Posuniak, II, Thomas Lee, Thomas Scroggs, Thor Olavsrud, Tiago Marinho, Tianxu (Tim) Guo, Tiffany Ross, Tiki, Tim Latshaw, Tim Mitchell, Tim Northcutt, Timothy Smith and Sara Biondi, Timothy Wochnick, TJ Wilson, Tobias "Urd" G., Tobias Mcnabb, Tom Ladegard, Tom Nguyen, Tom Van de Sande, Tonya Bezpalko, Travis Cook, Travis Mueller, Travis Prow, Tresi Arvizo, Trip the Space Parasite, Trok, Troy Orr, Troy Warrington, Trygve Lie, Twila Oxley Price, Tyler Henry, Tyler Lanser, Ukiah, Ukyou Strauss, Uncle Monty, Usotsuki, Vera Vartanian, Veronica Courage Wakefield, Vicente Cartas Espinel, Victor Fan, Victor Wyatt, Ville Siivola, W.J. Walton, Wade Griffith Sr., Walter Tolero Jr, warcabbit, Weiyi Guo, Werner Stiegler, Wesley T. Stigliano, Whatthefnu, Whitt., William B Ewen, William Gerke, William Lamming, William R. Brock IV, William Smith, Xander Kramer, Xavier Aubuchon- Mendoza, xK1, Zach Brown, Zach Welhouse, Zachery Neighbors, Zanwot, Zappique, Zereth, Zoot!

Residents

"They're All Dead" Dave, ~anon~, A. Emerson Rodrigues, Aaron "Azure" Julian, Aaron Kortteenniemi, Aaron Pothecary, AbeFM, Adam "Ferrel" Trzonkowski, Adam C, Adam Nemo, Adam V, Adán R., Adri, Adumbratus, Alan John Wilkinson (Cassius335), Alan Zabaro, Alberto Camargo, Aleks Krsch, Alex Bergquist, Alexa Ko, Alexander, Alexander Hawson, Alexandre "ShamZam" Piquet, Alexis Mirsky, Alistair C, Allan J. Sim, Amber Rene King, Amy Williams, Ana Silva, Andreas Ginter, Andrew Attwell, Andrew Bastien, Andrew Gill, Andrew Seiple, Andrew Van Rooy, Andy Hill, Angeyja Winter, Anika Page, Anonymous please, Anthony Mello, Antoine Bertier, Antonio Rodriguez, Arkane Loste, Arlene Medder, Arsenio A. Rafael IV, Asen R. Georgiev, Auri & Zach, Austin Conley, Avery Wilson, Aymeric P., B. Wertz, Backer not appearing in this list, Balázs Oroszlány, Barac Wiley, Baradaelin, Bard Bloom, Bastian Dornauf, Beau McCarrell, Belinda Kelly, Ben "Legendary" Bernard, Ben Bonds, Ben Pharn, Ben-David Kirsten, Benjamin Bangsberg, Benjamin Hager, Benjamin Loh, Benjamin Sousa, Benly Arizona, Bettina Tan, beyondkawaii, Billy Long III, Blastia, Bobby Billingsley, Bowie Tsang & Hilda Sze, Bradley Zakany, braincraft, Brian "The Minty" Curtis, Brian Auxier, Brian Browne, Brian LaFever, Brian Little, Brian Pitt, Bryan Jeal, Bryan P. Chavez, Bryce van Dyk, burningcrow, C. Starr, Caleb Haddix, Caleb Osborn, Calvin Snowden, Cardinal Esox Lucius, Carl Jenno Ganzon, Carl L Gilchrist, Carlos Daniel Muñoz Diaz, Cassandra James, Cayman Engel, Ceili Smalara, Chad "Arahoushi" Cooper, Chad Johnston, Chad Smith, Charles Mitchell Lord, Charles Taylor, ChazLie, Chris Allison, Chris Angelini, Chris Blondin, Chris Coates, Chris Czerniak, Chris Fitzsimmons (The Dragons Eye Games), Chris Lazenbatt, Chris Marsh, Chris Martin, Chris Michael Jahn, Chris Privitere, Chris Starr, ChrisB, Christian Hollnbuchner, Christophe SAURA, Christopher D. McDonough, Christopher Hunter, Christopher 'Red' De'Ment, Christopher Stringari, Chuck Henebry, Cliomancer, Craig Hackl, Curtis Hogg, Curufea, Cyn, Cyrus Chow, D F White, D McGrady, D.Graham, Daanyaal du Toit, Dan Gerold, Dan Wentzel, Dani Lynette, Daniel "Zøvnig" Kold, Daniel A., Daniel B. Taylor, Daniel Gonzalez da Costa Campos, Daniel M Luz, Daniel McKenna, Daniel Rachels, Daniel Sacdpraseuth, Daniel Solis, Daniel Tornsten, Daniele Di Rubbo, Danielle Linder, Dave Cake, Dave Cheetham, Dave Desgagnes, Dave Sherohman, David, David, David "Shiro" Martinez, David A. K. Lichtenstein, David Bowers, David Chart, David E Mumaw, David Grinton, David M., David Morrison, David S Pfaff, David Shore, David Snow, David Starner, David Thackaberry, David W Shelley, David Woodlock, DDRJake, Dean Glencross, Dennis Pruitt, Derek C, Desmond Wong, Di Zhilan, Diana Stoneman, Dirtch Koloblicin, Doc Chronos, Dominic Verrier, Dominik Denker, Don Hill, Don Kosak, Doubleclick, Doug Hagler, Doug Ruff, Douglas Justice, Drew (Andrew) South, Dylan Schokman, Ed Fields, Edward Saxton, Edward T Wang, Elaugaufein, Electronic Old Men, Elemiel, Elizabeth Creegan, Elizabeth Mitchell, Elyandel, Emanuele "∞" Vulcano, Ender, Eric Goh, Eric Rossing, Erica Greenblatt, Erich Vereen, Erik Amundsen, Erik Grunsten, Erin Alice Sanders, Erwin Burema, Ethan King, Evan Ringo, Evgeniy "Jamie" Vasin, evil bibu, Eyal Teler, Fabio Succi Cimentini, Flo Hoheneder, Fortinbrace, Fowlor, Fran Sivers, Franck Michaux, Francois Schnell, Frank Crist, Frederic Toutain, G. Hartman, Gabriel Westelius, Gaërouant, Galen, Gareth Tan Wen-Liang, Gary "Madu" Montgomery, Gaston Keller (aka Gurtaj), Geoff Watson, George Austin, George Wilkinson, Gerald Cameron, gia, Gilbert Podell-Blume, Gillian McCorriston, Giringiro, Glen Green, Gonzalo Dafonte García, Good Ol' Mike Sugarbaker, Grant Brownlee, Grant Greene, Graypawn, Greg Ferrell, Greg Leatherman, Greg Osborne, Guilherme Vieira Honorato, Guy Milner, H. M. 'Dain' Lybarger, Hap Perry, Hein Ragas, Helder Araújo aka Pistoleiro do Diabo, Henning Wollny, Henrikus Freeman, Herman Cillo, Hernan Kowalsky, Hiveul, Human Person Games, Iain A. McGregor, Ian V, Ianaandru Meredith, Icas, Igor Bone, Imran Inayat,

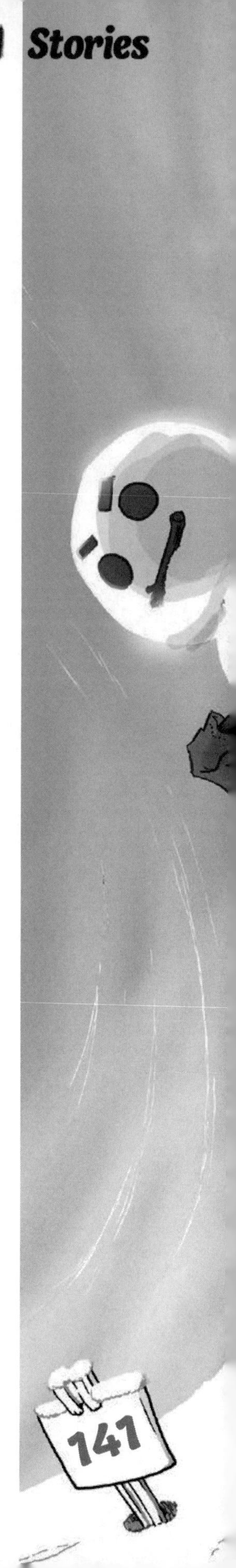

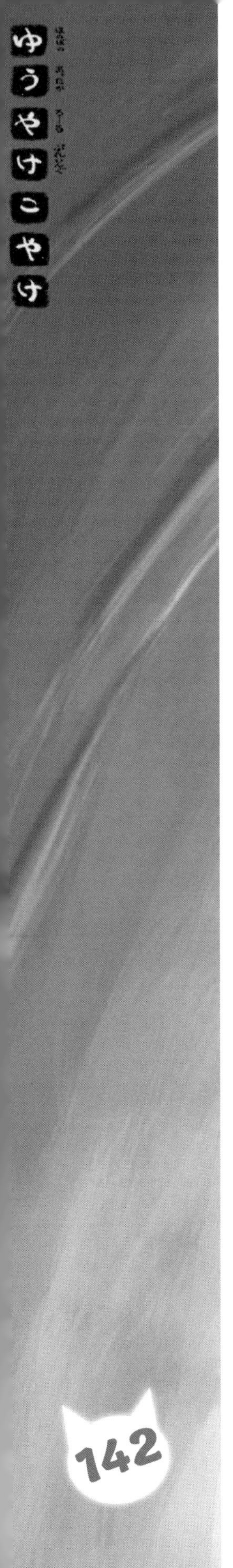

In Memory of Chris Brashier, Isaac 'Will It Work' Dansicker, Iso Stein, J M Simms, Jack Fractal, Jacob, Jacob Drosselmeier, Jacquelyn Manduley, Jake Kuska, Jake Mears, James "Jragon" White, James Abbott, James Cartwright, James Fleming, James Husum, James Nguyen, James Reid, James Robertson, James Sinnett, Jamie Dickson, Jamie Macey, Janet Houck, Jan-Pierre Jaspers, Jared Cassady, Jaroslaw "Vestin" Surowka, Jason Berry, Jason Dzillack, Jason G. Anderson, Jason Joyce, Jason Pitre, Jason Poynter, Jason Tocci, Jason Wright, Jau (Andrew Dunne), Javier Barroso Gil, Jay Shaffstall, Jay Steven Uy Anyong, Jaydee, Jayle Enn, Jean H, Jean-Olivier "Volsung" Ferrer, Jefferson Watson, Jeffery Patton, Jeffrey Mancebo, Jen Kitzman, Jennifer Kathleen, Jeremy Fridy, Jerry Sköld, Jesica O'Black, Jesse Anderson, Jessica Hammer, Jessica Pink, Jim Burdo, Jim Zub, João Mariano, Joe Ark Sun, Joe Maron, John H. Donahue, john hayholt, John LeBoeuf-Little, John M. Portley, John Powell, John Swan, Johny Fight, Jon Bristow, Jonathan Agens, Jonathan Korman, Jonathon Hodges, Jordan Cormier, Jordi Rabionet, Jorge "Simaehl" Idarraga, Jose "Magicstorm" Velez, José Carlos Domínguez, José Miguel Giménez, Joseph Still, Josh Einstein, Josh Greenberg, Josh Lithgow, Josh Medin, Joshua Beale, Joshua Estrada, Joshua Ferdinands, Joshua Hoskins, Joshua Straub, Julianna Backer, Julien Delabre, jyChin, Kai Tave, Kai Yau, Kairu, Kaja Hanson, Karl Maurer, Karl The Good, Katherine Russell, Katie Zenke, Kaylee and Xander Denton, Kayleigh Jones, Kelton, Ken Ringwald, Kevin, Kevin Crocilla, Kevin Harrison, Kevin M Sullivan, Kevin Moreno, Kevin R Z Reeves, Kiith, Kirt Dankmyer, KMKB, kounch, Krystina Metalis, Kyle Morton, Kyle Simons, Ladran, Lady Ruthface, Lapsed Pacifist, Lark, Larry The Roommate, Lasse DK, LawnPygmy, Leonard Tai, Lester Smith, Ryan Lew Zhe Zhang, Liam Eyers, LievreOkami, Lippai.Peter, Lloyd Ash Pyne, Lorenzo Urbano, Lou-Ann Pouderoux, Lucas Wright, Lucio Maron, Luis Antonio Avalos, Lunaticked, M Alexander Jurkat, M. Alan Thomas II, M. P. O'Sullivan, Maarten Engels, Maik Schmidt, Manu Marron, Manuel Quick, Marc 'Spike' Eichenberger, Marcelino Soliz, Marco "_Journeyman_" Bignami, Marcus "Zyfie" Beyer, Margana, Marisu, Mark B, Mark Green, Markku Tuovinen, Markus Widmer, Martin Wick, Martino G., Matic Kačič, Matt Wetherbee, Matthew Bannock, Matthew Bynoth, Matthew Couch, Matthew Gollschewski, Matthew Laughlin, Matthew Power, Matthew Robinson, Matthew Rolnick, Matti Rintala, Max "Ego" Hervieux, Max W Chase, Maxim Maganet-Yurov, Melissa Barbour, Mich Woo, Michael Amirault, Michael Aylen, Michael Brewer, Michael Burtner, Michael Cambata, Michael Creidieki Crouch, Michael Gebhard, Michael Holcombe, Michael Nichols, Michael Pagel, Michael Palacios, Michael Staib, Miguel Zapico, Mikael "Otaku Mike" Brodu, Mikael Knall, Mike Brodahl, Mike Lazo, Mircea Ungureanu, Miscavish Family, Miszczak Axel, Mitosis, Mook, Morgan Ellis, Morgan Gilbert, Multimaster, muskets, N. Falconer, Nate Lawrence, Nathan Chambers, Nathan Dunn, Nathan Hicks, Nathan Olmstead, Nathan Pannell, Nathan W. Morgan, Neil Ng, Neil Rall, Neil Smith, Néstor Villarrubia, Niall O'Donnell, Nicholas Bidler, Nigel Wong, Nihar Nilekani, Nikki Jeske, Nina Fabiano, Nique, Noah Figueroa, Noe Kotaku Newell, Nomadotto, Nyrreah, Oh Seung Han, Ok, Oliver and Jennifer Swan, Oliver 'Chase' Horton, Olivier Descamps, Olna Jenn Smith, Omy, Orlando A. Francis Jr., Oscar "ToPeace" Simmons, Oscar Ulloa, Ozymandius, Pablo Doba, Pablo Palacios, Paolo Ramello, Para Arianne, de Javier, Pat R, Patrice Hédé, Paul Baugh, Paul Mansfield, Paul Rickert, Paul Zimmerle, Pavel Zhukov, Paweł Michalik, Pedro H. Ferro, Peiblit, Per-Erik Rundqvist, Peter Bemis, Peter L Ward, Peter Smith, Péter Tóth, Peter William Gerkman, Peter, Kristin, & Jason Childs, Philip "Kyubey" Lam, Philip 'xipehuz' Espi, Philippe Debar, Phoenix Sun Marino-Ramer, Pierre Gavard-Colenny, Pierre Toulouze, Powgow, R. & J. Friend, R. R. Michael Humphreys, Rachel Ross, Rafe Ball, Raiden Drake, Rainer Wagner-Ballner, Ralf Wagner, Ralph Lettau, Rand Brittain, Reeve T. Shields, Remo di Sconzi, Renato Ramonda, Reverance Pavane, Rhett L. Frakes, Richard Armstrong, Richard Howe, Richard Pleyer, Riley McDonald, RJ Stewart, Rob Donoghue, Rob Ferguson, Robert Clayton Wyatt, Robert Fisher, Robert Gaither, Robert Iken Lee, Robert Rees, Robert Short, Robert Stehwien, Robert W. Whitehouse, Robertson Sondoh Jr, Rosie DM, Ross Willard, Rune Vendler, Ryan Kent, Ryan Riojas, Ryan Upjohn, S J Jennings, Sabine Lueck, Sakib Choudhury, Sam Ledwich, Sam Wright, Samarkin Dmitriy, Samuel L Sutton, Sangjun Park, Santtu "Japsu" Pajukanta, Sara Neagley, Sarn Aska, Scott Dockery, Scott T. Morgan, Sean Curtin, Seán Joesbury, Selene O'Rourke, Seth Harris, Seto Konowa, Seubpong J., Severian, Shannon Flesher, Shaun Clamp, Shimrod the Clever, Earl of Coalchester, Siaw Hsien Yang, Silverhawk, Silvio Herrera Gea, Simon "Zinic" Madsen, Simon* jf. Hunt, Siriondil, Some Guy, sparky1479, Spike Padley, Stacy E. Braxton, Stan Taylor, StarArmy.com, star-star, Stéphane, Stephen Esdale, Stephen Joseph Ellis, Stephen Sauer, Steve Jasper, Steven Bartalamay, Steven Hanlon, Steven Robert, Stew Wilson, Stuart Leonard, Sunil Segu, SuperBunnyBun, Svend Andersen, T.E. Rodham, Tad Kelson, Tadashi Kyle Hayakawa, Tako, Tamra Green, Tamsin Mehew, Tatiana Alejandra de Castro Perez, tavernbman, teeter, Teppo Pennanen, Termody, Thalji, the Encaffeinated ONE, The Handsome Dandy, The Roach, The Szczawinski's, TheFinnicle, Theo, Thomas Glorieux, Thomas Irvine, Thomas Previte, Tim Franzke, Tim Hodge, Tim Jensen & Willow Palecek, Tim Leard, Tim Newman, Tim Ryan, Timo Schiller, Timon Nelson, TJ McCrea, Tobbun, Tobias Romer, Toby Gleeson-Stack, Todd Zircher, Tollymain, Tom Fitzsimons, Tom LaPille, Tom Wilkinson, Tony Love, tosxyChor, Travis Scott, Tunod D. Denrub, Tyler Neff, Tyris, Cortle and Stent, Ubiratan Pires Alberton, Ulf "McWolfe" Andersson, usha maru, Varit R., Vaughan Cockell, Velenir Oriona, Venatius, Vicki Hsu, Victor Eichhorn, Victoria Stephenson, Victoria Uney, WaHi Council, Wallace the TimeLord of Forsaken Hollow, Hsieh Wei-Hua, Wibble Nut, Will Iverson, William Buchanan, William Cook, William Corbett, William Hatchman, William J. Norcutt, William J. Russell, William Mansky, Wing L. Mui, Wyldstar, Yannic Buty, Yelta Sumasu, Yoshi Creelman, Youngjun Ko, Yragaël, Zachary Patrick, Zalzator, Zed Lopez, Zethar - Yukari no Takauji, Zhuang Zhou David, Zuhur Abdo, 井隼理央, 笑男子

Tourists

Alison & Sela, Alistair, Anderson, Andreas Larsson, Christopher "PolarPhantom" Kirkman, Dado Viciado, Daniel J. Wyn, Daniel M Molina, Eric Damon Walters, Hayley Penny, Imran Siddiq, J.D. Dresner, Jake "VaneFox" Miller, Jamal forbes, Jason "jivjov", Jim Ryan, Jim Sweeney, Justin Smith, Martin H.L., Matteo Sasso, Nanasu Nana, Naomi McArthur, Nicholas H. Hollander, Niko Geyer, Odessus Naito, Patrick Runyan, PAXX LTD, Richard E Hughes, Rodrigo Garcia Carmona, Saul Al. Roberts, Simon Linder, Solomon Lee, Tainted Gaming Co., Three Fates Games, Tuyen Nhat Vo

CONNECTION CONTENTS TABLE

Contents	Description
Like	You like them, for whatever reason. *Note:* The strength of this kind of connection can only go as high as 2. If you want to raise it to 3 or higher, you'll have to change its contents.
Affection	You like them. You're lonely when they're not around. You want to be with them.
Protection	You want to protect them. You feel you need to be there for them.
Trust	You trust them. You go to them when you need help.
Family	You've lived with them for a long time. You understand them very well.
Admiration	You want to be like them. You want to be like that too.
Rivalry	You don't want to lose to them. You see them as a rival. You see them as competition.
Respect	You think they're amazing. You think they're great.
Love	You're in love with them. You love them a lot. Just thinking about them makes your heart pound. *Note:* This kind of connection must be of strength 2 or higher. If it has a strength of 1, you'll have to pick a different contents.
Acceptance	You accept them; you give them a place to belong. *Note:* This is only for the town and local gods. You must have the narrator's permission to select it.

ACTION CHECK GUIDELINE TABLE

#	Guideline
2 or Less	You probably don't need to do a check.
3-4	Well, I'm sure you can get by.
5-6	You can manage if this is something you're good at.
7-8	Normally, this'll be impossible.
9+	No way!

COST TO STRENGTHEN CONNECTION

To	Costs
1	5 Dreams (0 with Impression Check)
2	5 Dreams (0 with Impression Check)
3	5 Dreams
4	8 Dreams
5	12 Dreams

SURPRISE TABLE

#	Effect
1-2	The person cries out then and there.
3	The person runs away as fast as they can.
4	The person is paralyzed and can't move.
5+	The person faints and falls down.

TRANSFORMATION COST TABLE

Time of Day	Form (Except Birds)	Form (Birds)
Morning/Daytime +4	Completely Human +4	Completely Human +4
Evening +0	Tail +2	Small Wings +2
Night +2	Ears and Tail +0	Wings That Look Like They Can Be Used to Fly +0

Heart-Warming Role-Playing

GOLDEN SKY Stories

RAIT

Human Form :

Name :
True Form :
Age :
(Boy / Girl)

Powers

________ ( ) ________ ( )
________ ( ) ________ ( )
________ ( ) ________ ( )

			Weakness		Additional Power	
HENGE	( )	*Mysterious Powers*				
ANIMAL	( )	*Run, Feel, Hide*	● ________	↔	○ ________	( )
ADULT	( )	*Use Machines, Knowledge, Hide Feelings*	● ________	↔	○ ________	( )
CHILD	( )	*Play, Wheedle, Get Protected*	● ________	↔	○ ________	( )

TRUE FORM

DREAMS

CONNECTIONS

	Contents		Contents	Partner
YOU	( )	■■□□□☆□□□■■	(Acceptance)	TOWN
YOU	( )	□□□□□☆□□□□□	( )	________
YOU	( )	□□□□□☆□□□□□	( )	________
YOU	( )	□□□□□☆□□□□□	( )	________
YOU	( )	□□□□□☆□□□□□	( )	________
YOU	( )	□□□□□☆□□□□□	( )	________

WONDER

FEELINGS

THREADS

Partner	Contents	Partner	Contents
________	( )	________	( )
________	( )	________	( )
________	( )	________	( )
________	( )	________	( )

Memories :

Transformation Cost
Day : +4
Evening : +0
Night : +2
Human : +4
Tail : +2
Ears & Tail : +0

Raising Connections
1 : 5 Dreams*
2 : 5 Dreams*
3 : 5 Dreams
4 : 8 Dreams
5 : 12 Dreams
* free with Impression Check